Dark Guardian Found

THE CHILDREN OF THE GODS
BOOK ELEVEN

I. T. LUCAS

FOLLOW I. T. LUCAS ON AMAZON

Eva

5 years ago
Bayshore Towers
Tampa, Florida

"Please don't cut me, I'll do anything, please..."

Eva sat bolt upright in bed, whipping her head around to look at the man sleeping next to her. Did he hear that?

A split second later the cobwebs of dreams dissipated, and she remembered who and what she was. Fifty years of living with that shit, and she was still waking up every morning thinking she was a normal human being and not a freak with supernatural senses.

No one aside from her could hear the pleading coming all the way from the other side of the corridor. Not unless they were in that same apartment with the bully and his terrified victim. The luxury building had excellent soundproofing between the residences, ensuring the privacy of its wealthy occupants—ordinary people couldn't hear a thing from the neighboring apartments. But Eva was as far from ordinary as it got. She'd learned to tune out most of the intruding sounds, like the guy snoring next door, but the urgency and distress in the girl's voice had managed to penetrate her shields.

The nearest article of clothing Eva could see was her one-night stand's dress shirt. Lifting it off the floor and shrugging it over her shoulders, she debated whether to wake Wilbert Whitmore the Third and tell him to call the police.

No time.

Not even to find her panties. They must be hiding somewhere under the bed.

A girl's life was on the line and every second counted. Besides, Eva could probably handle the situation on her own. After all, she was a trained DEA agent, and subduing some drunkard bastard shouldn't be too difficult. Never mind that the last time she'd had any training was thirty-something years ago. Hopefully, the moves she'd learned were still hardwired into her brain, and the muscle memory was still there. As to her level of fitness, she had nothing to worry about—along with the enhanced senses, her body had somehow mutated into a never-aging, fast-healing, efficient machine.

Saving the girl should be easy, but it needed to be done quickly. Eva was there on an assignment, and couldn't afford for Mr. Wilbert Whitmore the Third to start asking questions. She was supposed to be a random hookup, and not some superwoman playing hero and saving young girls from bullies. Ideally, the rescue would be done in a few minutes, and she could get back in bed, pretending that nothing had happened. There was a fat check waiting for her if she coaxed more details out of Wilbert about the business deal he was negotiating on behalf of his father.

A quick in and out. Scare the shit out of the guy, get the girl away, and that's it. Nothing overly ambitious or fancy.

Not bothering to fasten more than the minimum number of buttons necessary, Eva grabbed a candleholder from the coffee table, a container of mace spray from her purse, and a lock-pick set from a hidden compartment in her left boot.

Prepared to snoop around Wilbert's apartment, she'd brought the tools of her trade. Seducing him hadn't been part of her original plan, but one thing had led to another, and she'd ended up going home with him instead. It wasn't her normal mode of operation as a corporate spy—hooking up with her targets wasn't part of the deal—but the guy was single, decent-looking, and she hadn't been with a man in over a month. The decision had been easy. A sweet deal, actually. While charging her client extra for going above and beyond their original arrangement, she'd scratched a troublesome itch.

Wilbert had passed out too soon to satiate her hunger, but that was nothing new. Most men didn't. In fact, she could remember only two who had, and both of them had been jerks. Her record with men sucked, including her cheating, lying, ex-husband.

But at least none of them had been physically abusive. Not that Eva would've tolerated even a hint of violence.

As she rushed to the scene unfolding in the apartment down the hall, her footfalls almost soundless on the luxurious carpet, Eva was once again reminded that things like that were tragically common. When she'd first started her detective agency, she'd dealt mainly with gathering evidence on cheating spouses. Her clients hadn't been the downtrodden variety, and yet in some cases she'd discovered that spousal abuse happened behind their fancy closed doors. As evidenced by what was going on right there, in one of the most prestigious addresses in Tampa, violence and bullying existed in the most affluent of places, crossing lines of social standing, level of education, and financial means.

"You little bitch, I'll do whatever the fuck I want to you. I own you."

"Please, Marty, I beg you, I'll be good. I'll do anything you want, please!" The girl was sobbing hysterically.

With an efficiency born of years of practice, Eva picked the lock and dropped her toolkit on the floor before the guy finished his next sentence.

"Damn right, you will. Because I'm going to teach you a lesson you're never going to forget."

Eva didn't need X-ray vision to know that the psycho was about to cut the girl. Mace in one hand and candleholder in the other, she burst in and rushed toward him. The element of surprise worked to her advantage. Regrettably, the size of the room didn't. Even as fast as she was, she couldn't cross the distance fast enough.

Looming over the kneeling girl, her hair fisted in one meaty hand, a switchblade clutched in the other, the guy had his back to the door. But even though he was clearly high on something, his reflexes were intact. Still holding onto the girl's hair, he turned around and pointed the knife at Eva.

At the sight of his half-naked would-be attacker, the snarl twisting his lips transformed into an evil smile.

Idiot.

He had no idea who he was dealing with. To him, Eva was just another female he could easily terrorize.

Big mistake, mister.

Eva kicked the door, and it slammed shut behind her. There was no going back. She was committed to wiping that grin off the asshole's smug face.

Holding his gaze with a smile of her own, she closed the rest of the distance in one leap and brought her candleholder down on his wrist, sending the knife clattering to the floor. The idiot hadn't expected her to move so fast, and the surprise in his eyes quickly turned into a murderous rage. With another smile, she lifted the mace and sprayed.

Bellowing his pain and fury, the guy dropped the girl and clutched at his face.

"Run!" Eva commanded.

But the girl didn't move. As soon as the jerk had let go of her hair, she'd crumpled down to the floor.

Did she pass out?

Her face was badly bruised, and blood was oozing from a shallow cut on her cheek, but those were superficial injuries—not enough to cause loss of consciousness. Except, the bastard might have done more damage than that. If he'd kicked the girl, she might have internal bleeding or damaged organs. Broken ribs were also a possibility.

That complicated things.

Eva's plan had been to scare the guy and help the girl get away, but the situation had turned out more complex than the run-of-the-mill domestic violence case.

This wasn't a normal couple. Not that beating up and cutting a partner could ever qualify as normal.

It was more than that, though. The girl lying unconscious on the floor looked underage, and the guy was a brutal thug with a lot of money.

The thing was, the bastard didn't seem as out of it as Eva had initially suspected, and he didn't look scared either. In fifteen minutes or so, he'd get over the temporary loss of vision and give chase.

Already, he was trying to grab her, reaching for her blindly. "I'm going to fucking kill you, bitch. You can run all you want, but I'm going to find you, and I'm going to cut you into tiny little pieces and send them one at a time to your family. And I'll do the same to that little bitch." He pointed at the girl on the floor.

An involuntary whimper betrayed the girl. Apparently, she wasn't passed out, just pretending to be.

Eva shuddered. The vehemence in his tone suggested those weren't empty threats. She wasn't afraid for herself, there was no way he could ever find her, but the girl was another story.

She would have to whisk her out of there and hide her. Make her disappear. The thing was, Eva needed more time than a fifteen-minute head start.

"Did you hear me?" The guy was practically foaming at the mouth. "I'm going to cut you up piece by piece, and I'm going to start with that little shit." He pointed at the floor. "While you watch. And then I'm going to do the same to you."

Eva wasn't the type to lose her temper, and her training had taught her to ignore taunting, but this one was pressing all her buttons. Every one of her suppressed motherly instincts was screaming at her to protect the young girl.

As the guy leaned forward, his hands grasping air while he tried to grab her, again, she glanced at the candleholder still clutched in her hand and, without giving it any thought, swung it full force, hitting the thug at the back of his skull. A sickening crashing sound followed, and he fell forward like a toppled tower and stayed down.

"Did you kill him?" the girl whispered.

"I don't know," Eva admitted. That hadn't been her intention—she'd only meant to knock him out to give them enough time to escape—she hadn't realized how much muscle she'd put behind that swing. Not that she was sorry to end the scum's life.

Not at all.

A monster like that didn't deserve to live and harm people just because he could.

The lack of remorse surprised her. Eva had never killed before, and taking a life should've shocked her. But it didn't. In fact, all she felt was enormous satisfaction. She'd just made the world a better place.

Later, she'd pray for God's forgiveness.

Crouching beside the prone body, she checked for a pulse.

There was none.

"He's dead." She glanced at the girl. "Are you sorry?"

The girl huffed out a breath. "The only thing I'm sorry for is that it wasn't me with that candleholder. I should've done something like that a long time ago, but I was too scared."

"I'm glad you didn't. He would've killed you."

The girl didn't look strong enough to lift the heavy candleholder, let alone swing it with deadly force.

An unnatural force.

Even in the hands of a strong man, the thing shouldn't have fractured the guy's skull.

"What do we do now?"

Good question. She could call the police and claim self-defense. Accidental manslaughter. The thing was, even if they believed her, which was doubtful, Eva couldn't afford the publicity a case like that would garner. All her careful planning and ingenious track-covering would be blown to hell.

No way.

She could disappear, but what about the girl?

"What's your name?" As partners in crime, they should at least get to know each other's names.

"Tessa." The girl got up on shaky legs and offered her hand.

"I'm Veronica." Eva chose one of the many different names she used.

"Thank you, Veronica. You should go. I'll say that I did it. I'm dead anyway." Tessa sounded like an old woman resigned to her fate, not a young girl with her entire life still ahead of her.

"What do you mean, you're dead anyway?"

"Martin is... he was a major drug dealer. Whoever takes his place in the organization will make sure to finish me off to teach the others a lesson."

Poor girl. She wasn't making any sense. Probably the trauma.

"Others? Like the other girlfriends or wives?"

"Slaves. Martin bought me."

Yep, definitely trauma. And if not, whatever the story was, this wasn't the time or place to discuss it.

"Get dressed. If you have a scarf and sunglasses to cover your bruises, wear them. Don't take anything. I'm getting you out of here."

The girl's shoulders slumped. "I have nowhere to go."

For some reason, Eva had been expecting that. Tessa had that lost, helpless and hopeless look about her. "Nonsense. I'm taking you home with me."

Tessa opened her mouth to say something, but then she shut it and ran to do as she was told.

Smart girl.

Eva grabbed a dishrag from the kitchen and wiped the candleholder clean, then repeated the process with the door handle. By the time she was done, Tessa had come back with a scarf wrapped around her head, hiding her bruises and cut cheek, and a pair of big sunglasses covering her swollen eyes.

"Follow me. Keep quiet as a mouse until I tell you it's okay to talk. Got it?" Eva said as she closed the door using the dishrag. She was going to keep the damn thing with her until she could burn it.

The girl nodded.

Back at Wilbert's place, Tessa waited by the door as Eva put the innocuous-looking candleholder on the coffee table.

As she left the girl on the couch to go retrieve her things from the bedroom, Eva had the passing thought that for years to come neither Wilbert nor his guests would suspect what that decorative piece had been used for.

Thankfully, Wilbert was a sound sleeper and didn't wake up as Eva gathered her stuff and tiptoed out.

She'd left him a souvenir, her panties that were lost somewhere under his bed, and a note with a phone number to call her. In order to collect her fat check, she still needed to get more details about the deal he was cooking. Wilbert would call, she had no doubt about it. He'd want a repeat of the mind-blowing sex.

This side gig as a rescuer, or perhaps vigilante, shouldn't affect her performance on the job. Eva's reputation as one of the best corporate detectives in the area was on the line.

"Tessa, have you confirmed my flight reservations and checked me in?" Eva asked more out of habit than necessity. Tessa was an excellent personal assistant—organized and methodical—and there was no way she'd forgotten.

Tessa's smile was part sweet and part indulgent. "Your first-class seat on Copa Airlines to Rio De Janeiro is confirmed. It leaves as scheduled at six forty-five."

"Thanks. You're the best." And so was her client who was footing the bill for the ticket and the luxury hotel.

The first time Eva had flown to Rio had been on an assignment for the same client, except it hadn't been about his business. The guy had hired Eva to spy on his much younger wife, whom he'd suspected of cheating on him while visiting her family. The client had been so relieved when Eva reported the woman innocent, that he'd paid her a nice bonus and had been using her services to spy on his business competitors ever since.

Eva owed him for introducing her to that lucrative niche market. The pay was much better, and no family drama. Win-win for Eva.

"You're welcome, and thank you for the compliment."

"It's well deserved. You're a life saver."

"Ditto."

Five years ago, when Eva had rescued her and taken her in, Tessa hadn't known how to use a computer: shocking for a sixteen-year-old, though understandable given her tragic circumstances. But she was smart and had caught up quickly, joining Eva's crews of misfits, as she liked to call her employees, slash tenants, slash adopted family. They could never replace her Nathalie, but to Eva, Sharon, Nick, and later Tessa meant much more than just people working in her detective agency.

She treated them as if they were her kids, which they thought was hilarious because Eva looked no older than twenty-five.

God, it was hard to believe she'd just celebrated her eightieth birthday—probably because most of the time she felt as young as she looked.

"You should start getting ready," Tessa said.

"I know."

"Here, I made you a list of things you need to pack. You always forget something." She handed Eva a printed page.

At the top of the list, the words PHONE CHARGER were typed in capital letters. Without fail, Eva always forgot to pack it and had to buy a new one at the airport.

"Did Sharon say when she'd be back?" Eva hated to leave without saying goodbye.

Tessa smirked. "She'll be here. Don't worry. She knows you want a hug before getting on a plane. And Nick is going to drive you to the airport."

"Good."

Instead of obsessing about leaving her "kids" home alone, she should be excited about visiting Rio after all that time.

Eva hadn't been back since pulling the clever maneuver almost seven years ago, leading whoever was after her all the way to Brazil, only to discover that her trail ended there. She'd gotten on a plane to Rio with her real passport as Eva Vega, but had returned to the States with a fake one. And the best part? All expenses had been paid by her paranoid client.

Lucky for her, the man who'd been in charge of producing the good stuff for the government back in her day was still alive. She'd approached him as Eva's daughter and told him a sad story about an abusive ex-husband who was after her. Having had a huge crush on Eva when she was still with the DEA, the guy couldn't refuse a plea from a daughter that looked like her identical twin. At a bargain price, he'd supplied Eva with several fake identities that were good for international travel.

Finished packing her suitcase, Eva threw the charger into her large satchel so she wouldn't forget it later. Her various passports, as well as other documents, were locked in a safe behind the mirror in her bedroom. She pulled them out, trying to remember which one she'd given Tessa to make the reservations. Veronica Soren? Melinda Bechek? Or was it Rachel Daigle?

The office was located at the front of the house, but instead of walking over she dialed Tessa's number. "Who am I this time?"

Tessa chuckled. "I don't know how you do what you do with such a shitty memory. You're Melinda Bechek."

"Thanks a lot. I give you compliments, and this is what I get back," she teased.

"Yeah, yeah. You know I love you. Sharon and Nick are back."

"I'll be there in a moment."

Eva closed the suitcase and hefted it off the bed down to the floor. Thankfully, the checked luggage weight limit for first class was generous. Her various disguises took up a lot of space, especially the padded one she used to make herself look old. Her makeup case alone weighed close to five pounds.

As Eva rolled the suitcase into the front room, Nick took it from her. "I'm going to put it in the trunk."

Sharon pulled her into her arms and squeezed. "Have a safe trip. And be careful."

"I always am."

Tessa was next, wrapping her skinny arms around Eva's waist. The girl was so small that she still looked like the sixteen-year-old Eva had found years ago. She'd tried to fatten her up, but nothing worked. Tessa couldn't gain weight no matter how hard she tried or how much food she consumed.

"I'm going to miss you," she said.

Yeah, she was going to miss all of them. They managed to plug a portion of that big hole in her heart. The missing piece that belonged to Nathalie.

Eva wanted to see her daughter so desperately, it was a constant physical pain. Leaving Nathalie had been the hardest thing Eva had had to do in her life. But she'd done it to protect her daughter. If she were ever discovered for the mutant she was, Eva wouldn't be the only one they would experiment on. They would want her child as well. Whoever they were. She didn't know whom she was hiding from, but she knew enough to stay hidden.

"One week is not that long. I'll be back before you know it."

Compared to the seven years since she'd last held her daughter in her arms, seven days was indeed nothing.

Bhathian

"Hey, Bhathian, what's up? You look in a nastier mood than usual." Anandur dropped his tray on the table and pulled out a chair.

"Bug off." Bhathian took a long swig from his beer. He should've known better than to take his lunch break in the keep's café, or Nathalie's as they all referred to it, the clan's new favorite place to hang out.

It was like waving an open invitation for unwanted company.

He wasn't in the mood for socializing. Hell, lately his dreary disposition had gotten worse. Bhathian had never been a cheerful sort of chap, not even in his youth, but he hadn't been grim. That first turn for the worse had come about thirty-one years ago when he'd let Eva slip from in between his fingers. Then six months ago, when he'd finally gotten a thread of information about her and followed it all the way to Rio, his hopes of getting her back had been shattered. Her trail ended there.

The woman was very good at running and hiding, leading him and whoever else she believed was after her to a dead end.

The sad part was that Eva was running from phantom shadows produced by her own mind. Not that Bhathian could fault her for that. The woman had no idea how and why she'd turned immortal and was terrified of anyone finding out, probably suspecting that the government or some secret organization had tampered with her genes.

If Eva had known no one was after her, she wouldn't have felt compelled to disappear and could've stayed in touch with their daughter.

But that was water under the bridge. By doing such an excellent job of covering her tracks, Eva had doomed herself to eternal running. She'd never learn the truth about herself, and he would never get the chance to make it up to her for deserting her in her time of need.

Dimly, Bhathian was aware that he was wallowing in self-pity, but he lacked the fortitude to pull himself out of that sinkhole, offending the Fates by his lack of gratitude. They had been kind enough to let him find the daughter he hadn't known he had—a dormant daughter who would soon join her immortal family as one of them. Not having to watch his child grow old and die while he lived on, he was already luckier than any other immortal male.

As soon as she delivered his granddaughter, Nathalie would go through the transition.

Bhathian couldn't wait for either.

The grandchild would be his chance to experience everything that he'd missed while his daughter had been growing up. And as soon as Nathalie recovered from giving birth, her husband was going to induce her transition, making her indestructible. The gnawing fear Bhathian was suffering every moment of every day while she was still a fragile human would finally be put to rest.

Damn, he'd been so sure he was going to find Eva and give being a family a try.

Naive wishful thinking.

Even if he had found her, he doubted Eva would've wanted anything to do with him.

He'd messed up big time.

After that one fateful hookup they'd shared over thirty-one years ago, when Eva had found him and told him she was carrying their child, he'd offered to pay for an abortion. When she'd refused, he'd offered her money.

No wonder Eva had disappeared and had never bothered to find him again and tell him about his daughter.

The guilt sat heavily on Bhathian's shoulders.

He should've suspected that Eva was an immortal, and not only because he'd been drawn to her like he'd never been drawn to any woman before. Her resistance to thralling should've been a big clue.

Except, it had never even crossed his mind because it was impossible.

The idea that she'd been a Dormant who'd been unknowingly turned by a random immortal male was preposterous. There were no other immortals aside from his clansmen and their sworn enemies, the Doomers.

When Bhathian had come back from Brazil empty-handed, he'd interrogated every male of his clan. But looking at Eva's picture, none of them remembered ever encountering her. And it wasn't as if a male could've forgotten a woman like her. She was unforgettable.

As for the Doomers, over thirty years ago there had been none in the area.

That left the incredible possibility that it had been some random immortal who'd somehow survived the ancient cataclysm that had wiped out their kind, or a descendant of one.

Was there another secret group of immortals outside the two warring camps?

Except, Bhathian and his clansmen had been searching for centuries, and had never found even one. And yet, someone must've turned Eva. She'd been a carrier of the immortal genes, but she'd been born human.

He'd seen her birth certificate.

"So, Nathalie is getting big." Anandur put his half-eaten pastry down. "I don't think she should be on her feet for so many hours a day. I thought Andrew told her to cut it down to four."

Bhathian glanced at his daughter. She was standing behind the counter, so her seven-months-pregnant belly wasn't on display, but he had to agree with Anandur. The child growing inside her wasn't small. Nathalie had already gained in excess of thirty pounds, and from now on the growth would just accelerate.

How the hell was she going to give birth to such a big baby?

Dr. Bridget should suggest a cesarean delivery. Ever since Nathalie had announced her pregnancy, Bhathian had read every book he could find on the subject, and it seemed that it would be much safer for both mother and baby not to go the natural way.

The thing was, Nathalie had dismissed his concerns, calling him a worrywart.

"Do you think a daughter of mine is going to follow her husband's instructions? She's doing whatever the hell she wants." Bhathian crossed his arms over his chest. He was proud of her independent spirit, but he wished she'd listen to reason from time to time. A talk with Dr. Bridget seemed like the best way to go. She was the only one who could talk some sense into Nathalie.

"I see." Anandur lifted the small cappuccino cup and took a few sips, then put it down and bit into his second pastry.

What was that about? Anandur was like an old yenta—an unrepentant gossiper. "What do you mean?"

Anandur rolled his eyes as he swallowed. "Isn't it obvious? When Nathalie first opened the café, Andrew used to hang around here and help her out every free minute he had. Have you seen him lately? Because I haven't. The only way I know that he comes home at night is seeing his car parked next to mine."

Bhathian cast another glance at Nathalie and frowned. Her smile looked a little forced. He'd noticed that before but had assumed it was the effort it took to work long days while hauling around that belly.

On second thought, it couldn't have been about the pregnancy. Nathalie was doing very well, considering the size of the baby, even thriving, and she was excited about becoming a mother. Her new coffee shop in the lobby of the keep's high-rise was a huge success, full of immortals who were either too lazy to cook for themselves, or just liked hanging out with fellow clan members.

Were Andrew and Nathalie having marital problems?

Not the social type, even Bhathian had noticed that Andrew never showed up in the gym or joined the guys for beers anymore. But that was understandable. The guy had a very pregnant mate at home and didn't want to leave her alone to hang out with the guys.

Up until recently, Nathalie used to invite Bhathian over once or twice a week, and he would spend some time with both Andrew and her. But she'd stopped doing so lately. She was too exhausted after work. Besides, he saw her every day at the café, so there was no need.

Anandur must've heard something. The guy was always snooping for gossip and could extract information from the most reluctant sources. "If you know something, just spill it."

Anandur shook his head. "Sorry, man. I don't. But I can smell trouble. I think you should talk to her. Or maybe give Andrew a call at work."

Uncomfortable with the subject, Bhathian glanced around to check if anyone was paying them any attention. Thankfully, Anandur had been uncharacteristically low key, and it seemed that those sitting around them were busy with their own conversations and tuning everything else out.

"I'm not going to stick my nose where it doesn't belong. They are both adults and can work out whatever problems they have on their own." The idea of approaching Nathalie or Andrew with questions about their marriage horrified him. Bhathian had a hard enough time with regular conversations, let alone touchy subjects.

Anandur took another sip from his cappuccino. "Do you think it has to do with his fangs? They should be fully active by now, venom and all. I know I would be frustrated as hell if I had to fight the instinct to bite."

Frustrated was too mild of a word for that. Bhathian couldn't imagine doing so on an ongoing basis. If that was the problem, then it was a huge one, and Andrew needed help.

He ran his fingers through his hair. "The only solution I can think of is an induced coma. That or stasis."

"I agree. Andrew should do it before he loses it and bites Nathalie."

Bhathian knew Andrew would never harm Nathalie or their unborn child intentionally, but immortals often had trouble controlling their animal urges. Especially a newly turned immortal like Andrew. "They shouldn't be left alone in the same apartment."

"Yeah, but who is going to tell them that?"

"Bridget."

Anandur nodded. "Are you going to talk to her?"

Bhathian pushed up to his feet and threw his empty bottle into the trash bin. "I was planning on seeing Dr. Bridget about something else. I might as well bring this up while I'm there."

Eva

"Look, Mom. Don't you just love this top? You should try it on." Eva turned her head to look at the American tourist.

The older woman smiled knowingly at her daughter. "It's too hip for me. But it will look amazing on you."

"You think so?" The young woman pretended that it hadn't been her intention from the start.

"I'm sure. Let's go in."

Eva couldn't help the envy. Hot and intense, it squeezed at her heart. She longed for moments like that with her Nathalie; shopping together, meeting for coffee or for lunch, just regular stuff mothers and daughters did.

Instead, she was the outsider, watching from across the street, listening in on their conversation while sitting by herself in a café and sweating buckets in her old woman disguise. The padding that made the thing look so realistic was worse than a thick coat, and Rio was just as hot and humid as Tampa. She wondered if heatstroke could count as a professional hazard and if she could charge extra for that.

As long as she delivered the goods, her clients never argued about any charges she added to the bill. Her prices were reasonable for the quality of work she was delivering, and she never charged extra if it wasn't justified.

The one thing she never compromised on was keeping her identity secret. None of her contacts—clients, targets, or snitches—had ever seen her without some sort of a disguise. In fact, she rarely left the house without one.

Paranoia was a good trait for a private eye, and in Eva's case it was doubly justified. The number of people who knew who she was and what she looked like could be counted on the fingers of one hand.

Take the guy she was spying on, Mr. Dwain Watson of the L&W investment group. Even if she happened to bump into him on the street, which was a possibility since his business was based in Tampa, he would never recognize her.

All the way at the back of the café, Mr. Watson was wheeling and dealing with his Brazilian associate, while Eva listened and took notes. The big advantage of having superior hearing was that listening devices were not needed; the big disadvantage of not using electronics was that she had to record everything using old-fashioned shorthand—but not one any court clerk would recognize. The one she'd developed looked like unintelligible scribbles.

When the waiter passed by, she ordered coffee and cake just so she could ask for another glass of water without annoying the hell out of him. She'd been sitting there for hours, and the guy looked like he was ready to kick her out.

Hopefully, Mr. Watson would be done soon, and not just because Eva was sweltering and people were waiting in line for her table. She already had all the information her client was interested in, but she couldn't leave in good conscience until the two businessmen shook hands on the deal. For what it was costing him, her client should get every last tidbit she could garner.

Several minutes later her wish was granted.

Eva waited until the two were picked up by their respective drivers, then folded her notebook and put it in her roomy satchel. Mission accomplished, she lumbered out, annoying the rude waiter on purpose. He looked like he was going to explode if she didn't hurry up.

At the next corner, she turned into the intersecting street and hailed a cab to take her back to the hotel.

Eva sighed as soon as she entered the lobby. *Bless the inventor of air conditioning.*

Salvation was near, and in a few minutes her ordeal would be over. She was going to peel off the padding and take a long, cool shower.

Refreshed, she got dressed in a simple long skirt and a boxy shirt, then donned a blond wig, blue contact lenses, and a pair of glasses. Perfectly blah. Even though blondes normally stood out in a country of mostly brunettes, no one would give her a second glance. She was just as invisible in her plain housewife attire as in her old lady one. The minimizer bra squashed her breasts, so they were almost invisible under her loose top, the khaki skirt was a size too big and made her ass look huge, and the shoes were flat Oxfords.

"Have a wonderful outing, Ms. Zelinger." The girl at the front desk smiled and waved.

Eva waved back. She'd registered the room to two occupants, a mother and daughter, and no one thought anything of her coming as one and leaving as the other.

The doorman summoned the first taxi out of the ever-present line in front of the hotel. His smile was cordial and polite as he helped her, very different from what she was used to when in her own skin or with a disguise that wasn't meant to make her look unattractive.

Men were such shallow creatures. But then she'd arrived at that conclusion a long time ago.

What happened to adorable little boys when they grew up and became men?

After Nathalie, Eva had hoped against hope to conceive again and have a boy, but it hadn't worked out. Her dreams of a house full of kids fizzled and died.

It was better that way.

Abandoning one child had been hard enough. Besides, a freak like her had no business being anyone's mother. When she'd been blessed with Nathalie, Eva hadn't known the extent of her mutation. The extraordinary senses had been weird, but she'd had all kinds of theories as to why. A brain tumor had been one of them. Not aging, however, wasn't something she could explain.

A curse or a blessing, she still wasn't sure.

In either case, God had different plans for her, giving her these strange abilities so she could do some good, and kids had no place in that grand design.

The best she could do was provide financial support for a few of the lost ones. Orphans no one wanted because they didn't fit the image prospective adoptive parents desired.

A flutter of excitement rushed through her as she gave the cabbie the address of the orphanage. She hadn't been back since she'd signed over her pension seven years ago. Her intention hadn't been purely philanthropic. Hiding her trail had been her top priority.

Anyone with good hacking skills could've followed the monthly deposits to their final destination.

Still, knowing that her contribution was supporting such a worthy cause was wonderful, a penance for her dark deeds. But even though she trusted the nuns to make good use of the money, she was curious to see what it was providing the children with.

The place looked the same as it had seven years ago, and so did Sister Juliana.

"Dona Eva, so good to see you again. It has been a long time." Sister Juliana's smile was welcoming and genuine.

It had been one of the rare instances Eva had given her real name; an unavoidable necessity when transferring the rights to a banking account registered to Eva Vega.

"You look as lovely as ever, Sister Juliana." Compliments always worked, even on a nun. After all, she was still a woman. Besides, it was the honest truth. Sister Juliana had that ageless look of someone who was at peace with herself and the world.

"Thank you. It's very kind of you. Would you like to see all the improvements we've made since you've last been here?"

Eva shook her head. "I would love to, but I hate going in there and seeing the hopeful looks disappear from the children's eyes when they realize I'm not there as a prospective parent. It breaks my heart."

Sister Juliana nodded. "I understand. Would you like to see pictures? I can show you a couple of the latest yearbooks and tell you some nice stories."

"That sounds perfect."

Sister Juliana opened a file cabinet and pulled out a glossy, colorful book. "This is one of the things your money made possible. We didn't use to have nice ones like this."

"I'm glad."

She handed the yearbook to Eva. "Because yours is a monthly contribution, we use it for everyday expenses. Clothes, shoes, books, school supplies. It certainly makes our lives easier and gives the kids a sense of normality. You'd be surprised what having new clothes instead of only hand-me-downs can do for a child's self-esteem."

"I'm happy to help," she said while flipping through the pages. "They are so adorable, I wish I could adopt all of them."

"So why don't you? Obviously not all, but one or two?"

Eva's reasons weren't the kind she could share with the good Sister. "Maybe one day, when I'm married, that is." That sounded like a good excuse to give a nun. The church wasn't too happy about single parent families.

With a smile, Sister Juliana leaned against her desk, crossing her ankles and her arms. "That reminds me; about six months ago someone came looking for you. A very handsome young fellow."

Eva's gut twisted into a hard knot. What she'd been waiting for had finally happened. They were looking for her. "What did you tell him?"

"The truth. I told him that I don't know where you are, and that the last time I'd seen you was almost seven years ago." She chuckled. "I know it's strange coming from a nun, but if he is an ex-boyfriend, I would give him another chance. Such a handsome man, and so polite. You don't see good manners like that anymore. And to come all the way here to look for you, he must still have strong feelings about you."

Yeah, obviously. Discovering someone with a genetic mutation resulting in immortality would be one hell of a motivation to go look for her. The right people would pay a fortune to get their hands on her. A rare specimen to experiment on so they could replicate it and sell it. Naturally, she couldn't tell Juliana any of that and had to go with the ex-boyfriend scenario.

Whatever name the guy had given was probably fake, so there was no point in asking for it. "Can you describe him to me? Maybe it would jog my memory."

Juliana lifted her arm, holding her hand about two feet over her head. "He was tall, four or five inches over six feet." She spread her arms wide. "Big shoulders. Very muscular. He frowned a lot, but I couldn't fault the poor man for his bad mood. Coming all the way from Los Angeles to look for you and finding a dead end must've been disappointing."

If she hadn't known better, Eva would've thought the nun was describing Bhathian. But the guy, if he was still alive, was probably in his late seventies—not the young, handsome man Sister Juliana was describing.

She shook her head. "I don't remember anyone like that, but then I meet a lot of people in my line of work. He might've been a business associate." It was horrible to tell a nun one lie after another, but there was no way around it.

Sister Juliana slapped a hand over her forehead. "I don't know what's wrong with me lately. Must be old age. I almost forgot that he left a letter for you in case you ever came back." She hurried to the other side of her desk and started sifting through the content of her drawers. "Aha, found it." She lifted an envelope. "It's addressed to you, but also to another person. Unless Patricia is your middle name."

Eva fought the urge to snatch the envelope from Juliana's hand, waiting for the nun to hand it to her. "No, it's not. Maybe he was asking about a different Eva."

The nun nodded. "Possibly. You don't match his description. He was talking about a brunette with amber eyes who was unforgettably beautiful. Did you color your hair?"

Sister Juliana was having a hard time reconciling the guy's description with the plain woman in front of her while desperately trying not to offend her.

"I started to see gray hairs." Eva patted her wig. "It was time."

"That explains it."

Envelope in hand, Eva turned around and tore it open, then pulled out the small paper square that was inside. It was folded twice as if that was supposed to add a layer of protection to what was written on it. There was nothing on the top flap, but as she turned it in her hand, things got blurry for a moment, and she felt faint for the first time in forever.

There were only two lines of writing—a simple to and from. To: Patricia or Eva. From: Bhathian.

How could it be?

It couldn't have been her Bhathian, Nathalie's biological father who had rejected her and his daughter all those years ago. The only explanation Eva could think of was that Bhathian had indeed written the letter, but someone else had delivered it—a son that looked a lot like his father.

Maybe Bhathian was on his deathbed, and his conscience was bothering him about the child he'd never gotten to know. Maybe he wanted to find his daughter before it was too late?

"Well?" Sister Juliana tried to peek from behind Eva's shoulder. "Is it for you?"

"Yes, it is." She turned around with a fake smile that was so well practiced no one would've known it wasn't genuine, and the lie rolled off her tongue. "It's a funny story. I once participated in an amateur theater production and my character's name was Patricia. Bhathian was the co-star, and for some reason I remembered him by his stage name, Reuben. We went out a couple of times, but it was nothing serious." Eva put the folded paper back in the envelope and stuffed it in her skirt pocket.

The nun's eyes followed Eva's hand. "Aren't you going to read it?"

Eva waved a dismissive hand. "I'll read it back in the hotel. It might be a silly love letter, and I don't want to start blushing and giggling like a schoolgirl in your office."

Sister Juliana didn't even try to hide her disappointment. "I understand."

"I should go." Eva glanced at her wristwatch. "I have a meeting later today, and I need to get ready."

"Of course." The nun offered her hand. "I'm delighted that you stopped by."

"Me too. I'll come again the next time I have business in Rio."

The nun frowned. "What exactly is it that you do?"

Eva put a finger on her lips. "I'm under contractual obligation to keep it confidential." At least she wasn't lying about that. Every contract she signed with a client stipulated confidentiality.

Bhathian

"How can I help you, Bhathian?" Bridget motioned for him to come in and take a seat.

Bhathian smoothed his palm over his short-cropped hair. This was going to be embarrassing.

Bridget leaned forward and smiled. "Just say what you came here to say. I never reveal anything my patients tell me."

"I'm not here for me. It's about Nathalie."

"Are you worried?"

He nodded.

"Perfect. That makes you a patient and therefore obligates me not to reveal anything you tell me. You came to receive treatment for anxiety. It qualifies."

Worked for him. And anyway, Bridget had misunderstood. His embarrassment had nothing to do with the subject of what he came to talk about and everything to do with his shitty communication skills.

"Nathalie is getting really big," he started.

"Yes."

"The baby is going to be big."

"Go on."

"I think a cesarean section delivery will be safer for Nathalie and for the baby."

"And that's your medical opinion?"

Bhathian felt his ears warm up. Bridget was making fun of him. He wasn't well educated, or even well read in other subjects, but he sure as hell had read plenty about pregnancy and delivery. He wasn't an ignoramus. "I've read a lot. And big babies can cause trouble for the mothers. I want my daughter to be safe. Whatever scarring she'll have because of the operation will disappear after the transition. Her body will be as good as new."

Bridget shook her head. "When it gets close to her due date, I'll determine what's best for Nathalie and for the baby and explain the options. It's her body and it's her decision."

That wasn't what he wanted to hear. If the choice were left up to Nathalie, she would never agree to even consider an operation.

"Can't you at least talk to her? You're the only one she might listen to."

"The only thing I can promise you is that I'll give her my best professional advice. And if I think she needs a C-section, I'll strongly recommend it."

"Thanks. I hope she'll listen." It would have to do. Hopefully, Bridget's recommendation would carry weight with his stubborn daughter.

Bridget smiled. "Don't worry. I have plenty of experience dealing with stubborn patients. Your Nathalie will listen. Anything else I can help you with?"

Bhathian shifted in his chair. "Yeah, there is. I think Andrew's fangs are functional, and that he is trying to get through the last months of Nathalie's pregnancy relying on his willpower and self-discipline. But we both know that he can't risk it. If he ends up biting her and inducing her transition while she is still pregnant, it will kill the baby and maybe even her."

It was Bridget's turn to look uncomfortable. "What do you want me to do? I can't force him to agree to an induced coma or entombment."

"I think we should ask Edna to issue a court order. He is dangerous to Nathalie and to his unborn daughter."

"That's not a bad idea," Bridget said, her tone and her expression showing surprise as if she'd never expected to hear anything clever from him.

Bhathian got that a lot.

People assumed that big muscles equaled a small brain. He wasn't very smart, but he wasn't stupid either. "So you'll talk to her?"

"First I need to see what's the deal with Andrew."

"Yeah, of course." He pushed up to his feet.

"Sit down, Bhathian," Bridget commanded.

For such a small female the doctor packed authority. Bhathian obeyed immediately, the soldier in him responding to an order. Hey, maybe Andrew would react to Bridget the same way. He was a soldier for many years before being forced off active duty and becoming an analyst. In the military, a doctor carried the same authority as a commanding officer. On the other hand, Andrew and Bridget had had that fling before he'd met Nathalie, and he might view her in a different light.

"Yes?" He arched a brow.

"I want to talk to you about your depression."

"I'm not depressed." He was, but it was nobody's business. In time, he'd snap out of it.

Bridget sighed. "Look, Bhathian, I know it's hard for a male like you to admit a weakness, especially a mental one. You're a Guardian, and you guys are supposed to be hard and resilient and basically indestructible. The best warriors in the world."

Bhathian straightened in his chair. "We are."

"But you're not. Not in your current state. Depression slows your reaction time, makes you less observant. In short, it can get you killed or let down those who depend on you for protection. I want you to talk to Vanessa. She can help you."

"I'm not talking to a shrink."

A mask of determination slipped over Bridget's porcelain doll face, her red brows dipping low. "You either haul your ass and plant it in Vanessa's office chair, or I'm grounding you."

He answered with a growl that was known to intimidate grown men, but not the doctor. She handed him a business card. "You can growl all you want all the way to her office. Here are her address and phone number. Call her."

"Fine." Bhathian took the card and stuffed it in his back pocket. Whatever, he could pretend he was going to do it to get Bridget off his back.

She smiled. "I'm going to call her in an hour and check if you made an appointment. If you didn't, my next call will be to Onegus."

"Stubborn woman."

"Yes, I am. It's for your own good."

Eva

The letter was burning a hole in Eva's pocket, but she didn't want to read it in the taxi. A few more minutes until she got back to her hotel room wouldn't kill her.

How the hell had Bhathian's son found her? An ordinary citizen couldn't have the necessary resources to track her money. Maybe he was an agent? Or a hacker? Or had access to one?

The chance of anyone tracking the money trail through the loops she'd created had been remote, a long shot, and deciding to close that last loop had been born in part out of her paranoia, but the extra precautions she'd taken donating her pension to the orphanage had paid off.

The nuns had no idea where she lived, and her trail ended there.

Yeah, no need to worry. Everything was working exactly as she'd planned it. And yet, she couldn't get rid of the churning unease in her stomach.

Was it the letter?

Was it her old life catching up with her?

Eva paid the cabbie, leaving him a big tip because she didn't want to wait for change, then hurried up to her room.

But she wasn't ready yet. Dropping the fake glasses on the bathroom vanity, she started pulling out the pins holding her wig in place. Too impatient to get them all out, she tore the thing off, the remaining pins clattering down to the tiled floor.

Only after shaking out her long hair and running a brush through it was she ready to read the letter. She needed to do it as herself and not one of her multiple personalities.

Eva sat down on the bed and pulled out the letter. Opening the thing and reading it, though, was another story. She sat there, holding it in her hands for God knows how long, just staring at it.

Come on, Eva, you're not a coward. He is not going to jump out of the paper and attack you.

The thing was, she didn't want to know.

For years upon years the memory of Bhathian had stayed fresh in her mind. Sometimes she'd remembered him with a pang of longing in her heart, but most often with bitter resentment. In both scenarios, though, he'd been young and healthy and single.

Eva didn't want to face the reality that he might be dying, or that he was married and had other grown children, half brothers and sisters to her Nathalie.

With trembling hands, she pulled out the carefully folded square and smoothed it out.

To Patricia, or Eva, or whatever name you're going by now.

From Bhathian.

First, I wanted to let you know that I found our daughter. Nathalie is a wonderful young woman. She is smart and capable and a devoted daughter to her adoptive father. And beautiful. Lucky for her, she looks more like you and only a little bit like me.

Fernando is not doing so great. His dementia is getting worse. He doesn't know who I am of course. We didn't tell him because of his condition and because we didn't know if you'd told him that he wasn't Nathalie's father.

The second thing I wanted to tell you was that I never stopped looking for you. I came back to that bar searching for you, and when you didn't show up, I kept looking everywhere. But you were very good at covering your tracks. I was resigned to never finding you and the child we conceived together. Until I met Andrew, who later became Nathalie's fiancé. He works for the government, and I asked him to help me. Without him, I would've never found Nathalie or uncovered your trail.

But it looks like it ends here.

Nathalie will be so disappointed.

I wanted to find you in time to tell you that she and Andrew are getting married and are inviting you to their wedding. We all want you to be there, though it would've been weird with Fernando around. He thinks that you guys are still married.

The other good news is that Nathalie and Andrew are expecting a baby. Can you believe it? We are going to be grandparents!

I'm probably writing this letter in vain, and you'll never get to see it. But I pray that you do and that you'll call me. If you get to read it in the next few days, you could still make it to the wedding. But whenever you get this letter please call me. There is so much more I need to tell you. Nathalie misses you and needs you.

Yours always,

Bhathian

. . .

Shoot. Eva noticed that she was crying only when fat tears hit the sheet of paper and the ink started to dissolve. Quickly, she wiped them away with her hand, and then patted the paper dry with a corner of the comforter.

Nathalie was married and was having a baby.

Eva's heart ached so bad it felt like it was going to explode. There was nothing she wanted more than to be with Nathalie and witness her grandchild's birth. But the best thing she could do for her daughter and her baby was to stay away and not bring danger to them.

Maybe she could take a peek, though?

Wearing one of her more elaborate disguises, she could sit in Fernando's café and have her fill of looking at Nathalie. Maybe Andrew, her husband, would come to visit her at work and she could get a look at him as well.

Staring at the phone number, she knew she wasn't going to call. She had nothing to say to Bhathian. Her curiosity about what his life had been like wasn't worth the reopening of old wounds.

Besides, she preferred remembering Bhathian as he used to be. Young and handsome and so damn sexy that he'd melted her panties away.

In the back of her mind, she wondered what would have happened if he'd found her. Would he have offered to marry her? Become a father to his daughter?

Not likely.

He'd only wanted to ease his conscience by paying her off. Nothing more. That day when she'd told him she was pregnant, Bhathian had made it perfectly clear that he hadn't wanted anything to do with her.

Drained by the emotional turmoil the letter had brought about, Eva took off her clothes, tossed them on the floor, and crawled naked under the covers.

But sleep refused to come.

Instead, she was stuck in memory lane. Bhathian had been the best lover she'd ever had, and there had been many over the years to compare with, but there had been more than just sex between them.

There had been a connection.

Even before discovering the pregnancy, Eva had wanted to come back and look for Bhathian, but working undercover prevented any kind of a relationship. She needed to wait until her mission was over. But apparently Bhathian hadn't felt the same; otherwise he wouldn't have cast her out as callously as he had.

"Patricia, check out the passenger in 3a," Margo whispered in Eva's ear.

It wasn't Eva's first undercover stint, but none of her previous assignments had lasted that long. Three months into the job, and she was thinking of herself as Patricia Evans, a first class TWA flight attendant, and not Eva Paterson, a DEA agent.

Dang it, she was developing a case of split personality.

"What about him?"

"He's hot."

Eva pretended to peek. She'd noticed the guy as soon as he boarded the plane, it had been impossible not to. Well over six feet tall and heavily muscled, he was too handsome for his own good. Eva stayed away from guys who looked like that, not that any she'd met had come even close. The overly good-looking ones were bad news, thinking of themselves as God's gift to women and expecting to be worshiped.

If anyone were to be worshiped it would be her. Her dream guy would have eyes only for her, and adore everything about her. Trouble was, it was hard to meet anyone while working undercover, skipping from place to place, and pretending to be other people. Besides, she doubted her dream guy even existed.

"Let's invite him to go out with us tonight."

"You do it," Eva told Margo. The girl made a sport out of picking up the cutest guy on every flight, preferably one of those sitting in first class.

"What's the matter, Patricia? Too prim and proper to ask a guy out?"

"Pfft, please. I don't need to. If I'm interested in a guy, I can make him ask me out."

"Prove it."

Eva rolled her eyes. She was stuck working with a bunch of immature twenty-something girls. At forty-five, she was done with those kinds of games. Not that any of them suspected her real age. Eva was lucky to look the same as she had twenty years ago.

"Fine. I'll show you how it's done." When in Rome and all that. A good undercover agent had to fit in with her coworkers.

Sauntering from one passenger to another, she asked each about their meal preference and a few polite questions about the purpose of their trip. Out of the twelve seats, only eight were occupied, and no one was sitting next to the hunk in seat 3a.

She flashed him the perfect smile. Not too sexy and not too forward, but friendly and with a slight indication of interest. For most men it was enough. "Good afternoon, sir, did you have a chance to look over the menu?"

He turned away from looking out the window and regarded her with his incredible gray eyes. "I'm afraid not. Would you mind joining me for a minute and going over the selection?" He pointed to the vacant seat next to him.

Smooth. The guy had just earned himself several bonus points. She wasn't supposed to, but a first-class customer's wishes were not to be ignored.

"I'll be happy to."

"I'm Bhathian," he introduced himself.

She pointed at her name tag. "Patricia."

"A pleasure to make your acquaintance." He offered his hand.

Eva hesitated, and not because Bhathian's hand was the size of a frying pan. Sitting so close to him, she could almost feel the magnetic pull between them.

There was no doubt in her mind that the moment their hands touched sparks would fly.

Not that she had a choice. To refuse would've been rude. Eva forced a smile. "The pleasure is all mine."

His hand closed gently around hers, and instead of sparks, a soft wave of warmth spread through her, intensifying rapidly into an erotic inferno.

With a gasp, Eva pulled her hand away.

By the confused look in Bhathian's gray eyes, he'd felt it too. For a long moment they just stared at each other. Eva was the first to shake it off. With a

Herculean effort, she schooled her features into a professional expression and asked, "The menu. What would you like to know?"

Carol

"What's today's special?" Anandur asked.

Carol cast him an annoyed look. "You can wait another thirty seconds until I'm done writing it on the board."

"I'm hungry."

"So? I'm making only one main dish a day. You'll eat whatever I've made."

"True. But I want to know what it's going to be."

She took a step back from the blackboard to admire her handwriting. "As you can see, we are serving spaghetti. One with meat sauce and the other one with a vegetarian sauce."

"Spaghetti? What happened to the fancy stuff you were cooking before?"

Carol shrugged. "I'm not a professional cook, and I'm having trouble with the huge pots. It was fine to cook elaborate dishes when the quantities were smaller, but as more of you guys went for it, I had to scale up and things didn't come out right. I decided to move to easier things and get more ambitious once I got the hang of it."

He patted her shoulder. "Smart move."

"Yes. I'm a genius ain't I?" She grimaced and glanced at Robert who was sitting by himself at one of the tables and pretending to read a newspaper.

Right. She knew exactly what he was doing. Trying to make her jealous. It hadn't taken long for the other clan females to realize that there was no great love between her and Robert, and the floozies had decided that he was up for grabs.

Robert hadn't gotten that much female attention in all his years put together, and the bastard was having the time of his life.

The girls had a serious case of hero worship and didn't care that he was an ex-Doomer, or that he was as boring as a dry stick. Robert had proven himself worthy by rescuing Carol from his sadistic commander. Helping her escape, he'd saved her life while sacrificing everything he had. After his treasonous act, there was no going back for Robert.

Guilt had become Carol's constant companion. The three months she'd promised him in exchange for his help had come and gone, and she was still with him, not because she wanted to be, but because she felt like an ungrateful bitch every time she thought of leaving.

In her heart Carol knew she would be doing Robert a favor by setting him free. As the only immortal male around who wasn't a relative or already taken, he was the object of desire of every single clan female, which apart from Amanda meant all of them. No wonder the girls had started clamoring for his attention the moment they'd sensed he was up for grabs.

But he wasn't. Carol hadn't released him yet.

She sighed. Robert was a decent guy, handsome, devoted, hardworking, and Carol owed him her life. For the past six months she'd made a real effort to make their relationship work, and sometimes it hadn't been all that bad. But she was getting more and more frustrated with him and with the new lifestyle she'd been forced into because of him.

The administrative job Kian had given Robert was easy, and all of it was done sitting on his butt, while Carol sweated over pots and pans in the basement kitchen.

She wanted her old, carefree life back.

Never mind that it had been her idea. It had seemed such a good one. She loved to cook, so when Nathalie had mentioned that more than pastries and sandwiches were needed on the menu, Carol had offered to cook the dish of the day. It had been okay at the beginning, and she'd even had fun, basking in all the compliments on how amazing a cook she was.

But now that the entire Los Angeles clan—or at least those residing in the high-rise or keep as some of the old timers still insisted on calling it—was showing up for lunch, the task had become too demanding.

She needed help.

The thing was, Kian didn't want any humans working in the café, except Nathalie of course, but then she was Bhathian's daughter and Kian's sister-in-law. Besides, Nathalie wasn't going to remain human for long.

None of the other clan members wanted the job of an assistant cook. Carol's only option was to admit that she'd gotten in over her head and that the dish of the day had been a bad idea. Sandwiches for lunch were perfectly fine, and those who wanted more could eat out somewhere else. There were plenty of restaurants in the area they could go to.

"You want to talk about it?" Anandur offered. "You look upset."

She was tempted. Out of all the Guardians, Anandur was the only one she really liked. Kri, the girl Guardian, was okay, but she was a tomboy and her size was intimidating. Brundar was scary, and so was Bhathian. Yamanu was just weird, and Arwel was always drunk.

Carol didn't know Onegus well enough to form an opinion, but she had a feeling that the overly charming chief Guardian was too full of himself.

The problem with Anandur, however, was his big mouth. Telling him anything was like announcing it to the whole clan.

"Do you know anyone who wants to work in the kitchen? I need help."

"You can ask Amanda to lend you her butler."

"Onidu? She will never agree to part with him." The Odus were some sort of biomechanical robots. There were only seven of them, all serving the goddess and her children. Too rare and valuable to be borrowed by a lowly clan member like herself.

"Try her. Amanda is gone most of the day, and Onidu has nothing to do other than stare at Dalhu painting in his studio." Anandur chuckled. "Talk about watching paint dry."

She snorted. "True."

"Anyway, if you let him go a few minutes before she comes back from the university, Amanda wouldn't even feel his absence."

It all sounded very reasonable except the part about talking to Amanda. Carol was a nobody who'd gained some questionable fame after getting abducted and tortured by the Doomers, but that didn't mean she could just walk up to Annani's daughter, the princess, and ask to borrow her butler for a few hours a day.

"Could you do it? I mean ask Amanda."

Anandur arched a brow. "Why?"

She shrugged. "I'm a nobody. Why would she want to talk to me?" If Amanda were a male it would've been different. Carol knew how to handle men, even those she was related to. They were so easy to manipulate, especially by a fragile-looking, pretty girl. Amanda was a beautiful woman herself, and smart, a neuroscience professor. Carol's feminine charms would not work on her.

"It's nonsense, but if it makes you so uncomfortable, I can ask her."

Carol stretched up on her tiptoes and kissed Anandur's cheek, or rather his bushy beard, which felt like kissing a scrubbing brush. "Thank you, you're the best." She rubbed her lips. "But you really should shave that mop off. It's scratchy."

Anandur smoothed his thumb and forefinger over the dense, red hair. "Why? I don't hear any complaints from the ladies."

She chuckled. "They must be thralled."

"That's an insult. I don't thrall women before the sex, only after."

Carol rolled her eyes. "It was a joke, you big dummy. Of course you don't. You're a Guardian. There is no way you'd break one of the most important clan laws." Unlike her, who'd done it on several occasions, getting drunk or high and talking too much. Blurting out stuff that could endanger the clan was a serious offense. She'd even spent time in solitary confinement for it. The first time Carol had been caught flapping her mouth in a bar, she'd gotten away with a warning, but the second time Kian hadn't been that lenient.

Anandur pointed a finger at her. "That's right. I always follow the rules."

"For some reason I doubt it." Anandur might obey the law, but she was sure he bent it as far as he could.

"Smart girl. By the way, why don't you go to a culinary school? Or at least take a course? You should learn the basics of working in a professional setting."

Carol shook her head. "I don't have patience for that. I'm more of a hands-on kind of girl."

Anandur slapped his forehead. "Of course. Why didn't I think of it sooner? You can ask Gerard to be an apprentice in his kitchen. What better way to learn how it's done than to observe the best chef in town?"

That sounded wonderful for so many reasons. Watching Gerard work his culinary magic would be amazing. But more than that, she was dying to see his clientele. From what she'd heard, Gerard's restaurant—

By Invitation Only—attracted millionaires, movie stars, and high-ranking politicians. Getting access to that kind of crowd was a dream come true for a woman like Carol. So many successful men she could seduce. The best part, though, was getting away from the keep and from Robert at least for a few hours every day.

"You think he'll agree?"

Anandur rubbed his beard again. "He is a prima donna. Perhaps you should ask Kian to talk to him. You know that he and Gerard are partners in that restaurant?"

"I didn't know that."

"They are. And the way I see it, it's in Kian's best interest to have you train with the guy. After all, he is Nathalie's partner as well."

Carol's shoulders slumped. "I can't leave her alone here. She has no one else to help her in the café, and she can't handle it by herself. Not in her condition."

"We'll get Onidu to help Nathalie. With you gone, there will be no more cooking in the basement, so he can help here."

"Did anyone tell you that you're brilliant?"

Anandur's grin stretched from ear to ear. "Yeah, once or twice."

Robert

"How is it going, Robert?" Kian entered Robert's office.

He'd been given an actual room, and not a closet or a pantry like what he'd had at Sebastian's base. On the other hand, at the Doomer base he'd been second in command, while here he was a lowly clerk.

Did he miss his previous status? A little.

But he sure as hell didn't miss the Doomer lifestyle of endless battles, or serving under his sadistic commander. Not that Sebastian, aka Sharim, had mistreated Robert or any of the other soldiers. As a commander, Sebastian had been one of the best to serve under, but the bastard had tortured Carol and numerous other females over the years.

Clerking wasn't so bad. It was peaceful, and working in such luxury was a treat. His office was freshly painted and came equipped with a brand new desk, top of the line computer, and all the office supplies he could think of.

The only problem was spending his long workdays alone. Other than Kian, and occasionally Kian's assistant Shai, no one stopped by to talk.

"Good. I negotiated a discount from the windows supplier. The interior doors vendor refused to budge on the price, but I got him to upgrade instead."

The clan was building a new stronghold somewhere in Malibu, and Robert had been given the job of purchasing building materials. Regrettably, Kian didn't trust him yet to leave the keep and visit the building site, but Robert had access to the blueprints, so the clan's cautious regent must've deemed him at least somewhat trustworthy.

It was an impressive project, and once completed, it would provide a more secure stronghold for the clan. The idea was to split its population between the two locations. Some would remain in the high-rise, and some would move into the new "village" when it was ready.

"Any trouble? Anything you need help with?"

Robert shook his head. "I've got it."

Kian surprised him by pulling out a chair and sitting down. Usually, he would stop by, ask a couple of questions, and leave.

"How are you acclimating here?"

Strange question. Kian didn't strike him as someone who was interested in people's personal lives.

"I'm doing fine."

"Made any friends?"

Robert shook his head.

"I see. How about Dalhu?"

"He doesn't want anything to do with me. I remind him of a life he wishes to forget."

Robert had tried to approach the only other Doomer who'd ever crossed over to the clan, but the guy had made it clear he preferred Robert stayed away from him. Perhaps Dalhu was uncomfortable associating with someone who'd outranked him in the Brotherhood, or perhaps he was uncomfortable with Robert for another reason. Dalhu, who used to be a warrior, had become an artist. Not something that would've garnered him respect in the Doomer camp. The Brotherhood didn't consider art as an appropriate occupation for a male.

Kian raked his fingers through his hair, looking uncomfortable. "And how are things with Carol?"

Now Robert was certain it hadn't been Kian's idea to come and ask him all those questions. He narrowed his eyes. "Why? Did Carol say something?"

"No. But my wife seems to think that you guys need some help. Maybe talking to Vanessa or something like that."

"Who's Vanessa?"

"Our psychologist."

So it had been Syssi's idea. If Robert weren't an ex-Doomer, she would've probably come to talk to him herself. Instead she'd sent her husband.

Robert found it ridiculous that even a man like Kian, the clan's formidable regent, bowed to his woman's dictates. It should've been the other way around. According to the teachings of Mortdh, women were supposed to obey their men.

Except, it didn't work that way, and Robert was basing this on his own experience. There was a big flaw in Mortdh's philosophy, or rather a missing part.

Men craved their women's approval and affection and were willing to go to great lengths to get it. The best examples of that were sitting across from each other in his office.

The thing was, Robert wasn't seeking Syssi's approval and therefore didn't need to accept her suggestions.

"We don't need it."

"But you're not happy together. She's not happy, and you're not happy."

"So what? Who said everyone needs to be happy all of the time?"

Kian grimaced. "I know. It's a modern concept. It used to be about survival; now it's about being fucking happy."

So true. "I'm not giving up yet, and neither is she."

"Good for you." Kian pushed up to his feet, looking relieved to be done with his task. "If you need anything, come see me. I mean it. My office door is open to you."

The guy seemed sincere, and Robert decided to plunge ahead with what was bothering him most about his relationship with Carol. "What happens to me if I'm no longer with Carol?"

Kian chuckled. "You'll need to hide in your apartment because there will be a stampede of immortal females chasing after you."

Robert felt his face warm up. "I'm not such a great catch. And I wasn't asking about that. Would I still have a home here?"

"You are a great catch because there is only one of you. And this is your home independent of your relationship with Carol. I can't let you go even if I wanted to. You know too much."

"There are many ways to let go of someone." Robert made air quotes around the "let go" part.

Kian's face darkened. "It seems that you've learned nothing about us during the months you've been here. I'm not in the habit of giving my word and then going back on it, or repaying kindness with betrayal."

Robert hadn't seen that side of Kian yet. The guy was terrifying when angered.

Offending the regent had been a big mistake. Robert should've known better. As a Doomer, he'd learned to keep his mouth shut and think twice before saying anything that might be perceived as insolent by his superiors.

Robert stood up and bowed. "I apologize. I've misspoken and inadvertently offended you, my benefactor. I'll accept any punishment you deem appropriate."

Kian shook his head. "There will be no punishment. You need to adjust your way of thinking, Robert. You're no longer in the Doomer camp, and no one here gets punished for saying something someone doesn't like."

Robert should've been relieved, but he wasn't.

It would've been better to suffer through some sort of punishment than Kian's disapproval. "I hope you accept my apology. It was sincere. I'm grateful for all you've done for me, and I should've thought things through before blurting out nonsense."

"Apology accepted."

Eva

Eva parked her rental car a block down the street from Fernando's café, and with a heavy sigh heaved her bulk out of the rental.

Like a method actress, she always stayed in character when wearing a disguise, even if no one was paying her any attention.

Lumbering up the street, her shoulders slumped and her back slightly bowed, she almost felt as old as she looked. Hell, she was as old. If not for her mutation, the old lady get-up would not have been a costume to be discarded at the end of her performance.

Eva stopped in front of the café and peeked inside. The place hadn't changed much as far as the decor, but everything else about it had.

Nathalie was nowhere in sight, and neither was Fernando. A young man was in charge of the register, and another one was waiting on the customers.

She took a step back and looked at the sign. It hadn't changed. It was still Fernando's café.

Had Nathalie sold the place and the new owners kept the name?

One thing was evident, though; these people knew how to run this place better than Fernando. Eva had never seen the café so packed. Not at three o'clock in the afternoon. It used to be busy during breakfast and lunch, but other than that not so much.

Time to ask some questions.

Eva pushed the door open and shuffled inside.

"Welcome to Fernando's café." The handsome young man greeted her with a charming smile.

Maybe that was the secret. An attractive guy to lure in the female clientele. A discreet glance confirmed her suspicion. Women of all ages filled the booths, with only a couple of guys sitting in the back.

"Thank you." She smiled, flashing him a set of fake teeth that matched the rest of her appearance. "What happened to Fernando? I used to come here a lot before moving to Florida, and it was always Fernando standing at the cash register, and his lovely daughter Nathalie serving the customers."

The young man regarded her with suspicious eyes. "Fernando retired, and Nathalie is married now and expecting her first baby." With the charming smile gone, the handsome guy in front of her didn't look as harmless as before. In fact, he seemed menacing.

What was wrong? Did her wig sit crookedly? Had some of the prosthetics gotten unglued?

"Excuse me for a moment, but I need to use the restroom. Is it still in the same place?"

"Yes."

"Good. An old woman like me always needs to know where to find one."

His smile looked forced.

Damn it.

Heading to the bathroom, Eva made herself go slow. Something must've gone wrong with her costume. It was the first time someone wasn't buying it.

Everything looked fine. The fake loose skin of her latex mask was just right, and the makeup that hid the transition between the mask and her eyes was intact. She stretched on her tiptoes to take a look at the rest of her body. Maybe her fake boobs were askew. It happened sometimes and would've been a dead giveaway. But everything was in its right place.

When she got out, the guy watched her as she shuffled back up front. "Would you like a booth, ma'am?" he asked.

"Yes please."

He showed her to her seat and even offered his hand to help her in. A surprisingly polite move for a product of this generation, or the few that came before it. Respect for the elderly hadn't been part of their education.

"Thank you."

"You're welcome. What can I get you?"

"I would like a cup of coffee and a Danish. Are they as good as Fernando's? His used to be the best in town."

This time the guy's smile was genuine. "I'll bring you one, and if it's not as good as Fernando's, it's on the house."

He was good, a natural born salesman. "You've got yourself a deal, young man. What's your name?"

"Jackson." He offered his hand.

Damn it. She couldn't let him touch her. Her gnarled hand looked real, but it felt like latex, not skin. Eva grabbed a napkin from the dispenser and pretended to sneeze into it. "I'm sorry, must be my allergies flaring up. I'm Hilda." She crumpled the napkin in her hand and grabbed another one.

Jackson retracted his. "Nice to meet you, Hilda. I'll let Fernando know that you stopped by."

"Thank you. That's very nice of you. I hope he remembers me. It's been a few years."

Hopefully, the real Hilda, who'd retired to Florida more than eleven years ago, hadn't passed away in the meantime. But even if she had, Fernando would probably not remember her. According to the letter, his dementia had progressed since the last time Eva had seen him. Nathalie, however, might.

"Do you have a phone number he can call you at?"

She waved a hand. "It's not important. I'm just an old customer. He probably doesn't remember me."

Jackson nodded, but his eyes remained suspicious.

Was he one of those people who possessed a strong sixth sense?

She should ask him.

That was how Eva had collected her other misfits. Whenever she encountered someone who struck her as different, she looked into that person's eyes and asked a simple question: "What makes you special?"

For some reason, she'd always gotten an honest answer.

Sharon could predict what people would say next with uncanny accuracy. She claimed it was easy because people were predictable and she could easily read their facial cues. But Eva suspected it was more than that.

Nick had a way with computers and electronic devices that seemed almost magical, so much so that Tessa and Sharon nicknamed him the wizard. He believed it was just an acquired skill, but Eva had seen him tackle stuff he'd never encountered before and figure it out as if he'd seen the schematics and memorized them.

Eva had the same feeling about Tessa. The girl was different all right, but when asked that same question she'd claimed there was nothing special about her. Maybe her traumatic youth had stunted her natural talents. It sure as heck had stunted her growth. At twenty-one, Tessa could pass for a twelve-year-old, and she'd done it once when Eva needed a kid for an undercover stint.

Jackson was different too, though with him it was something physical. The way he moved, fluid and graceful like a dancer, projected a magnetic sexuality that belied his youth. He could not have been more than eighteen, and yet every woman in the café, regardless of age, couldn't take her eyes off him. If she believed in mythical creatures, Jackson would've fit the role of an incubus.

Eva could sense it, but remained unaffected. It was just an observation. He was a pretty boy to look at, that's all. Perhaps she was too jaded to feel the attraction the others did.

Men in general left her indifferent even though she was a shamefully lustful woman. Not that she had a thing for other females, although it would have made her life easier if she had. She loved sex, just not the entanglement that came with relationships, or the feelings of guilt that came with hookups.

She'd been raised in a religious home and had been taught that good girls didn't do it outside of the marriage bed. Things hadn't worked out for her that way, but she still felt a smidgen of guilt after every meaningless sexual encounter.

Most of the time Eva took care of her own needs without a partner. She picked up a guy no more than once a month and would've gladly skipped that as well, but the need to touch and be touched became overwhelming after a while.

Like with food, going for too long without resulted in mindless binging of whatever junk she could put into her mouth. Her one-night stand with Bhathian thirty-one years ago was a perfect example of lust overpowering good judgment.

> *"You're gorgeous," Bhathian whispered in her ear as they rode the elevator up to her hotel room.*
>
> *God, she couldn't wait to get him naked. The hours they'd spent at the bar had been such a waste of time, but neither had wanted to be the one to suggest sex.*

Eva was too much of a lady to let him know she was burning, and Bhathian had taken his sweet time torturing her with one slow dance after the other. Swaying to the music, they'd kissed and touched each other everywhere they could without getting arrested for indecent behavior. One thing was sure, after that public make-out session, none of her fellow flight attendants would ever call her prim.

Her hands shook as she tried to insert the room key into the lock. Bhathian took it away from her and opened the door, then kicked it closed while practically tearing her clothes off of her. In seconds, she found herself without a stitch of clothing on, sprawled on the bed and panting in anticipation.

Burning with need after hours of build-up, Eva was more than ready and ached to be filled. She wished Bhathian would forgo foreplay and just pounce on her. They'd done enough playing around on the dance floor.

"Just look at you," he hissed through clenched teeth.

They hadn't turned the lights on, but she had no trouble seeing him in the dark. Those strange enhanced senses of hers often came in handy. What she wondered, though, was how Bhathian could see her, and why the hell did his eyes look like they were glowing from the inside.

Such a beautiful man. "Let me see you," she said.

"Do you want me to turn on the light?"

"In the bathroom." He'd misunderstood her meaning, but she had to go with his interpretation. After all, she couldn't admit seeing perfectly well in the dark.

Bhathian flipped the switch on and left the door open a crack. Undoing just the top buttons on his shirt, he pulled it off and tossed it aside.

Wow. The guy had the kind of chest a girl wanted to sink her nails into. Not an ounce of fat, he was all hard muscle covered by smooth skin.

Nathalie

"You seem in a good mood. Was it something Anandur said?" Nathalie asked Carol.

The immortal was a great help, and her dish of the day was a big success, but she wasn't happy. Not with her job working for Nathalie, not with living at the keep, and not with Robert. Sadly, those two didn't belong together.

As one who'd fallen in love recently, it hadn't taken Nathalie long to realize that Robert and Carol weren't meant to be. They hardly talked to each other and rarely touched. That wasn't how people in love acted. When Nathalie had met Andrew, they couldn't take their hands off each other and had talked nonstop into the night.

With a quick sidelong glance at Robert's favorite table, Nathalie found him doing the same thing as every other day at lunchtime—sitting alone and reading a newspaper because he had no one to talk to.

Poor guy. He was like that ostracized kid who sat alone in the school cafeteria.

Both he and Carol were miserable, but lately so were Nathalie and Andrew. They weren't enjoying the marital bliss everyone thought they were. Things between them were strained and getting worse by the day.

It was tough to maintain a loving relationship without a smidgen of intimacy.

Andrew was so terrified of succumbing to his urges and biting her, that he wouldn't even hold her hand. As soon as he was back from work, he would go on a drinking binge, pass out on the bed in the spare bedroom, and not wake up until the next morning. The only way she could even talk to him was calling him at work.

It wasn't anyone's fault, but it sucked.

"He had a wonderful idea," Carol said.

Confused, Nathalie tried to remember what she and Carol had been talking about. "Who?"

Carol looked at her with pity in her eyes. "Anandur... Is that what pregnancy does to a woman? The bigger your belly grows, the more absentminded you get?"

There was something to it.

The child inside her was getting more and more active, letting Nathalie know she was there by kicking around with her tiny feet or maybe punching with her tiny fists. It was distracting, but in the best possible way.

With a smile, Nathalie rubbed a hand over the side of her belly. She'd just felt a little bump. Moments like that reminded her that having her child was worth all of the sacrifices she and Andrew were making. Besides, it wasn't going to last forever. Only nine more weeks to go.

They would survive.

"Why are you smiling like that?" Carol looked into her eyes as if checking for dilated pupils.

"I think I'm high on pregnancy hormones."

"Are you? Is that how it works? Makes sense. Otherwise why would women subject themselves to that?" Carol pointed at Nathalie's stomach. "And then that." She crouched a little and grimaced in mock pain.

Nathalie chuckled. "I guess you're not in a hurry to become a mommy."

The expression of horror on Carol's face was hilarious. "No, no, and no." She shook her head, her blond curls bouncing from side to side around her face. "Not this girl, not ever."

Nathalie backed into the stool she kept behind the counter and took a load off. Carrying an extra thirty pounds was taking a toll on her legs and her back. "So what was Anandur's idea?"

"Oh, well. He asked about the dish of the day, and I told him spaghetti. And then he asked why not the fancy stuff I used to make at the beginning, and I told him that figuring the right quantities was over my head and that it was too much work. And then he said I should intern with Gerard in his restaurant. I've never been to By Invitation Only, but I heard it's the best."

Sheesh, when Carol was on a roll, she was on a roll. The entire speech was delivered in such a rush that Nathalie had to replay it in her head to get what Carol had been trying to say.

Apparently, pregnancy was also slowing her brain.

"I think it's a wonderful idea. But who is going to fill your place? I can't manage all by myself."

"Onidu. Anandur said he has nothing to do while Amanda is at work."

Hmm, interesting idea.

Now that she knew the "butlers" were a sort of super-duper advanced robot, Nathalie had less of a problem with asking them to do things for her. Syssi was loaning her Okidu to help out with cleaning her apartment. Nathalie even let him do the laundry. Mainly because she had no choice. Running the café was using up all of her energy. At the end of the day, all she wanted to do was to put her feet up and vegetate on the couch.

"Are you going to talk to Amanda about it?"

Carol shook her head. "I asked Anandur to do it. She intimidates the hell out of me."

"Why?" Amanda's beauty was off-putting to most women, but Carol was gorgeous in her own way. In fact, as impossible as it seemed, she was sexier than Amanda. Her beauty was softer and more feminine.

Carol straightened her apron, brushing off invisible crumbs. "I'm a simple kind of girl, a pleb, while she's Annani's daughter, a princess, and a big shot professor."

"I hear you. But she's nice, not stuck-up at all."

"Whatever. I'm glad Anandur agreed to ask her for me. I still have to talk to Kian about interning with Gerard, and I'm trying to summon up courage for that."

Nathalie patted her shoulder. "You can do it. You're the toughest woman I've ever met, and everyone respects the hell out of you. No one is going to refuse you anything."

That seemed to boost Carol's confidence. "You know what? You're right. I'm not above using their misplaced feelings of guilt to my advantage."

"Can someone make me a cappuccino or should I come back later?" Ingrid smiled at them from the other side of the counter.

"I've got it." Carol patted Nathalie's arm. "You just sit and rest for a little bit."

"Thanks." Nathalie leaned her back against the counter, trying to get comfortable, when her phone vibrated in her apron's pocket.

With an effort, she reached around her belly and pulled it out. "Hey, Jackson, what's up?" Hopefully nothing, because she didn't have the energy to deal with a single thing.

"We had a strange visitor in here, and I thought you'd want to know about it."

"Strange how?"

"An old lady came in, asking about Fernando and you. She said she used to be a customer before moving to Florida."

"What's her name?"

"Hilda."

"I remember a Hilda. She moved to a retirement home in Florida over a decade ago. Why do you think she's strange? She's just an old lady."

There was a quiet moment before Jackson answered. "She looks like an old lady, and she sounds like an old lady, she even acts like an old lady, but she doesn't smell like one. She smells like a young woman and a lot of latex."

"A disguise?"

"Yes. Professionally done. If I weren't who I am, I would've never noticed a thing. And she has the act down to perfection. Meryl Streep has nothing on her."

There were quite a few movie studios in Glendale, so it might have been an actress testing out her costume and her acting skill on unsuspecting coffee shop patrons.

"This is Los Angeles, Jackson. She is probably an actress."

"Who knew to ask about you and Fernando by name? And who pulled out an old customer's name that you actually recognized?"

He was right, a random actress wouldn't have known that, and Nathalie didn't remember having any regulars from the nearby studios.

Who could it be?

Her next guess was so preposterous that Nathalie berated herself for even thinking it. Her mother wouldn't just show up out of the blue, and although she used to dress older than she looked, Eva had never resorted to such elaborate costumes.

Besides, Nathalie would've recognized her own mother no matter what she was wearing, and Eva would've known that. A daughter would know her mother's voice, her syntax, her mannerism, and no actress was good enough to hide all of it.

Eva couldn't have known that Nathalie wouldn't be there when she showed up, and if she'd gone to such length to hide her identity, she wouldn't have risked it.

But what other explanation could there be?

"Is she still there?"

"No, she left but said that she might be back later. She even asked to see the dinner menu. I have a feeling she was hoping I'd call you, and that you would come."

Did she dare hope?

"I'll be there."

"I thought you would."

Nathalie's first instinct was to call Andrew and have him come pick her up, but then she reconsidered. Bhathian should be the one to accompany her.

God, she would hate to get his hopes up for nothing. Again. But going without him was out of the question.

Taking a deep breath, she dialed his number.

He picked up immediately. "Nathalie, is everything all right?"

She rolled her eyes. "I'm fine, Bhathian. Can you take a break and drive me to my old place?" Hopefully, he wasn't teaching a class.

"Sure. When?"

"As soon as you can. Right now would be good."

"What happened, did Jackson mess up?"

"No, everything at the coffee shop is fine too. I'll tell you on the way."

"Give me ten minutes to wrap things up."

"Okay."

She clicked off and put the phone on the counter, then turned to Carol. "I hate to leave you alone here, but I need to go to my old place for a couple of hours."

Carol waved a hand. "Don't worry about it. Worst case scenario I'll put up the 'we're closed' sign and get rid of everyone." She winked.

Not funny. Knowing Carol she would do it without batting an eyelid.

Nathalie took her apron off and bent down to get her purse from the bottom drawer under the counter. Damn it. It had been difficult enough on the way down, but straightening up on her own was impossible.

"Here, let me give you a hand." Carol came to her rescue.

"Thanks."

Nathalie pulled out a compact mirror and a foldable brush from her purse. While working, she always kept her hair in a tight braid so it wouldn't absorb the smells, but she wanted to look her best in case she was really about to see her mother, and having her hair free of the braid and brushed was all she could do. Makeup didn't really do much for her, and all of her maternity clothes were functional and comfortable but not flattering.

Nathalie snorted. As if anything could make her look good with the huge belly walking a few feet ahead of her. She needed a wheelbarrow to carry that thing.

Brushing out her hair wasn't going to improve her appearance by much, but Nathalie was anxious, and it gave her something to do while waiting for Bhathian.

Shit, he might be pissed that she hadn't told him to change. Coming straight from class, he was probably wearing his nylon training pants and T-shirt. Not the impression he would want to make on Eva after not seeing her for more than thirty years.

When she saw him coming out of the elevator, Nathalie realized her worries had been uncalled for. Bhathian was impressive no matter what he was wearing. With his height and his muscles and that chiseled jaw, he was every woman's dream. And those gray eyes... Eva would find him just as irresistible as she had that first time.

Nathalie shook her head.

That old woman hadn't been her mother. Maybe Jackson's sense of smell had gone haywire. Maybe he'd smelled someone else that had been standing next to the very real Hilda.

Heck, if it were really Hilda, Nathalie should take Fernando with her, not Bhathian.

Eva

Across the street, from behind the used books storefront window, Eva watched Fernando's café, listening in through an earpiece. Her bat hearing had its limits. Two closed doors with a wide street in between them was too much even for her. But that was what technology was good for.

She'd left behind a small listening device, gluing it to the front counter's underside with a piece of gum. The dinner menu Jackson had handed her was the perfect size to hide what she'd been doing under it, while her body was blocking the view from behind.

No one had seen anything.

The bookstore's owner was getting annoyed with her for sitting in the only chair and pretending to read for the past hour, but she knew he wouldn't dare say anything.

That was the beauty of her disguise.

Telling an old woman to beat it would've been rude. Besides, no one wondered about her earpiece.

Eva was excited. She had no doubt that the boy had called either Fernando or Nathalie. Most likely Nathalie since Fernando was incapable of driving in his condition. She'd seen Jackson duck into the kitchen the moment the door had closed behind her, but even though she'd put on the earpiece as soon as she'd exited the café, she hadn't heard him make the call. He must've gone out the back to make it.

A shame, she was curious about what he'd said.

How he'd known something was off about her still mystified Eva. Maybe it was in the same way that she'd known there was something different about him. Perhaps one misfit could sniff out another.

A car stopped and then eased into a parking spot a few doors down from the café. The driver got out—a tall and muscular guy with a military buzz cut. Hurrying to the other side, he moved with surprising fluidity for such a big man.

There was something familiar about him, but his face was turned around, and all she could see was his impressive back.

Yum.

Eva's hands practically itched with the need to run up and down that muscular back...

Enough!

She wasn't on an official assignment, but she wasn't sitting in a club and looking for a hookup either. A pity, though. And she couldn't blame her shameful wantonness either. Any woman would have wanted her hands on that.

Eva sighed.

The difference between her and most other women was that they would just drool and daydream, while Eva would have no problem getting him to go with her. When a woman had lived as long as she did and was reasonably attractive, she knew that men were simple creatures and not much was needed to lure them.

Not in her current getup, though. The only way a guy like that would touch an old lady was to help her cross the street.

Waiting impatiently to see if the face was as handsome as the rest of him, she was disappointed when he bent low to open the passenger door and helped a woman out.

A very pregnant woman...

"Oh my God!" She gasped, sudden tears flowing in rivulets down her latex cheeks and making a mess of her careful makeup.

"What's wrong, ma'am?" asked a worried teenager crouching beside her. "Can I help you? Do you need me to call a doctor or something?"

She patted his head while pulling a large handkerchief from her satchel and holding it in front of her face. "Thank you, young man. But I'm okay. It was just such a sad story." She pointed to the book lying face down in her lap.

His expression relaxed and he smiled. "You're sure you're okay?"

"Yes, yes. Off you go." She shooed him away. "Let an old woman enjoy her romance novel."

"You scared the crap out of me, lady," he said and walked away.

Thank God.

But not soon enough.

Her Nathalie and the young man who'd helped her out of the car had already entered the café, and Eva had missed her chance to see his face.

Was that Nathalie's husband?

Guilt assailed her for thinking lustful thoughts about her daughter's man. One thing was apparent, though. She and Nathalie had similar tastes in men.

"Hi, Gordon, where is Jackson?" Eva heard Nathalie's voice through the earpiece.

More tears came gushing out.

"On a supermarket run. He should be back in a few moments," the guy named Gordon answered.

"We'll wait for him upstairs."

"I'm sorry that we don't have a table available for you."

"Don't be. Business is good."

Her sweet, smart Nathalie. She'd always had a good head on her shoulders.

"Do you want me to bring you something?"

"No, thank you. I'll just grab a couple of bottles of Pellegrino on the way."

Eva braced her hands against the chair's armrests and pushed herself up, then lifted the handkerchief to her face.

"Do you have a restroom here I can use?" she asked the owner.

He grimaced and snatched a key from under the counter. "Follow me." He led her to the back and unlocked the bathroom door. "Here you go, ma'am."

"Thank you." *What a nice guy.*

Eva locked the door behind her and lowered the toilet lid to put her satchel on top of it. Pulling out several jars of makeup, she lined them up on the small vanity and started fixing the damage she'd done.

With Nathalie and her husband gone from the vicinity of the listening device, Eva had no more use for the earpiece and removed it. She wondered why Nathalie's husband hadn't said a word, not even hello.

It wasn't as if she had a problem with that, Eva liked the quiet types. Men who kept on jabbering annoyed her—like Fernando before the dementia. The man had been spending entire days on his feet, working from before sunrise to sunset, and still had had the energy to talk nonstop with his customers.

They'd loved him for it. Eva couldn't stand it.

But then hearing one's husband flirt with other women could have had something to do with it. He hadn't known she'd been aware of his whispered endearments and the responses they had garnered. For Fernando's and Nathalie's safety, Eva's strange abilities had to remain hidden from everyone, including her husband and daughter.

Pretending to be clueless about Fernando's extramarital activities must've been the best performance of her life.

With a sigh, Eva examined her work from several angles. The disguise was once again flawless, but would it fool her own daughter?

It should.

More than a decade had passed since Nathalie had seen old Hilda, and Eva had done a good job of reconstructing the woman's appearance from memory. Height was the only thing Eva couldn't disguise, but that was why she'd chosen Hilda. They were both about five foot seven inches tall. Hilda might have been a little taller, but she had a hunched back.

Aside from her amber-colored eyes, nothing of Eva's own face was recognizable, and she had a solution for that as well—tinted contact lenses. They irritated her eyes, but she had to put them in. If she wanted to see her daughter up close, there was no other way. Dark sunglasses didn't go with the old lady costume, and certainly not indoors.

As to her voice, she could rasp. Hilda had been a heavy smoker.

Bhathian

"I'm going downstairs to check on the table situation." Bhathian pushed off the couch. The waiting was killing him. The old woman Jackson had described probably wasn't Eva in disguise, but on the remote chance that she was, Bhathian wanted to see her as soon as she came in.

If she ever came back. She'd told Jackson that she might. But that had probably been just polite talk.

Nathalie lifted her feet and put them on the ottoman Jackson had added to the room's furnishings. "We've been here less than five minutes."

Bhathian glanced at his watch. It seemed longer. "It wouldn't hurt to check."

"Fine. But don't scare the customers away with your scowl."

That was exactly what he was planning to do. If there was no table available, he was going to stand there and glower until there was.

Jackson met him on the staircase. "I was just coming up to call you guys. Gordon has a booth for you."

"Good." Bhathian reversed course and went back to what used to be Nathalie's den and was now Jackson's bedroom.

He offered her a hand up. "Come on. We have a booth."

She let him pull her to her feet and groaned. "I feel like a beached whale. I can't even tie my shoes anymore."

Bhathian patted her shoulder. "Just a little bit longer." He wasn't good at that father thing, or giving support, and not for lack of trying. Fernando, even in his current diminished mental state, was doing a better job, constantly giving Nathalie compliments on how glowing she looked, and how proud he was of her. The guy was a natural. Or maybe he just benefited from years of practice doing the father gig.

The booth Gordon was saving for them was the last one in the back of the coffee shop, but it was next to the front window. Bhathian could watch the street for anyone approaching the café's front door.

"What can I get you?" Gordon asked.

"Coffee," Bhathian said without taking his eyes off the street.

"For me too. And a glass of water," Nathalie told the boy.

"Are you going to keep staring out the window the entire time we are here?"

"Yes."

Nathalie chuckled. "In that case, I'm going to entertain myself by reading a book on my phone."

"Go ahead." He waved a hand.

It was good that Nathalie was taking the whole thing so calmly, but he couldn't understand why. How come she wasn't excited, or anxious?

Maybe because she didn't believe it had been her mother either.

It didn't make any sense for Eva to suddenly show up one day after so many years. The woman was so paranoid her picture should've been next to the dictionary definition of the word.

Bhathian watched an old woman slowly cross the street. Cars coming from both directions stopped, waiting patiently for her to pass at the snail pace she was progressing. The poor woman was carrying a large canvas handbag, and her feet were so swollen that they were overflowing her worn-out shoes. Her uneven gait implied achy joints.

Humans had it so rough. Even if they managed to live to an old age, they weren't enjoying it.

Finally, after long minutes had passed, the woman made it to the other side. Taking a breather as if she'd just finished a long journey, she glanced at the coffee shop with a pair of sharp eyes.

For some reason, Bhathian's heart sped up as he watched that focused gaze scan the faces of those sitting in the booths next to the window.

When she reached him, her hand flew to her chest, and he knew it was her.

This was his Patricia, his Eva.

He prayed that was indeed an elaborate costume and not the actual state she was in. Because if what he was seeing was real, she only had a few years left in her.

He saw hesitation in her eyes and was about to get up and give chase in case she decided to bolt, but then she nodded as if reaching a decision and approached the front door.

"She is here." He slid over on the bench and got up.

Nathalie bent sideways and turned to look behind her. "The old lady?"

"It's her." He didn't wait to explain and strode toward the front, reaching the door in time to open it for Eva.

She gasped and staggered back. "You look just like him." Horror filled her eyes, and she braced against the doorframe. "Oh my God! Tell me you're not Nathalie's husband."

"Of course not. You know who I am." He'd wanted to say that he was Nathalie's father, but given that he looked younger than his daughter, the humans in the café who knew Nathalie would've thought he was nuts.

Eva closed her eyes and breathed out. "Thank God."

Bhathian reached for her hand. "Let me help you to our table. Nathalie is waiting."

She nodded and let him lead her, keeping up the pretense of an old woman needing assistance.

He leaned down and whispered in her ear. "You can stop pretending."

She lifted a pair of shocked eyes at him. "How do you know that? And how did you know who I was?"

"I'll explain everything later."

Nathalie was probably going crazy waiting. He was surprised she hadn't run up to them already. Maybe she was stuck in the booth, her belly trapping her in place.

He tugged on Eva's hand, forcing her to walk faster. When they reached the booth, Nathalie was still facing the back wall. She didn't turn to look at them.

He touched her shoulder. "Nathalie?"

She lifted a tear-stained face to look at him. "Is it her?"

Confused, he glanced at Eva, finding her huddling behind him. He tugged on her hand again, almost toppling her as he pushed her in front of him.

"It's me," Eva whispered and then broke into heart-wrenching sobs.

Damn, everyone was looking, and it was up to him to save the situation. Mother and daughter had just fallen apart.

Bhathian glanced back. "Jackson, I need you here."

The boy rushed over, immediately taking in the situation. "Come on, ladies. Let's continue the happy reunion upstairs."

He offered his hand to Nathalie and helped her up. "I know you haven't seen Aunt Hilda in ages, but that's no reason to cry, Nathalie." He led her along the center aisle, smiling at the gawking customers. "Women. They cry when happy, they cry when sad. I don't get it." He shook his head, getting a few understanding nods from his audience.

Bhathian followed behind with Eva, admiring the ease with which Jackson was manipulating the onlookers. The best Bhathian could've accomplished would've been to scare them off with a growl and tell them to mind their own business.

On the stairs, Eva dropped her act and climbed with ease, while poor Nathalie was huffing and puffing by the time she reached the landing.

"Here we go." Jackson helped her to the couch. "Sorry about the mess, ladies. I wasn't expecting guests." He grabbed a couple of pillows and a blanket, tossing them aside to the floor.

Eva sat beside Nathalie and took her hand in both of hers, then dropped it. "I'm wearing latex gloves. Are you allowed to touch latex when pregnant? I don't know. Some people are allergic. It wasn't an issue when I was pregnant with you." She was blabbering, but at least she'd stopped crying.

Nathalie grabbed her hand back. "It's fine. I'm not allergic." She chuckled. "If not for Bhathian, I wouldn't have recognized you. That's one hell of a disguise. You actually look like Hilda."

"How did you know it was a costume?" Eva's eyes shot to Bhathian. "How did you recognize me?"

"Because you almost fainted when you saw me in the window."

She nodded. "You look so much like your father, it's startling. You're even named after him. Right?"

"I don't know. Maybe. I never asked."

Eva tilted her head and regarded him with a puzzled look. "Your father's name is Bhathian. Isn't it?" She shook her head as if to clear it. "You brought me a letter from him. You left it at the orphanage in Rio. And you look exactly like he did thirty-one years ago."

It dawned on him then. Eva thought he was his son. Of course she would think that. She had no clue about what was going on.

"No, Eva. I'm Bhathian, the one and only original Bhathian you met thirty-one years ago, the one who fathered Nathalie. Just like you, I'm an immortal."

Eva opened her mouth to say something, then closed it and shook her head.

"I think some strong liquor is in order," said Jackson, who everyone had forgotten about.

"Yes, definitely, please," Eva said.

Eva

Was it a trap?

Eva took a sip from the drink Jackson had handed her, some fruity liqueur she didn't care for, and looked at the two guys sitting across from her on what looked like folding tray tables.

She searched their faces for signs of deception.

In her profession, she'd learned the telltale signs of lies and nefarious intentions, but these two were good. Their sincere, slightly concerned expressions looked genuine.

Were they expecting her to admit what she was so easily?

Would her own daughter participate in the attempt to deceive her?

Maybe they were threatening her with something and she had no choice?

That would explain her tears. But then Eva had cried too. How could she not? She hadn't expected to see her daughter ever again. Not face to face, anyway. She'd fantasized about watching Nathalie from afar often enough, at least once a day and sometimes more. But she'd kept reminding herself that the sacrifice was necessary to keep her child safe.

Had she ruined everything by coming here?

Eva narrowed her eyes at the man who called himself Bhathian. "I don't know what you're talking about."

He chuckled. "I understand your caution. You have no idea what's going on. But you're safe and you're not the only immortal out there. Jackson here is one too." He pointed at the young man who smiled and bowed his head. "Nathalie's husband was turned immortal a few months ago, and as soon as Nathalie delivers our grandchild, she will go through the transition herself."

Right. Next he would tell her that they were all aliens, and that she'd been kidnapped and infected with their alien germs. But she could humor his nonsense for a few more moments. "So what are you trying to tell me, that it's contagious and that I caught it from you when we... made Nathalie?" They were all adults here, and they had bigger issues than her hookup with Bhathian all those years ago. She wasn't sure about Jackson being an adult, but she had no doubt that he was old enough to know all there was to know about sex.

Bhathian shook his head. "No, it's not contagious, and you were already an immortal when we met. I didn't know you were, and apparently neither did you. Our lives would've been very different if we had." He sighed.

"How so?"

"When you told me you were pregnant, I couldn't do anything about it. We keep our existence secret and our relationships with humans down to brief encounters. I'm sure you can understand that. You have been running and hiding for so long for the same reason."

He looked at her, probably waiting for her to agree with his assessment, but Eva kept her expression neutral. Not that it was all that difficult with the mask she was wearing. The range of emotion she could express was limited by the latex.

Bhathian continued in a soft, wistful tone. "If I had known you were one of us, I would have never let you go. We could've been a family."

He was good, playing on her emotions like that.

"I'm still not sure what you're talking about."

She felt Nathalie's hand on her knee. "He is telling the truth, Mom." She looked at Bhathian. "You need to prove it to her."

"Yes, you're right. Why haven't I thought of it?" He smiled. "Fortunately, our daughter inherited your smarts."

Nice try.

Flattery wasn't going to work.

Bhathian bent down and pulled out a wicked-looking knife from an ankle holster.

Eva spread her arms, shielding Nathalie behind her. "I'm not as helpless as I look," she gritted.

He grinned. "I know you're not. Don't worry. I'm just going to make a little cut in the palm of my hand to show you how quickly I heal. This should convince you that I'm telling the truth because you've probably experienced the same rapid healing yourself."

Yes, she had.

"Okay. But no sudden movements, or I'm going to take you down."

His grin got even wider, and the gleam in his eyes looked suspiciously like arousal.

Bhathian moved in exaggerated slow motion. Extending his palm so she could see it, he brought the tip of the knife to rest against his skin and pressed down until blood welled. He didn't even twitch. The cut wasn't deep, but it must've hurt. Still going in slow motion, he lowered the knife and put it back in the holster while keeping his palm up for her inspection.

Now that the weapon was tucked away, she allowed herself a good look at the small wound. Just as he'd said it would, the cut was already closing. She pulled a tissue out of her satchel and handed it to him. If he healed as fast as she did, by the time he wiped off the blood there would be nothing left of the wound.

"Good as new." He presented his healed palm.

Eva sagged, letting the couch cushions absorb her weight, and covered her face with her hands. Now that she'd determined Bhathian had been telling the truth, she let herself power down, and the tears came back full force.

Nathalie patted her latex-covered hand. "Don't cry, Mom. Because if you start again, so will I." She sniffled.

Eva opened her arms. "I need a hug. I've been dreaming about one since the moment I left."

They embraced, not an easy feat given Nathalie's pregnant belly and Eva's padded body suit, and the tears flowed despite their best efforts.

After what seemed like a long time, Eva pulled back and wiped her latex-covered face with her sleeve.

"Ugh, gross." Nathalie recoiled. "Now that the makeup's rubbed off, I can see the mask."

"Sorry about that. I would've taken it off, but I still need to make an exit and get back to my hotel looking the same way I left. I'll fix it later."

"You're really good with that. It looked so real before you ruined it with the tears."

Eva chuckled. "Years of experience."

"Is that why you left? Because you weren't aging and didn't understand why?"

She nodded. "I thought I'd been part of some secret experiment without my knowledge. It started with the enhanced senses. My hearing and vision became so acute I was getting headaches. And the smells—I'm sure I can smell better than a dog. It was strange, but could still be explained away. For a while, I was afraid that a brain tumor was causing it, but I was too scared to have it checked because if that wasn't the case, the doctors might've thought I was crazy and locked me up. The aging thing didn't start bothering me until my mid-fifties. I thought I was just lucky. But I never got sick either. I don't know how I managed to go so many years without even a scratch, but when I finally accidentally cut my finger and put it in my mouth to dull the pain, when I pulled it out the finger was as good as new."

"You must've freaked out," Nathalie said.

"I did. I was convinced that I'd been experimented on and that my immortality was an unexpected side effect. Otherwise they, whoever they were, would not have let me get away. A mutation like that would've been researched, experimented on. I lived in constant fear of discovery."

"That's why you ran?"

"I had to. I hid it as long as I could, but eventually people were bound to find out. And once they got me, I knew that they would come after my child." She looked at Nathalie. "I did what I thought was the best thing for you. As long as I was gone, you were safe."

"No one is after you, Eva," Bhathian said.

"But what if someone discovers I'm immortal?"

"I didn't say you don't need to hide who you are. Just that right now no one knows about you and no one is after you. It wasn't some weird government experiment that turned you. It had been done by an immortal male you must've met in your youth."

"What?" That made even less sense than her experiment scenario.

Bhathian smoothed his hand over his cropped hair and sighed. "I'll try to explain as best I can, but I'm not the right guy for that."

"Just tell me in your own words."

"You'd better start at the beginning," Nathalie said. "It's so damn confusing when you guys tell it one a piece at a time."

"Okay. So you know about the gods from mythology?"

Eva nodded.

"They were real. And just as it says in your Bible, they had to mate with humans because there weren't enough of them. The gene pool was too limited. The children that were born were not as powerful as the gods but they were still near-immortal."

"Wait, so we are not immortal? We can still die?"

"We can be killed. It's just harder to do than with humans. The second generation after that, the product of near-immortals and humans, were born with no powers at all. But the females carried the genetic code and could transfer it to future generations of females."

"What about the males?"

"A male born to a dormant female, that's what we call those who carry the dormant genes, is a carrier and can be turned. But he can't transfer it to his children. So any child I would've conceived with a human woman would not have been a Dormant and couldn't have been turned into an immortal."

This was so over her head, it wasn't even funny. She would need days to process it. Some basic information was still missing from Bhathian's story.

"How is a Dormant turned? If I understand what you're trying to explain, I was a Dormant who somehow got activated by another immortal."

"Exactly. The males of our species have venom glands and fangs. The venom facilitates the transition."

"Fangs?"

Bhathian opened his mouth and pointed at his canines. They looked longer and sharper than normal but they weren't fangs.

She chuckled. "You're not a very convincing vampire."

He looked offended. "They elongate during fights and during sex."

He was really asking for it. "What about sex after a fight?"

"What about it?"

She couldn't help herself and snorted. "Do they get even longer?"

His smile turned predatory. "I don't know. But I'm willing to give it a try."

Damn it, the man was too sexy for his own good and was making her tingle in all kinds of places.

Jackson cleared his throat. "People, please, get a room."

Nathalie giggled, and Bhathian's smile got broader. This time the fangs were unmistakable. They must've elongated in response to their little sexual banter.

Hot. The tingling had gotten way worse.

Jackson pushed up to his feet and walked over to Nathalie. "How about we give your parents a little privacy? Let me get you a cup of coffee." He offered her a hand up.

"Stay," Eva commanded. No way were they leaving her alone with Bhathian. "I need to hear the rest of the story."

Jackson looked at Nathalie and she shrugged. "They will have plenty of time to catch up later."

"As you wish. But I'm out of here."

Eva frowned. "What's his problem?"

Bhathian's fangs seemed to have grown even longer. "You're an immortal female, Eva, and he is a young immortal male. I'm sure you get the picture."

"He's a baby! And I didn't even look at him! And look at me! Do I look like someone a boy his age would fancy?" She looked like Jackson's great-grandmother.

Bhathian looked uncomfortable. "Nathalie, would you give us five minutes? I feel really awkward talking about things like that in front of you."

"I'm a grown woman, and I will not freak out because my parents are talking about sex. But whatever. I'll give you a few minutes. Help me up?"

He did. "Thank you."

"No problem." She left the room, her heavy footsteps rattling the wooden staircase.

"I didn't want to embarrass you in front of our daughter. But you need to know a few things about us. About yourself."

"I'm listening."

"We all have an exceptional sense of smell. You've gotten a little aroused when I showed you my fangs."

Eva rolled her eyes. Hell would freeze over before she admitted that. "Pfft, please..."

"It's nothing to be embarrassed about. You're an immortal female, and your body craves my bite. It's just chemistry."

She crossed her arms under her fake boobs. "I want no such thing."

"I could smell your arousal and so could Jackson. He couldn't help his response, so he hoofed it out of here."

Embarrassing didn't start to cover it. But Eva wasn't some blushing virgin. "So any time a female immortal feels horny all the males around her go wild?"

"If she is unattached and not related to them, then yes."

"How would you know if I was attached or not?"

"If you were attached to a human, I wouldn't. But if it were another immortal male, your scent would've alerted me to the fact."

"Fascinating."

He nodded.

"Can I come in?" Nathalie knocked on the doorframe.

"Yes, dear. Bhathian just finished explaining about the birds and the bees immortal-style."

"Good, I'm glad that's out of the way. We need to decide what to do next, though. I vote for you to come stay with us at the keep. Get to know the rest of the clan."

"There is a clan?"

"Yes. But first I need to call the boss and ask permission. Would you excuse me for a moment?" He pulled out his phone and walked outside.

"If you want to talk privately, you'll need to get out of the building," she called after him.

"I know."

Eva patted her mask and grimaced. She probably looked horrible. "I'd better go fix that."

"The bathroom is that way." Nathalie pointed in the same direction Bhathian had gone.

"I changed my mind. I'd better wait for Bhathian to come back or he'll think I want to eavesdrop."

"I wouldn't," he said as he entered. "We have a green light."

Eva lifted her satchel. "I don't want this to be the first impression I make." She waved a hand over her getup. "I need to go back to my hotel room and change."

"We can drop you off and wait in the car."

No way. She didn't want Bhathian to know where she was staying. "It will take a long time. You can give me the address, and I'll drive myself, or you can wait for me here."

"We'll wait for you here."

"I'll try to be quick about it." Eva gave Nathalie a hug because she couldn't leave without one.

Driving back to her hotel, Eva thought back to that one night with Bhathian. For years she'd been trying to reconcile everything that didn't make sense about it, wondering if her memory was faulty. His night vision, his glowing eyes, the insane attraction, the incredible stamina...

She'd always enjoyed sex, but no man had ever satisfied her like Bhathian.

Bhathian

As he waited for Eva to come back, Bhathian thought about the way Kian, the usually overcautious regent, had welcomed her wholeheartedly without even conditioning her arrival at the keep on a blindfold. As an immortal, and as Nathalie's mother, he deemed her safe. Eva, on the other hand, remained suspicious. A lifetime of hiding and keeping secrets had taken its toll. It would take a lot of time and effort before she could trust anyone.

"I wonder if she's changed at all," Nathalie said.

"Probably not much since you last saw her. But then you said that she always wore heavy makeup to make herself look older. She might look much younger than how you remember her."

Nathalie snorted. "She might look younger than me. That would be so weird."

"It's possible." Bhathian couldn't wait to see Eva without the disguise.

He still remembered her vividly. A bombshell—so sexy that one look was enough to knock a guy off his feet—a natural born seductress. The thing was, none of it had been manufactured, or even conscious. Eva had been quite naive for a forty-something-year-old woman. Back then, she hadn't been as guarded and suspicious as she was now. Though as an undercover DEA agent she must've seen the ugly and dirty part of humanity.

Of course, he hadn't known she was with the DEA when he'd first seen her on the plane. To him, the woman who'd called herself Patricia had been a flight attendant who'd flirted with him and whom he'd later seduced on the dance floor of a bar.

Holding her in his arms as they'd slow danced, Bhathian had wanted her with such an intensity that he'd had the fleeting crazy notion of taking her right then and there and thralling everyone in the busy bar to forget it. He'd barely held on until they had gotten to her hotel room.

She'd blown his mind.

He should've known that no human could have kept up with him all night as she had. And her resistance to thralling should've been the clincher. And yet he'd let her go because he was a dense dumbass who hadn't put those clues together.

Life had never been the same since.

Everyone wondered why he wore a permanent frown, or why he smiled so rarely. He hadn't admitted it to anyone, including himself, but he'd been living with a big yawning hole in his heart and a persistent ache in his gut. He'd known something was missing, but he'd refused to acknowledge that he'd been longing for a human woman he'd met twice and had sex with once.

The Fates had brought him a gift, and he'd been too blind to see it. Two immortals making a baby on their first try was unheard of.

Ever.

He'd never been a big believer in a higher power. When he invoked the Fates it was just as a figure of speech. But there was no way to regard Nathalie's conception as anything but fated.

After more than an hour had passed, Bhathian started to get anxious. What if she wasn't coming back?

It would be just like Eva to disappear again.

Could she be that cruel? He could understand if she hadn't wanted anything to do with him, but what about Nathalie?

She would be devastated if her mother pulled the same stunt again.

"I'm going to wait for her outside," he told Nathalie.

She cast him a pitying look. "Okay. Text me when she gets here, and I'll come down."

Bhathian nodded.

It was good to be outside and breathe fresh air as he strode up and down the street, giving an outlet to the nervous energy buzzing not only in his brain but his entire body.

His heart skipped a beat when he saw Eva's rental car slowing down. Seeing her come back made him dizzy with relief.

He was there the moment Eva eased into a parking spot and cut the engine. Wrenching the driver side door open, he almost tore it off the hinges, and as he bent to offer Eva a hand up, the buzzing in his head became deafening.

"Easy there." She regarded him with a wary look in her amber eyes as she placed her hand in his, sending an electrical current from his fingers down to his toes.

Gently, he pulled her up, his body quaking with the need to bring her flesh against him. It took an iron will to step back and give Eva some space.

She was even more beautiful than he remembered. Hair the same dark mahogany shade as Nathalie's cascaded in waves and big curls around her shoulders and down her back. And her lips... her skin... her everything... He couldn't verbalize what his eyes were seeing adequately to do her justice.

"Take a breath, Bhathian." She clapped him on the shoulder, leaving him rooted to the spot.

It took him a moment to shake himself and follow Eva to the café. She moved with the fluidity of an immortal female, but for some reason hers seemed more predatory, more confident. She gave off a dangerous vibe.

He had a feeling Eva wasn't a woman to mess with.

Before, when she'd told him she would bring him down if he dared do anything with the knife, he'd humored her, scoffing at what he'd considered an empty threat. Now he wasn't so sure.

Damn, he'd forgotten to text Nathalie.

It was probably too late for that. He rushed to catch up and open the door for Eva, earning an indulgent smile for his effort.

Indulgent, mocking, amused; he'd take any smile she threw his way.

"Wow!" Jackson took a step back. "That's one hell of a transformation."

"Careful there," Bhathian growled. If the boy was sporting a hard-on, he was going to punch him in his pretty face.

Jackson lifted his hands in the air. "Just saying, man. No disrespect."

"You look amazing." Nathalie waddled toward them from the kitchen. "Mo... my, oh my, you're a knockout." She swallowed the "Mom" at the last moment.

The humans sitting in the café weren't the same ones from before. Nevertheless, Bhathian didn't want any more unintended slip-ups. It was time to take this show on the road. "Let's go, ladies." He opened the door.

"Are we taking your car or mine?" Eva asked.

"We'll take mine, and I'll drive you back here once we're done." He was looking forward to having some time alone with her, but it was doubtful she'd agree to meet him without the buffer of company. He would have to be sneaky about snatching moments with Eva and getting her used to the idea that this time he wasn't going anywhere.

Nathalie

"Are all these people here for me?"

Eva's step faltered as they crossed the security checkpoint and stepped behind the thick bulletproof glass that separated the front of the lobby from the clan's private area in the back. The executive lounge, as Kian called it for the sake of those who wondered why the place wasn't open to the public.

A partition made from greenery hid the café from view, but it did nothing to block the murmur of excited voices.

Kian must've told everyone in the keep about Eva's arrival because it sounded like there was a crowd waiting for them. On second thought, he'd probably told Syssi, who'd told Amanda, who'd told Dalhu, who'd told Anandur, which was as good as putting it on the evening news.

Nathalie clasped her mother's hand. "Don't be mad. Everyone knows we were searching for you. They are happy for us and curious to see you."

Eva stopped and turned to Bhathian. "Does that mean that there will be a stampede of immortal males sniffing me out like a bunch of hounds?"

Nathalie giggled. The visual Eva's remark painted was just too funny.

Bhathian's body seemed to swell in aggression, and he wrapped his arm around Eva. "They'll have to go through me first."

Before he'd spoken, Eva had seemed unhappy about his display of affection, but what he'd said must've changed her mind. It was quite obvious she wasn't interested in rekindling things with Bhathian, but he was useful for fending off other potential suitors, whom Nathalie had no doubt would've been many.

Eva was the first unattached immortal female these males weren't related to. And she was gorgeous. A stampede was entirely possible.

As they cleared the partition, Kian was the first to approach, the others staying behind out of respect for their regent.

"Welcome to our clan, Eva." He offered his hand, and she shook it.

"Thank you," was all she said as she pulled her hand away.

Nathalie would have whispered in her ear that she had nothing to worry about with Kian, he was as taken as a guy could be, but it would've been futile to whisper given the bat ears of their audience.

Thankfully, Syssi stepped forward. "Hi, I'm Syssi." She offered her hand.

Kian smiled brightly and wrapped his arm around his wife's slim waist, pulling her close. "My better half."

Eva's shoulders relaxed, and she shook Syssi's hand. "Nice to meet you. Nathalie and Bhathian didn't have time to tell me anything yet, so I don't know who is who, but I'm sure you'll fill me in."

Next was Amanda, who gave Eva a very obvious once-over and then nodded her approval. "Now I see who Nathalie gets her good looks from because it's certainly not from him." She pointed at Bhathian.

Eva stiffened again.

"It's okay, Mom. They all know Bhathian is my biological father, but no one talks about it in front of Fernando. Papi is happily clueless."

Apparently, though, that wasn't what got Eva's hackles up.

With her four-inch heels, Eva was at eye level with Amanda who was wearing flats, and she hit her with a hard stare. "Thank you for the compliment, but you're wrong. I see a lot of Bhathian's beauty in Nathalie—a feminine version of it, naturally."

Amanda grinned like she'd just proven a point and offered her hand. "I'm Amanda, Kian's sister."

Eva took the hand she'd been offered and was immediately pulled into a bone-crushing hug. "You're family now. Handshakes are for strangers," Amanda said.

During the entire exchange, Bhathian had been doing a great impression of a statue. He hadn't even twitched. Like a sentry, he stood by Eva's side until the procession of welcomers ended.

"Thank God," Eva said as she plopped down into a chair. "My cheeks hurt from smiling. Not to mention my feet." She kicked off her shoes.

Amanda snickered. "I know, right? Heels make your legs and butt look great, but kill your feet. Anyhoo, I have to bid you goodbye. Hope to see you here often." She bent down and kissed Eva's cheek.

"It was nice to meet you, Amanda," Eva said and sounded like she meant it.

Amanda took some getting used to. Her over-the-top personality was off-putting at first, but once people got over that as well as her stunning looks, they discovered she was fun and kind and not stuck up at all.

Kian and Syssi joined them.

"What do you think of your daughter's new business?" Syssi waved a hand over the café.

Eva turned to Nathalie. "This is yours?"

"Theoretically. Kian put up the money for it, and I'm paying him back in installments."

Kian crossed his arms over his chest. "It's hers. Nathalie is just stubborn. I told her she doesn't need to pay anything, but she insists."

Eva swallowed, and the corner of her lip started twitching. Nathalie still remembered the signs heralding tears. Her mom was getting emotional.

"Thank you for welcoming my daughter and including her in your family. I'm so grateful to you all. My biggest fear was that Nathalie would be alone. Fernando and I had no other family. He got sick and I had to leave. There was no one she could turn to for help."

Syssi leaned over and patted Eva's hand. "I'm so glad Bhathian found her. I couldn't have hoped for a better sister-in-law. Nathalie is awesome."

Eva's eyes peeled wide. "You're Andrew's sister? But where is Andrew?" She turned to Nathalie. "Is he scared of meeting his mother-in-law?"

Nathalie was waiting for that to come up; luckily it wasn't six yet and Andrew was still at work, so she didn't have to invent excuses. "He is not back from work yet."

"Is he still working for the government?"

"Yes. He is an analyst in the anti-terrorism department."

"I understand that he was the one who found me."

"With some help from his friends. You were very difficult to track."

Eva leaned back in her chair. "And to think that I've spent all this time running and hiding for nothing."

"Not for nothing. Hiding what you are is of crucial importance," Kian said.

She nodded. "What I still don't get, among many other things, is how did you know about me? I mean about the immortality."

Nathalie shifted in her chair, trying to get into a more comfortable position, which was a futile endeavor. "It's a long story. Andrew has access to information most people don't. Bhathian asked him to do what he could to locate you. A friend of Andrew's who is a forensic artist drew your portrait from what Bhathian remembered about you. So when Andrew started digging and saw the picture I'd given the police after you'd disappeared, he immediately noticed that you haven't aged at all."

"Is that how Bhathian found you?"

"Yes, and he brought Andrew along for courage. That's how we met."

"Well, at least some good came out of it."

Bhathian frowned. "That's not the only good thing. Aren't you glad we found you? If not for my letter, you'd still be hiding and missing your daughter like crazy."

"You're right. I just need a day or two to absorb all of this. It's so overwhelming, and I still have so many questions, but Nathalie looks like she is in pain. Sitting here is not doing her any good." She looked at Nathalie with compassion. "You need to lie down and rest, sweetie."

She did, but she wasn't ready to let go. "I don't want you to leave. I've missed you so much and now that you're back I don't want you out of my sight."

Eva lifted Nathalie's hand and kissed it. "I'm not leaving yet. I'll come back tomorrow. I promise."

"In the morning?"

"How early do you want me?"

"Can you come at eight-thirty?"

"I'll be here. What should I tell security?"

"Don't worry about it." Kian waved a hand. "You're already on file as a guest. The facial recognition software will green-light you without you having to say a word."

Eva grimaced. "Like that's supposed to make me feel better. It's exactly the kind of thing I try to avoid, which is getting increasingly difficult with today's interconnected world. There is no more privacy to be had."

Syssi sighed dramatically. "Google knows who you are and where to find you. That's spooky. Like a big brother watching."

Kian seemed to be bothered by the exchange. "Everything we do here in the keep is encrypted and redirected. We have better cyber security than the Pentagon. You have nothing to worry about."

Eva lifted a brow. "What about hackers?"

"None are good enough."

She crossed her arms over her chest and smiled. "You want to bet? How much are you willing to lose?"

"Bring it on. No one can break through our security."

"Five bucks if my guy can penetrate your systems."

"You've got yourself a bet."

Eva

"I'm curious. How come you know a hacker?" Bhathian asked a few minutes into the drive.

They were alone for the first time since Eva's arrival, and it felt awkward as heck. The man was just as irresistible as she remembered him, but she had to remain strong. Under no circumstances was she going to succumb to his overwhelming masculinity and invite him to her hotel room.

She'd made that mistake before and had gotten burned.

The thing was, her traitorous body had ideas of its own, and to keep it in check, she forced herself to go over a list of recent cases in her head. In detail.

That tidbit of information about Bhathian's ability to scent her arousal was a strong deterrent to any naughty thoughts that might have crossed her mind.

"I have a detective agency. Nick is an employee."

Bhathian cast her a sidelong glance. "So you went back to your old occupation, but as an independent contractor?"

Obviously, if Nathalie's husband had found Eva's records, he'd also found out she hadn't been a real flight attendant.

"Not exactly. I'm not chasing drug smugglers, just unfaithful spouses and clandestine corporate maneuvers."

He nodded. "I'm glad you're not doing anything dangerous. Is there good money in what you do?"

Eva stifled a snort. Her day job wasn't particularly risky, but her after-hours hobby certainly was. Maybe not as much as she'd previously feared because apparently her miraculous healing worked on more serious injuries than accidental cuts and bruises. She hadn't known that it could handle bullet and deep stab wounds as well.

Today she'd learned that the only way to kill an immortal was to cut out the heart, chop off the head, or blow him or her into tiny pieces.

Splendid. From now on she could take on riskier cases and go after higher caliber targets.

"I can't complain. The corporate stuff pays well. It's a smaller and less competitive niche in the larger private eye field, and I'm very good at it."

"The disguise, it's something that you use on the job, right?"

"That's my best one. No one pays any attention to an old lady. I'm invisible when I'm wearing it. But it's uncomfortable. The body suit I wear under the clothes is heavy and hot, and the latex mask and gloves are no picnic either. Not to mention that it takes me over an hour to put it on and then apply the makeup."

This was a safe topic, and Eva debated whether she should keep going with it until Bhathian dropped her off at the coffee shop where she'd left her rental car. As it was, she had enough interesting stories to pass the time on a drive from Los Angeles to Las Vegas and back, let alone a short one like that.

"Any other employees besides Nick the hacker?" Bhathian asked.

"He's not only a hacker; the boy is a genius with all kinds of electronics. Then there is Sharon, who is doing preliminary research and gathers information for me. And Tessa who is my personal assistant."

Bhathian seemed focused on the road ahead of him, but he was listening. "You're fond of them. I can hear the smile on your face when you talk about them."

"I am. We are a little freaky family. I rent a house that serves both as my home and my office. The kids live and work with me."

"Don't they have their own families?"

"Tessa doesn't; she was a foster kid. Nick hates his father, and Sharon's parents live somewhere in the south and are very religious. They are overjoyed that her boss is a woman who also provides lodging for her."

They were nearing the café, and Eva couldn't wait to get out of Bhathian's car so she could finally take a deep breath.

Was he as nervous?

She glanced at his handsome profile and immediately looked away. That broad chin of his and those full lips were too much of a temptation.

As Bhathian eased the car into a parking spot, her hand hovered over the handle, and when he cut the engine, she unbuckled and pushed the door open.

"Wait." He put a hand on her thigh, sending goose bumps to every part of her body.

"Yes?"

"Don't go yet. We have so much to talk about."

"Not really." She pushed up to get out.

In a blink of an eye, he was on the other side of the car to assist. As if she needed it. But Eva had been raised a lady, and her good manners didn't allow her to refuse his hand.

When he got her standing, she could sense his inner struggle. He wanted to pull her against his body and hold her. Eva wasn't sure she would have the will to push him away if he did. Dressed as he was in exercise pants and a muscle shirt, every one of Bhathian's impressive muscles was on display, from his powerful calves to his bulging biceps.

She didn't dare check what else was bulging.

"I want to see you, Eva."

"You will. I promised Nathalie I'll come back tomorrow morning." Avoiding his eyes, she fixed her eyes on a spot over his left shoulder. For a woman who had no problem risking her life or taking the life of a target, she was showing uncharacteristic cowardice.

"I meant alone."

She shook her head. "That's not a good idea, Bhathian."

He hooked a finger under her chin and gently lifted her head, so she had to look at him. "Am I so repulsive to you that you can't even look at me?"

There was so much pain in his gray eyes that she didn't have the heart to lie and say yes. "Just the opposite, Bhathian. You're so handsome that I'm afraid I'll succumb to your charms again. But I can't. I've been hurt enough. I'm not looking for a repeat."

His smile was sweet, for lack of a better word. It wasn't conceited as she'd expected it to be, or even satisfied. He looked like a boy who hungered for affection and had just gotten a morsel of it.

"I'm not going to hurt you ever again. If you'd just give me another chance, I'll prove it to you."

Tempting. But she wasn't a naive girl that bought any of the lies men told. Some of them even meant the false promises at the moment they left their mouths, but not the next one.

Fickle creatures.

And what was even more absurd was that men called women shifty.

Doubtless it was true for some. Eva hadn't dated any women and was no authority on the subject, but the truth was that people in general were not trustworthy. In her line of work she got to see the ugly underbelly of humanity. The liars, the cheaters, the manipulators, and the abusers. Men didn't hold a monopoly on bad character traits though; she'd encountered a good number of female rotten apples.

"I don't think so. We have a daughter, so I guess we need to get along, but no more than that." She turned to leave.

He caught her hand. "Please."

Damn it.

Eva didn't know Bhathian well, but she had no doubt that the word 'please' didn't leave his mouth often.

She closed her eyes and sighed. "What? What would you have me do?"

His finger hooked under her chin again. "A kiss. One little kiss for old times' sake."

God, she wanted one too. "For old times' sake," she whispered.

His lips were soft and warm on hers, gentle and hesitant, not demanding at all. Exactly like she wanted, just a chaste little kiss.

Liar.

She wanted a real kiss to remember.

It was the only one she would allow herself, so she needed to make it count.

Her arms wrapped around Bhathian's thick neck, she pulled his head down and licked into his mouth.

He groaned, his big body trembling, either from excitement or from the effort it took to let her lead, Eva wasn't sure. As she plastered herself against him, he wrapped his arms around her waist, holding her gently.

The world and all of her troubles and concerns dissolved into nothingness, and all that remained was that kiss. Bhathian's lips, Bhathian's tongue, Bhathian's hands, Bhathian.

Amanda

"Did you go through yesterday's report?" Syssi asked the same question she'd been asking every morning ever since William's game went live.

"I'm ready to give up." Amanda leaned back in her chair and closed her eyes.

The game was working perfectly, but the scores of the best gamers were far from encouraging. It was true that the game tested only precognition, and that there were plenty of other paranormal talents out there it wasn't designed for, but with the thousands of people playing there should have been at least a handful who showed some promise.

She and Syssi had agreed to check out anyone who scored eight and above on the scale they'd compiled, but to date four was the highest score.

"Maybe we should lower our standards and check out the best from what we have," Syssi suggested.

"What's the use? A four means dismal talent. A potential Dormant would've scored higher."

Syssi pulled out a chair and sat across from Amanda. "What are we doing wrong?" She braced her elbows on the desk and rested her chin on her upturned palms.

"I don't know. I was so hopeful when I found Michael and you, but I'm starting to think it was a fluke. Almost a year later and we still don't have even one good candidate. But you know what bums me the most?"

"What?"

"The looks I'm getting at the keep. Everyone is waiting for me to discover the next Dormant, hoping it will be their destined mate. I hate to see the disappointment in their eyes."

Syssi snorted. "I don't know why. Finding a destined mate is even harder than locating a Dormant. Just look at Carol and Robert. Two eligible immortals who can't stand each other."

"True."

"Kian and I are so incredibly lucky."

Amanda sighed. "So am I with Dalhu, although I didn't think so at the time. Maybe Carol and Robert just need more time."

Syssi shook her head. "It's not the same. To be together, you and Dalhu had to overcome enormous opposition and eons of ingrained hatred. Carol and Robert have it easy. No one is trying to separate them or objecting to their union. It just simply doesn't work."

Amanda tapped her finger over her lips. "You'll think I'm being silly, but I'm starting to suspect that my research was just a vehicle for the Fates to bring you and Kian, and Kri and Michael together. I think all our efforts to find Dormants are futile. It will happen when the Fates decide it's time and not a moment before."

Syssi chuckled. "A very unscientific conclusion, Professor."

"Just think about it for a moment. In a city of millions, what were the chances of me bumping into Dalhu, a Doomer, on Rodeo Drive?"

"Not statistically significant, that's for sure."

"Exactly. But that's nothing compared with Nathalie's conception. Some random unaccounted-for immortal activates Eva, who meets Bhathian in a club, hooks up with him one time, and *boom*, she's pregnant with Nathalie. Immortal females can't conceive so easily. There are exceptions, like my oldest sister, but Eva isn't one of them. Nathalie said that Eva and Fernando wanted to have another child, but couldn't."

Syssi nodded. "I agree. It's too much of a coincidence. But what do you suggest we do? Go dance naked in the woods and chant prayers to your Fates?"

"If I thought that would work, I would do it in a heartbeat."

"Yeah, that's because you like being naked."

"And you don't?"

"Not in public!"

"What don't you want to do in public?" Hannah poked her head into Amanda's office.

"Dance naked in the woods," Amanda said.

"Ooh, sounds interesting. Are you girls planning a Wiccan ritual? Because if you do, I'm in."

"You're into Wicca?" Sissy asked.

Hannah shrugged. "I don't even know what it is, but I'm curious."

Amanda knew a little, and she could find more on the Internet. "You know what? We should do it. Just for fun."

Syssi cast her an incredulous glance. "Are you out of your freaking mind? I was just joking! I'm not going to dance naked outdoors. You can't pay me to do that."

"Coward," Amanda mouthed.

"Yes, I am. I'm not going to participate in your crazy ideas."

"What if we're not completely naked? We can wear white nightgowns or whatever else witches wear for their moon dances."

Syssi hesitated for a moment. "Fine, I'll come. But there must be more than the three of us there."

"Of course. Isn't twelve the right number? What do you think, Hannah?"

"I can check and prepare a list. After my date with William, that is. That's what I came to tell you. I'm leaving early today."

The thing between Hannah and William was troubling. The two had been going out steady for a while now. Like some couple from the Fifties, they were taking walks on the beach, going to movies, and having lunches and dinners together. But when Amanda pulled William for a little talk about overdoing it with Hannah and thralling her too many times, he'd said they'd never gotten that far.

How the hell was it possible?

Hannah was a sexually active adult woman, and William was an immortal male. There was no way these two weren't hooking up, and yet William had insisted that they didn't.

Since the guy was tight-lipped about the relationship, Amanda was planning on having a talk with Hannah about it.

She was still looking for an opportune moment to bring the subject up casually.

"Have fun," she told Hannah.

"I will. See you tomorrow morning, boss."

Amanda waited until she heard Hannah open the lab's squeaky door and close it behind her.

"I don't get what's going on."

"What do you mean?"

"Are they having sex or not?"

Syssi's cheeks pinked. "I don't think it's any of our business."

"If he is thralling her repeatedly it is. But he says he doesn't."

"Maybe they are just friends?"

"That's what it looks like. But I find it hard to believe that an immortal male can be 'just friends' with an attractive woman."

"As the saying goes: to every rule there is an exception. Maybe William is an exceptional immortal male?"

"That he is."

Was it possible that William's powerful brain could override his immortal body's urges?

If the answer was yes, then it was worth investigating. Maybe he could help poor Andrew.

Andrew

"Before you duck into the spare room with that bottle, I have something to tell you." Nathalie regarded Andrew with a pair of sad eyes. In preparation for the baby's arrival, they'd moved into a four-bedroom apartment. But Nathalie refused to call the additional room a nursery until the baby was born.

Every day when he returned from work he found her in the same position: sitting on the couch, her feet up on the coffee table with a throw pillow under them. And like every other day, he'd already eaten dinner out so he could lock himself in the spare room as soon as he came home, drinking himself into oblivion.

He was at the end of his rope, and it was taking every mental muscle he had to just survive from one day to the next. They'd talked about it, and Nathalie had agreed that it was the only way. Hopefully, she hadn't changed her mind and decided to move out, or conversely kick him out. It would crush him.

"What is it?" he asked.

"Can't you sit down with me for a minute?"

Andrew walked over to the chair facing the couch and sat on the edge.

The look Nathalie gave him was full of pity, but he wasn't sure who she was feeling sorry for, him or herself. She braced her hands on the couch and lifted to push herself up and sit a little straighter, scaring the shit out of him. It seemed Nathalie was getting ready for a serious talk.

"Jackson called earlier today to tell me about a strange old lady that came into the café, asking about my father and me."

Relieved, Andrew let himself slump in the chair. It wasn't about him.

"He said that she only looked old but smelled young."

That wasn't so unusual, given the nearby studios. "An actress in costume?"

"That was what I thought too. The old lady turned out to be my mother."

Did he hear her right? "Wait, what?"

Nathalie cast a wary glance at the bottle in his hand. "You're not drunk yet, right?"

"No."

"I need to backtrack a little. Before Bhathian left the Brazilian orphanage, he left a letter for Eva in case she ever went back there. Smart move on his part because she did. About a week ago."

"Must've been one hell of a letter to make her show her face back here."

Nathalie chuckled. "She didn't show her face. Her disguise was so perfect I don't think I would've recognized her. If not for Jackson's nose, she could've seen me without revealing herself, which was her original intention. Anyway, long story short, I grabbed Bhathian and he drove us there. She was so shocked to see him that she let her act slip. He confronted her and brought her over to me. One look and we were both crying like crazy."

It hurt a little that Nathalie hadn't thought of taking him with her, but Bhathian's part in Eva and Nathalie's life obviously superseded Andrew's. She could've at least called him, though.

"Where is she now?"

"Back at her hotel room. Kian agreed and we brought her here, after she'd changed of course. You should've seen it. So many came to greet her, the café was overflowing with people."

Yeah, he should have. "Why didn't you call me?"

"Would you have come?"

"Of course. What kind of question is that?"

She shrugged.

"Come on, Nathalie. You know I love you and that I have no choice about any of it. I'm doing the best I can under the circumstances."

The tear that slid down her cheek cut into his heart like a poisoned dagger.

"I know. And I love you too. But it's so hard, and I feel so alone. When I imagined you meeting my mom while keeping your distance from me, I just couldn't. I don't want her to think we are having problems."

It took a Herculean effort not to go to Nathalie and take her into his arms. But he knew better than to succumb to his longing. The smallest of touches could trigger his animal nature. He couldn't risk it. "We can explain what's going on. She would understand."

"Yeah, I realized that once I had a moment to think. That's why I wanted to ask if you can be late for work tomorrow. She'll be here around eight-thirty in the morning. We could have some quiet time with her."

"No problem. I'll be here."

"Sober?"

"Yes, but probably hungover."

Nathalie twisted the bottom of her maternity tunic between her fingers. "Are you sure there is no other solution?"

"Would you prefer me in stasis?"

"No, definitely not. I'll take you drunk over semi-dead any day."

"Me too. But it's getting harder. I'm terrified of waking up in the middle of the night and going after you. I would've stayed somewhere else, but then I'm terrified that you'll need me and I won't be there for you." He rubbed his hand over the back of his neck. "I don't know what to do."

"Maybe you should talk with some of the others. Not only Kian or Bridget, but maybe Edna or the other Guardians. Someone might know something. You'll never know if you don't ask."

"True. I think I'll go to the gym and see who I can corner." He lifted the whiskey bottle in front of his face and grimaced. "It's not like I'm eager to start on this." After this ordeal was over, Andrew swore he would never touch alcohol for as long as he lived, and given his near immortality it meant never. He hated the taste of it, he hated the drunkenness, and he hated the hangovers.

Bridget had refused to prescribe him the strong sleeping pills he'd asked for, claiming it would impair his faculties, making him too loopy to function at work.

For reasons he wasn't completely clear on, Andrew really didn't want to lose his job. The main one was the access to classified information, but it was more than that. His work was part of his old self, the human part, and he wasn't ready to give it up. In fact, his old office was the only thing affording him some sense of normality in a life that had gone crazy.

"Don't you want to hear why she ran out on us?"

Andrew had a pretty good idea. "Because she was afraid that once her immortality was discovered, she would be experimented on and so would you. She sought to protect you."

Nathalie pouted. "Yeah, that's about it. Still, she could've called to let me know she was alive."

"It was probably a risk she didn't want to take. If you had no idea whether she was dead or alive, you couldn't be questioned. Wouldn't you have done the same in her situation?"

She thought for a moment. "If I believed I was a risk to my daughter and that by leaving I'd ensure her safety, then the answer is yes.

I didn't have a chance to really talk to her yesterday. We were never alone. But tomorrow I'm going to."

He nodded and pushed up to his feet. "I'm sorry things have to be this way between us. I wish it could be different. You have no idea what it does to me not to hold you." He let his head drop. "Or put my ear to your belly and listen to our daughter's heartbeat up close. It's killing me."

As another tear slid down Nathalie's cheek, Andrew felt bad for sharing his suffering with her. But letting her think it was easy for him to keep away from her would've been worse.

"I love you, Andrew and we will survive this as we survived everything else."

"I love you more," he teased.

On an impulse, he bent down and kissed the top of her head, then forced himself to bolt out the door before doing anything stupid.

Down at the gym, Andrew was surprised to find William using one of the treadmills. Not running, just walking leisurely while reading a book, but that was more than Andrew had ever seen him do.

"Hey, William. What brought you here?"

William pushed his glasses up his nose. "I'm exercising."

Strolling at a speed of two miles per hour didn't qualify as exercise, but Andrew didn't have the heart to correct him. "Good for you," he said instead.

"I have a lady friend who likes to take long walks. I need to get in some sort of shape to keep up."

That was interesting. "Anyone I know?"

"I don't think so. She works at Amanda's lab, a post-doc. Very smart and very pretty."

Andrew rubbed his palm over his jaw, thinking of a polite way to ask the obvious. "She's human, of course."

"Naturally."

"Thralling a smart woman like her must be difficult."

"I'm not thralling Hannah. I would never risk damaging her beautiful mind."

Okay... "So she knows about us?"

"Of course not."

William was leaving him no choice but to be blunt. "How are you having sex with her without biting her and then having to thrall her?"

"Easy. I don't have sex with her."

Andrew's jaw dropped. "How? Aren't all immortal men horny beasts?"

"Not me. I'm more of a cerebral kind of guy. I enjoy a good conversation."

"But how do you fight it?" Maybe William had some trick up his sleeve that Andrew could use.

"Obviously, I'm not like the others. Just look at me." He waved a hand over his body. "I think it's because I'm so many generations separated from the source. The immortal genes get diluted."

Andrew shook his head. "Not likely. I'm certainly farther down the line from you, and every day is a battle for me."

William shrugged. "You're a newly turned immortal. It will probably get easier with time. I'm just grateful I don't have these kinds of problems. A strong sex drive is very distracting."

Tell me about it.

Even before the transition, the preoccupation with sex had been a problem, but then most men were in the same boat. Still, it had been nothing in comparison to what he was experiencing now. The only thing that seemed to numb the urges was a shitload of alcohol.

"How about stasis? One good bite and lights out until after your daughter is born. Problem solved."

Andrew shook his head. "I can't. For many reasons. If I don't show up at work for three months, I'll get fired. But more than that I want to be there for Nathalie when she needs me, and I certainly want to witness the birth of my child."

Walking slowly on the treadmill, William pondered the problem but seemed to come up with nothing useful. "Maybe your urges will subside soon."

That wasn't likely either, given that six months had done nothing to tone them down. On the other hand, he was still in the process of transitioning. His fangs had reached their full length only a month ago, and his venom glands had become active only recently. Who knew, maybe in a year or two he would be just as tame as William.

One could hope.

Eva

"I have the financials on the Greewald case ready," Sharon said as Eva walked into the office.

"Good, print them out and put them on my desk."

"It would be easier to send you the electronic file."

"I don't want to stare at a computer screen, I told you that a thousand times. Is it so difficult to just do as I ask?"

Sharon lifted her palms in surrender. "You're the boss."

Annoying girl. Sharon was so stubborn. But Eva was even more so. She liked going over reports the old-fashioned way. With a red pen on white paper.

Eva sighed and sat at her desk. She could've been nicer about it, though. Her reluctance to read things on the screen was a standing joke between them, and she shouldn't have snapped at Sharon.

Only a week had passed since Eva had parted with Nathalie, and already she couldn't wait to be back. Leaving her pregnant daughter and going back home to Tampa had been difficult, and if Eva was honest with herself, so was leaving Bhathian.

The worst part was that she couldn't share her great news with her crew. *Hey, guys, I don't need to hide anymore, and I have my daughter back.*

Eva needed to tell them something, though. Her mood swings were drawing worried glances. One moment she was happy because she had her daughter back, the next one she was sad because she couldn't drop everything and go to her whenever she felt like it.

Flying back and forth coast to coast in addition to her various business trips wasn't a solution. She needed to move her base and crew to Los Angeles. Her clients wouldn't even have to know. The only contact she had with them was via the Internet and the good old postal service. There was only one client who'd seen her, in disguise naturally, and he would be fine with the move. Most of the assignments he was sending her way weren't local anyway.

Eva glanced at Tessa, and as always the girl immediately felt it and looked away from her computer screen. "Do you need anything?"

"Did I tell you that I met a cousin of mine in Los Angeles?"

Tessa frowned. "No. I thought you didn't have any family."

That was what Eva had always claimed. "I didn't know I had a cousin either until I met her by chance in a coffee shop. She looks so much like me that I had to ask. Apparently, my grandmother on my mother's side had a sister and Nathalie is her granddaughter."

"Fascinating."

"I was so happy to discover that I had family, and she was so sweet, inviting me over to her apartment and introducing me to her husband. They are such an adorable couple, and they are expecting their first baby."

Tessa started doodling on her yellow legal pad, a nervous habit that popped up only when she was upset. "How come you didn't tell me about your cousin when you came back? Finding out about her doesn't seem like something that would've slipped your mind."

"No, but I had some thinking to do. I'm contemplating moving us to Los Angeles."

Tessa's hand stilled, and she looked up. "Really? Because of a distant cousin?"

Eva shrugged. "She's the only family I have. So yes. Besides, we can run this business from anywhere. I'm flying all over on assignments anyway."

"I guess. Did you say anything to Sharon and Nick?"

"Not yet. I made my decision five minutes ago."

Tessa scribbled 'Los Angeles' on her pad, then decorated it with flowers. "Do you want me to tell them while you're gone? Or do you want me to keep it a secret until you come back?"

"You can tell them. We'll talk about it when I'm back from this assignment. It has to be a unanimous decision. I don't want any of you to be miserable because I'm in the mood to move."

"I don't mind, and I don't think they will either. It's not like any of us have friends here that we will miss."

Sad but true.

Her crew of misfits, of which Eva considered herself a member, didn't play well with others. Maybe people sensed their oddity, or maybe they just felt different and didn't think they could fit in with the normals.

"You sure you don't want me to drive you to the airport?" Tessa asked for the fifth time.

"No, sweetie, you have work to do, and I already called a taxi. Come give me a hug." Eva kissed Tessa's cheek and then walked out, pulling her carry-on behind her.

For this assignment she didn't need her more elaborate costumes. A blond wig, blue contact lenses, and a tight dress would do. She had a scumbag to lure and eliminate.

Her crew didn't know that this time Eva wasn't going on a routine corporate espionage trip. She found it strange, though, that Tessa hadn't asked questions about an unscheduled assignment that neither Sharon nor Nick had done any prep work for.

Was it possible that the girl suspected something?

After all, it had all started with Tessa.

That first kill five years ago, which no one other than the two of them knew about, was what started Eva on her path. She'd finally realized why she'd been granted her special powers.

Eva had a job to do that others could not.

Get rid of scum.

The taxi pulled up to a stop in front of her house and the cabbie got out. "Good afternoon." He reached for Eva's carry-on. "Let me." He hefted it into the trunk.

"Thank you." She smiled at him when he opened the door for her.

Getting comfortable in the back seat, she didn't take off the dark sunglasses that covered half of her face, but she loosened the scarf she had wrapped around her head.

On that night, five years ago, all the pieces had fallen into place. Before, Eva hadn't known she could kill a man with such ease. Her strength and her super-hearing and her super-speed were gifts meant to be used for more than the simple detective jobs she was getting hired for.

And then there was her name.

Her mother had named her Evangeline, but her father hadn't liked it and they had compromised on Eva. The official meaning of the name was a bringer of good news, but Eva thought of it as having a very different meaning: an avenging angel.

There was nothing that brought her more satisfaction than freeing the world of the worst kind of vermin. Those who picked up little girls like Tessa off the streets, abused them horrendously, and then sold them to other vermin.

Eva was the avenger of lost girls. Those who were abandoned by everyone and missed by no one.

By herself, she couldn't go after the big fish—they never went anywhere without a horde of bodyguards. Not even to bring a hot date into their hotel room. Killing one of those without getting caught was difficult.

Instead, she went after the middlemen in the hierarchy of scum.

There hadn't been many. Each target required a thorough investigation she had to do on her own. Other than the snitches she paid for information, Eva didn't involve anyone else. The informants were left with the impression that she was searching for a lost girl. A client's runaway daughter. A perfect story, given her day job.

Eva chuckled. She was a private eye with an interesting side hobby.

At the airport, she didn't board a plane. Instead, she got into another taxi and headed for the Four Seasons. Her target wasn't staying at the fancy hotel, but according to her informant, he would be visiting a nearby club tonight.

Tomorrow, he would be found dead from a drug overdose, and no one would remember the "hooker" whom he'd taken to his room.

Nathalie

"Don't go the stasis route," Amanda said.

Andrew paced the length of their living room. "Then what do you suggest I do?"

The intervention had been Bhathian's idea. Kian and Syssi, Amanda and Dalhu, and of course Bridget had been invited to a brainstorming session to help find a solution to Andrew's misery.

And Nathalie's.

It wasn't only about all the things she was missing—Andrew's arms around her, his hands rubbing her back when it ached or massaging her feet after a long day at the café—all the sweet little things he'd been doing for her before his fangs became active.

Andrew was suffering and her heart was breaking for him.

He was getting worse, mainly because he was so terrified of losing it and attacking her.

There had been talk about Andrew moving out and staying at her old place, and Bhathian moving in so she'd have someone to help her in case of an emergency.

If no one came up with a better solution, Nathalie would not see Andrew until the delivery. He said they could talk on the phone, but she knew that regardless of where he was sleeping, he would get wasted as soon as he came home from work. Andrew was convinced that the animal urges of a newly transitioned immortal male were too powerful for his brain to control.

Nathalie would've dismissed his fears as gross exaggerations, but all the other immortals sided with Andrew.

Agh. She hated this kind of talk as much as the forced separation. Andrew and all the others were talking about him like he was some rabid dog. Not her wonderful, loving husband. Kian was convinced that Andrew's restraint would eventually snap and he would attack her. Was she fooling herself that he would never harm her no matter what?

Amanda crossed her arms over her chest. "Anything but stasis. Dalhu looked like a corpse after only a week. Imagine what you would look like after eight."

The image Amanda had painted wasn't something Nathalie wanted to revisit. "I agree with Amanda. I don't want you to do it either."

"Then the best idea is for me to move out."

Kian shook his head. "Risky. Nothing will stop you from getting into your car and driving over here in the middle of the night. I'll have to inform security not to let you in."

"Then do it."

"There must be something we are overlooking," Syssi said.

Dalhu raised his finger. "May I suggest something?"

Andrew stopped his pacing. "Please."

"The nice prison at the basement has a door an immortal can't break through. You can stay there. Still close to Nathalie in case she needs you, but safely locked away at night."

"That might work... What do you think, Nathalie?" Andrew asked.

Nathalie hated it, but it was better than the other idea. "I prefer this to you sharing a room with Jackson, that's for sure. And you'll be closer to me. But I still hate to see you suffering like that. What about an induced coma? With intravenous nutrition and whatever else goes in there."

Bridget looked thoughtful. "I don't even know if it'll work on an immortal. I've never tried keeping an immortal sedated for that long. But I can look into it and we can give it a try, see how it works for a day or two."

Andrew rubbed the back of his neck. "That's a last-resort measure, same as the stasis. I want to work for as long as I can."

"I think there is another option," Bhathian said. "I can move into the spare room with you. If you try to leave in the middle of the night, I'll stop you."

That was the best idea Nathalie had heard all evening. Bhathian would have no trouble subduing Andrew if he lost it. Not that she truly believed he ever would. They were all suffering from a severe case of paranoia. "I love it. That way I'll have all the men I love with me."

"What about your evening classes?" Kian asked.

"I can rearrange my schedule, so I'll be there when Andrew comes home from work, or I can have Anandur take my place when needed."

Kian pushed to his feet. "Then it's settled. And if this doesn't work, we can always utilize Dalhu's idea."

When the others left, Bhathian stayed behind. "Care to join me for a sandwich at the café?"

Nathalie glanced at her watch. "Carol is probably closing up. But I can whip us up something." With only the two of them working at the café, they had to limit the hours it was open. Nine to five-thirty on weekdays and closed on weekends.

Andrew nodded. "Good idea. I left work early to get here and didn't eat anything since lunch."

"You should eat dinner at the café every day," Bhathian said as the elevator doors closed behind them and the thing started its descent. "It's a public place, and there are always a few guys sitting around. You can spend some time with Nathalie knowing that they'll stop you if you try anything. If it makes you feel safer, I can be there too."

"That's a wonderful idea, right?" Nathalie glanced at Andrew hopefully. They could at least talk a little before he ducked into the spare room at night.

"It is." For some reason, Andrew didn't look convinced, but she wasn't going to push him.

Carol was still serving coffee and sandwiches when they got there. "Hi, you guys, what can I get you?" she asked.

"I can take care of it. You probably want to go home already." Nathalie felt bad for dumping more and more of the work on Carol. Onidu was supposed to start tomorrow morning after Amanda left for work, but Nathalie wasn't sure how well he was going to manage.

If he didn't, and Carol left to intern with Gerard, Nathalie would have to either further limit the hours the place was open, or turn it into a self-service.

"No, I don't. I'll close up after you're done."

"You're an angel," Nathalie said and meant it.

Having an immortal helper was great. Carol never got tired, and if she was cranky, it was because of Robert and not because her feet were killing her.

"Thank you for doing this for us," Nathalie told Bhathian.

"No need to thank me. It's not as if I have anything better to do with my evenings. If I'm not working, I'm sitting in front of the dumb box and watching sports by myself. Now I can watch with Andrew."

Andrew clapped Bhathian's back. "Thanks, man. And I'll have a drinking buddy. It sucks to drink alone."

There was something that didn't sound right with Bhathian's story. He didn't spend all his evenings alone in his apartment; usually he went out hunting at the clubs with the guys.

"What about the nights you go out?" she asked him.

"As I said, I can have Anandur or Yamanu take my place when needed."

For some reason Bhathian seemed embarrassed. It couldn't have been about her mentioning his prowls, they'd joked about it plenty of times, and it had never bothered him before. Was it because of Eva? Was he staying away from other females because of her?

It wasn't something Nathalie felt comfortable asking him about, and frankly, it was none of her business.

Waiting for Carol to serve their order, they sat in an awkward silence. Bhathian was never one for small talk, but she and Andrew had never been so distant with each other. After a few moments Andrew shifted in his chair. "You'll never believe who I met at the gym the other day."

"Who?" Nathalie asked. She missed the little tidbits of gossip Andrew used to share with her.

"Think of the last person you'd expect to find on a treadmill."

Bhathian snorted. "William."

"You got it. Granted, he wasn't running or sweating, only walking, but it's progress."

Good for him. Sitting in front of a computer all day wasn't healthy even for an immortal. "I've noticed that he lost some weight lately, but I thought it was the walks he was taking my father on."

"Not only Fernando. William has a girlfriend."

"Oh wow. That's great news." Or maybe not. If William was seeing a woman, he would have less time to hang out with her father, and she'd have to find Fernando another babysitter.

"Here you go, guys." Carol started unloading a tray, placing four plates loaded with sandwiches and sides of salads on the table. "I'll join you, if you don't mind. I put up the closed sign."

It seemed Carol didn't feel like going back to her apartment yet.

Bhathian pulled out a chair for her.

Carol waited with her sandwich in hand until they all had bitten into theirs. "What do you think? As good as Nathalie's?"

"Uh huh," Andrew mumbled with a full mouth.

Nathalie finished chewing and swallowed before answering. "Better. What dressing did you use?"

"I whipped up something new and wanted to test it on you guys."

"It's amazing. Are you going to keep it a secret or are you going to share it with me?"

"I'll show you what I did, but if I decide to bottle and sell it, I'm not sharing the profits." Carol winked.

"It could be a hit," Andrew said, wiping his mouth with a napkin. "It's so good I want another one."

Carol grinned. "No problem. How about you, Bhathian, another one?"

"Sure. You need to start super-sizing these sandwiches. That's not enough for a male to fill up on."

She was back with two more in under three minutes.

It must be nice to be so fast and tireless, Nathalie thought. She couldn't wait to transition and have as much energy and stamina as Carol. Just one little bonus on top of getting her man back in her bed.

For a few moments, Carol watched the guys wolf down the sandwiches with a satisfied smirk on her face, but then her expression became thoughtful and she started to wind a lock of her hair around her finger.

"I know it's none of my business, and I probably shouldn't even know about it. But I think I can help you with your problem, Andrew."

Damn Anandur. The blabbermouth had probably spread the rumor to every resident of the keep.

Andrew grimaced. "Living here is like living in a commune. Everyone knows everything about everyone else."

Carol snorted. "Yeah, tell me about it. I get unwanted advice about Robert and me all of the time. But I really think my suggestion can help. Have you ever tried pot? It takes the edge off. And if that doesn't work, I can recommend stronger stuff. I'm an expert of sorts."

Andrew shook his head. "I'm working for the government. Doing drugs is a sure way to get fired."

"How often do they test you guys?" Carol asked.

"I get a physical once a year."

"And when was the last one?"

"I think about six months ago."

Carol rolled her eyes. "So what's the problem? By the time they test you again you'll be clean."

"Damn, I didn't think about it. But can I even have a physical? What if they find something weird?"

Bhathian clapped him on the shoulder. "Then you thrall the nurse and alter the results."

Andrew frowned. "I don't think I can do it, thralling I mean. I didn't try it yet."

"Then it's time you learned. Tomorrow, come down to the gym after work and I'll have Arwel show you how it's done. He's a telepath, so he'll know if you're doing it right."

"Don't I need a human to practice thralling on?"

Nathalie raised a finger. "One human volunteer here..."

"No way," Bhathian and Andrew said almost at the same time.

"Just think about it, boys. It doesn't have to be anything too intrusive. Andrew can practice projecting a different image of himself. Like Anandur with his demon."

Bhathian's expression turned thunderous. "He showed you his demon?"

Nathalie shrugged. "I asked him to. I think it's a really cool trick."

"I'm going to kill that son of a bitch. That thing could've scared you into a miscarriage."

Nathalie laughed. "Don't be silly. I knew what was coming and was ready for it. Besides, his demon is kind of cute."

Andrew growled. "Cute?"

Jealous anyone?

"You know, like in not scary. But it sure is ugly."

Eva

The hectic pace of the last three weeks had exhausted Eva's crew, and the only reason she wasn't sporting dark circles under her eyes like the three of them was because she wasn't human.

"What do you think?" Eva asked no one in particular.

"It's small," Tessa said.

A four-bedroom house on a canal in Venice cost a small fortune in monthly rent, and the girl was complaining that it was small.

"It was either a big house inland, or a small house near the beach. I figured you guys would prefer the beach."

"The house in Tampa was big *and* close to the beach," Sharon said.

"Well, kids, what can I say, Tampa is cheaper than Los Angeles."

Nick was the only one who seemed to be happy about the move. "You can stand down here and nag, while I go upstairs and call dibs on the best bedroom."

"Second floor is yours, third floor is mine," Eva reminded him.

"I know." He lifted his suitcase and took the stairs two at a time.

Tessa grimaced as she looked at her own two suitcases and then at the stairs. "He could've at least helped me with these."

Eva patted her back. "Don't worry. He'll be back." She grabbed one of the suitcases. "I'll take this one up and send Nick for the other." She could've lifted both with ease.

Tessa grabbed for the handle. "I can do it myself."

"Right..." Sharon passed Tessa on the way to the staircase.

"Why is everyone treating me like a kid?"

Because you look like one. Eva wanted to say. "Go check out the office in the back and let me know if anything is missing." The movers she'd hired were top notch. They came to the house in Tampa, packed everything carefully and marked each box with detailed instructions where everything went. Supposedly, they'd unpacked and put everything in its proper place. She'd be surprised if they'd done as good a job as they'd promised. Not that she needed to check on it right then, but it was a good excuse to send Tessa away.

"Sure." The girl let go of the suitcase and headed toward the back of the house.

It was all about saving face.

Eva lifted Tessa's two suitcases and ran up the stairs, depositing them in the hallway between the bedrooms, then went back down for her own.

"You could've waited for me," Nick said as he saw her coming up the stairs again.

"Never too late. You can take this one." Eva pretended to huff as she handed him one of her suitcases.

"What a view!" Nick exclaimed as they entered the third-floor master bedroom. He put the luggage down and crossed the room to the French doors leading to the balcony. As he opened the way, the room filled with fresh sea breeze and a chorus of seagulls' cries.

Pure heaven.

For an undeserving sinner.

The guilt was uncalled for, she'd told herself as much a thousand times, but the fact remained that Eva walked on the dark side. Heck, she hadn't set foot in a church since that first kill, even though she truly believed she was doing her part in God's grand design.

But so did the Devil, and he wasn't a good guy.

"Wow, just look at this," Nick called. "You can see the ocean from up here."

She joined Nick on the balcony. It was on the smallish side, but roomy enough to accommodate a lounger and a tiny bistro table with two chairs. The picture of that balcony was what convinced her to lease the small house for the outrageous asking price.

"It's beautiful, but I need to take on an extra case or two a month to afford this place."

"So why did you do it?"

"Because of this." She waved her hand toward the horizon, where blue water met blue sky.

Nick shrugged. "You're the boss, and I'm not complaining about living accommodations next to the beach. I heard that California babes are the hottest, and I'm going to check them out."

Eva's phone buzzed in her pocket. She'd been waiting for that call. "Hi, Nathalie. We've just got in."

"Are you sure you want me to come over right now? You don't want to rest a little? Get comfy in your new place?"

"Sweetheart, I haven't seen you in a month, and I can't wait a moment longer. Unless you've gotten too big to travel. I can come over to your place if you prefer."

"No, I'm good. I'm dying to see the house you got. It sounds amazing. But I'll have to ask Bhathian to drive me because I can barely reach the steering wheel."

Eva had been hoping for time alone with Nathalie, and she wasn't ready to see Bhathian. The memory of that one kiss they'd shared was still fresh on her mind.

"I can come and get you."

"It's okay. Bhathian wouldn't mind."

I bet he wouldn't.

"As you wish."

"I'll see you shortly, Mom."

Eva cast a quick glance at Nick. It didn't seem as if he'd heard anything. He was leaning against the railing and enjoying the breeze ruffling his long hair.

"You're going to fit right in." She slipped her phone into her pocket and leaned against the railing next to him. "You already look like a surfer."

"Thanks."

She hadn't meant it as a compliment, but if he thought it was then why not. "I want to freshen up a little before my cousin gets here," she told him.

Nick got the hint. "I'm out of here."

Eva closed the door behind him and pulled out her phone again to text Nathalie a reminder.

You're my cousin. The granddaughter of my grandmother's sister. We've just met and don't know much about each other.

A moment later her phone buzzed with Nathalie's answer. *Sorry, I didn't know you had company.*

No harm done. Nick didn't hear a thing. I just wanted to remind you. Eva erased her messages before closing the phone. One could never be too cautious.

Eva took a five-minute shower, put on fresh clothes, and went downstairs feeling like a new woman.

"We need to go shopping," Sharon said. "Do you know where the nearest supermarket is?"

"Yes. But you'll need to do it without me. My cousin is coming to visit."

"Already? We can't even offer her coffee."

"Then I suggest you get moving." Eva pulled out a couple of hundreds and handed them to Sharon. "Take Nick with you to carry the bags."

"I feel like a pack mule," he grumbled.

Sharon slapped his back. "Stop complaining. There is a price to be paid for having a dick."

"Yeah, and there is a price for being the only guy working with three women. You all gang up on me."

"But you know we love you." Eva kissed his cheek. "Now get going. My cousin will be here any moment."

Half an hour later there was a knock on the door.

She ran to the door and yanked the thing open, then grabbed Nathalie and pulled her into her arms as far her belly allowed. "This baby is big."

"Tell me about it," Nathalie huffed as she walked inside. "Cute place."

"Hi, Eva," Bhathian entered behind their daughter, carrying a large box under his arm. He offered his hand. "It's Eva, right?"

She chuckled, thinking he was joking. But that wasn't like Bhathian. He didn't strike her as the humorous sort. He probably wasn't sure which name she was using. "Yes, it is."

A sharp intake of breath from behind her reminded Eva that Tessa was there. Turning around, she found the girl staring at Bhathian with doe-eyed fascination. A guy his size must've looked intimidating to her.

"Tessa, meet my cousin Nathalie."

The girl shook Nathalie's hand without taking her eyes off Bhathian.

"And this is her... her..." Eva stuttered, searching for a plausible familiar connection.

Bhathian stepped forward and offered his hand. "I'm Bhathian. Nathalie's cousin from her father's side."

Good save. Who would have known Bhathian had it in him.

Tessa placed her small hand in Bhathian's giant one and blushed. "It's nice to meet you." She cranked her head way up to look up at his face. "What did they feed you that you grew up so big?"

He winked. "Lots of eggs."

Nathalie waddled to the couch and plopped down. "Do you have any plates? I brought pastries."

Bhathian let go of Tessa's hand and patted the box under his arm. "You're in for a treat. Nathalie bakes the best ones."

Tessa shook her head as if she needed to dispel a thrall. "I'm going to check if the movers unpacked them."

Bhathian put the box on the coffee table and lifted the lid. "I vote for eating straight from the box. We brought napkins."

Tessa ran off to the kitchen anyway, probably to splash some cold water on her flaming cheeks. Eva cast Bhathian a sidelong glance. He was handsome, very handsome in fact, but she'd never seen Tessa react like that to a guy. Throughout the years they'd been together, Tessa had never shown any interest in the opposite sex. Perfectly understandable given her past. Except that was exactly why her reaction to Bhathian was so surprising.

"I'll see if she needs help." Eva followed the girl to the kitchen.

She found Tessa leaning against the counter and fanning herself with her hand.

"Nathalie's cousin is hot," she whispered.

Eva chuckled. "Yes, he is. I would've thought that a guy that big would scare you."

Tessa shook her head. "Not at all. He has a protector's vibe. Having someone like him around would actually help me sleep better at night."

Eva caressed Tessa's cheek. "Why didn't you tell me the nightmares were back?" she said softly.

Tessa leaned into Eva's palm and sighed. "You've done so much for me already. I didn't want to burden you. Besides, there is nothing you can do."

"Not true. You could sleep with me like you did at the beginning. Remember? You couldn't sleep without me cuddling you."

Tessa smiled a sad little smile. "I was a kid then, and I thought of you as this grown-up, strong woman. But now I'm a grown woman too. I can't sneak into your bed like I used to."

"Yes, you can. You're welcome whenever you can't sleep."

Tessa's eyes filled with tears and she brushed them away with the back of her hand. "I owe you my life, Eva. You're the best person I've ever met. I love you."

If she only knew...

Pulling the girl into her arms, Eva kissed the top of her head. "I love you too, sweetie."

Bhathian

Bhathian knew he was making Eva uncomfortable, staring at her like some lovesick puppy, but he couldn't help it. Everything she did was sexy. The way she lifted the pastry up to her mouth, putting it between her plump lips, the way she laughed at the silly jokes Nick the wonder boy hacker was making.

It was a relief to sense no attraction between Eva and Nick. The boy was a scrawny geek, and it was no wonder that Eva didn't feel anything for him, but that the pup wasn't attracted to her was strange.

No healthy male could've helped it.

Maybe Nick was pitching for the other team?

Bhathian hoped so. One less male to worry about.

"We should head back, Bhathian." Nathalie patted his thigh. "Andrew is probably on his way home, and I want to be back in time to have dinner with him."

He pushed to his feet then offered her a hand up. "It was nice to meet you all," he said.

"Same here." Nick got up and offered his hand. "I hope you guys will come visit often and bring those delicious pastries with you."

Sharon slapped his back. "Nick, that's not polite."

"What if I say please?" He steepled his hands and put on a pleading expression.

Nathalie laughed. "You guys should visit my old café. You'd like Jackson. He is the one who's in charge now that I can't work." She patted her belly. "He and his friends are using my father's recipes to bake these."

Eva lifted a brow. "You didn't make them?"

"No. The guys bake double the quantity and deliver half to the ke... I mean the executive lounge. There is very little I can do these days."

Eva hugged her daughter gently. "You shouldn't be working at all. You huff and puff when getting from the couch to the door."

"That's what Andrew and I have been telling her too. She doesn't listen to us, but maybe she'd listen to you." Bhathian crossed his arms over his chest and glared at Nathalie.

She sighed. "Two more weeks and then I'm going to leave it all to someone else. But I know that with nothing to do I'll go crazy from boredom."

Eva laughed. "Enjoy your free time. You're going to miss it once this little one is out and demanding every moment of your day and night. I still remember..." She caught herself in time. "I still remember babysitting for my neighbor when her child was born. Poor woman, she didn't get any sleep. I took care of her little girl so she could grab a nap."

Eva's crew was eyeing her as if she'd sprouted horns. "What?"

Sharon shook her head. "I don't know. It's just weird to think of you holding a baby. You're so..."

Eva narrowed her eyes. "I'm so what?"

"Worldly and mysterious?"

She smirked. "I can live with that. Let me walk you to your car." She hooked her arm through Nathalie's.

"That was a close one," Nathalie said when they were a few feet away from the house, walking to Bhathian's car.

Eva nodded. "More than one. A couple of them."

"Do you think they suspect something?"

"I don't think so, and if they do, so what? They would never guess what the real deal is. Let them speculate."

Bhathian clicked the remote, then opened the passenger door for Nathalie. "Give me your hand. I'll help you get in."

Nathalie sighed. "I feel like an elephant."

"You're beautiful." Bhathian kissed the top of her head before helping to lower her into the seat.

"When are we going to see you again, Eva?" Nathalie put the emphasis on the name. "I'd better get used to calling you that."

"I'll give you a call tomorrow. I need to get settled and organize my caseload."

Nathalie looked disappointed.

Eva leaned inside and kissed Nathalie's cheek. "I promise I'll come over. I just don't know when yet."

"Okay."

Bhathian closed the door and glanced at Eva. She looked uncomfortable again, not sure what she was supposed to do next. He was no better. They were like a couple of teenagers trying to figure each other out. At least he was. Maybe for her it was something else.

Eva hadn't given him any indication that she was even attracted to him other than that kiss almost a month ago. But then he hadn't seen her in the interim.

If he had any chance to win Eva over, he would have to work hard at seducing her.

"Are all the guys that run Fernando's café immortal?" Eva asked.

"Jackson and Vlad and Gordon are. They recently hired a human girl to waitress."

Eva nodded. "I think I'll take my crew there and introduce them. It would be good for them to hang out with some young people. Maybe the guys can recommend popular clubs."

"I'll give Jackson a call and tell him to play nice."

"He seems nice enough."

Bhathian grimaced. "Yeah, a charming little bastard who'll get into your girls' panties in no time at all."

"I'm not their mother. Besides, they sure can benefit from a good tumble in bed. Sharon, that is. Tessa is a different story."

"Why? What's wrong with her?" Bhathian asked.

"It's her story to tell, not mine."

Bhathian shifted his weight to the other foot and offered his hand. "I don't want to keep Nathalie waiting."

"Goodbye, Bhathian." Eva shook his hand. He was about to pull her into him and steal another kiss, but he felt as if they were being watched and glanced at the house. Sure enough, Nick was standing on the balcony of the third floor and looking down at them.

"I'll see you tomorrow." He let go of her hand.

She nodded and turned on her heel, but not before Bhathian caught a fleeting look of disappointment on her face. She'd wanted him to kiss her, and if not for the little bastard on the balcony he would've.

Damn.

Bhathian got behind the wheel and slammed the driver's door shut.

"What's the matter?" Nathalie asked.

"I want to strangle that Nick fellow."

"Why?"

"Look in the rear-view mirror. The little prick is standing on the third-floor balcony and spying on us." Bhathian eased out of the tight parking spot.

"I can't see anything," Nathalie said, cranking her neck to look at the mirror.

"Never mind. I don't want you to strain a muscle."

He needed a strategy. Hell, he needed coaching on how to court a woman. Maybe he could use his mandatory sessions with the therapist to ask for her advice. Or, if he wanted a male's perspective, he could ask Jackson.

Yeah, not in this lifetime or in the next.

Andrew, however, would know a thing or two, and he wasn't a snotty teenager.

"What made you fall in love with Andrew?" he asked Nathalie.

"He's a great guy. Any woman would've wanted him."

Bhathian growled low in his throat. If he didn't tell her why he needed to know, Nathalie would keep talking in generalities in an unnecessary attempt to spare his fatherly feelings. Humans had all kinds of hang-ups about things of that nature. "I need to learn how to charm a woman."

"You mean my mother?"

"Yes."

"And you want my advice."

"You know her better than I do. I hate to admit it, but I don't know how to go about it. I've got the seduction part down, but that won't be enough to win Eva over. I need to know what Andrew did to make you fall in love with him."

Nathalie chuckled. "It started with the physical attraction. I wanted him so badly, and the silly man was trying to be a gentleman. Eventually, I just told him to stop treating me like a breakable doll or something."

"I don't get it. Are you telling me I need to just go for it?"

She shook her head. "No. I knew that Andrew was treating me like that because he was afraid of scaring me off. I was too important to him. He admitted that he'd never behaved like that with any of his other girlfriends. So even though I was impatient and I wanted him to make a move, I appreciated what he was trying to do."

Bhathian shook his head. "I'm never going to understand how women think. So you wanted him to initiate sex, but you were glad he didn't."

"Yes."

Hopefully, Andrew's side of the story would make more sense, because Nathalie's didn't.

Eva

"Hello, Jackson." Eva smiled at the young immortal managing her ex's coffee shop. "I have some hungry customers for you here." She waved a hand at her crew. "My employees. Sharon, Nick, and Tessa."

Jackson bowed his head. "Welcome to Fernando's café. You came to the right place. Can I start you off with some cappuccinos?"

"Yes, please." Sharon pushed past Eva to get a better look at the hot guy behind the register.

He's too young for you, sweetheart, Eva wanted to whisper in Sharon's ear. But then Jackson would've heard it.

"I'll pass for now," Nick said. "Maybe after I eat."

Everyone turned to Tessa, who hadn't said a thing and was hiding behind their taller frames and trying to stay out of Jackson's view.

"What would it be for you, Miss?" Jackson leaned forward and flashed the girl a charming smile. "A cappuccino? Tea? Me?"

Tessa blushed redder than Eva had ever seen her blush before. Not that the girl blushed often, and certainly not because of a handsome guy flirting with her. Other than that one blush Bhathian had elicited yesterday, all the others had been due to embarrassment over mishaps at work. Tessa was scared of making mistakes as if Eva was a horrible boss who would chew her up for every little thing.

"Do you have herbal teas?" Tessa asked in a tiny voice, looking at the shelves behind Jackson, probably to avoid looking at him.

"We have a nice selection." Jackson dropped his flirtatious tone, replacing it with a gentle and coaxing one. He was talking to Tessa as if she was a skittish mare who needed to be handled with care. "I'll bring you the box so you can take your time and choose what you like."

She abandoned the shelves and dared a quick glance at the boy. "Thank you."

"My pleasure. I suggest you guys snatch that booth over there before someone else does." He pointed at the only free one up front.

"Can I grab a few menus?" Eva asked as her crew took ownership of the booth.

Jackson leaned over the counter. "I'd rather bring them over myself if you don't mind." He winked.

Eva narrowed her eyes and whispered. "Aren't you a little too young to be flirting with adult women?"

He shook his head. "There is no age limit on flirting. Besides, the little one is younger than me."

"She's not. Tessa is twenty-one."

Jackson's smile was so bright it could've blinded someone less jaded than Eva. "Perfect, then she's legal."

Oh, the boy was asking for trouble. "But you're not."

"Yes, I am. I'm eighteen. She can have me any way she wants me without breaking the law."

Eva leaned, so her nose was practically touching the boy's. "Tessa is not for you, Jackson. She is fragile and needs to be handled with extreme care."

Jackson's expression turned serious. "I know. I'm not blind. But she looks like she needs a friend. Someone to make her laugh. I'm good at that."

Eva lifted a brow. "A friend? I wasn't born yesterday, Jackson. I know what boys your age want, and being just friends with a girl is not it."

"But I'm not a regular boy." He winked. "Don't worry. I promise to be on my best behavior."

Who did he think she was? A naive soccer mom? "Like that's supposed to make me feel better? What's your best behavior? Waiting for the second date to make a move?"

Jackson frowned. "Why are you getting so worked up about it? I'm not some evil incarnate who's out to harm your employee."

Shoot, he was right. Jackson wasn't the enemy. He was a charming young man, and the fact that he was younger than Tessa was actually an advantage. Tessa had been brutally forced to grow up too quickly. As a teenager, she'd been snatched before having a chance to flirt with boys her age. Maybe Jackson was exactly what she needed to get over the trauma that had stalled her growth, physical as well as emotional.

"I'm sorry I overreacted. You're a nice guy, Jackson. It's just that Tessa is..." How could she say what needed to be said without saying too much? Tessa's past was her own, and she had the right to tell it to whomever she deemed trustworthy. To this day, the only one who knew the whole story was Eva. Sharon and Nick had been told a censored version with the worst parts omitted.

"You were saying?" Jackson prompted.

"Sensitive."

"Got it. Fragile and sensitive and needs to be handled with care."

"Exactly." She smiled at him.

As Eva slid into the booth next to Sharon, the girl eyed her suspiciously. "What were you talking about with Jackson?"

"This and that. He took over for Nathalie, and I was wondering how a guy this young is handling running a business." After many years of working undercover, Eva was an expert liar. Trouble was, Sharon had a talent for sensing things like that. Fortunately, it seemed not to work where Eva was concerned. Sharon never asked her about the solo, off the books, missions Eva was running from time to time.

None of her crew ever had.

The lie worked, and Sharon seemed satisfied. "What's the story with that? How come she lets a kid run the place?"

Over the course of the long month Eva had been away, she and Nathalie had chatted on the phone at least once a day. Nathalie told her how the whole thing had started with Bhathian and Andrew one day showing up at the café and everything that had followed.

As long as she omitted the immortal part, there was no harm in telling them. "Nathalie was running the place basically on her own. Her father, the original owner and the one who'd come up with the recipes, was diagnosed with dementia, and she had to take over."

"What happened to her mother?" Nick asked.

She is sitting here in front of you.

Eva shrugged. "She disappeared. So one day, Bhathian, the cousin you met yesterday," *who isn't her cousin but her real father,* "came to visit, and when Nathalie complained about her waitress quitting, he suggested a distant relative of his who just graduated from high school."

"Jackson," Tessa said.

"Exactly. He started as Nathalie's helper. Despite his young age, Jackson proved a savvy businessman, and Nathalie ended up relying on him more and more, especially as her pregnancy progressed and it became difficult for her to work. He brought over two of his friends, and eventually she let him run the place so she could take some time off before the delivery and later to be with her baby."

Jackson had probably been listening to Eva telling the story, and waited for her to be done before showing up with the tray.

"One cappuccino for Sharon." He placed the cup in front of her. "Another one for Eva." He handed her the cup. "And tea for Tessa." He put down a large wooden box and then a steaming teapot. "And the menus." He handed them out.

Tessa mumbled a quiet thank-you and lifted the lid, avoiding looking at Jackson while sifting through the assortment of teas.

"You're welcome," Jackson said softly.

"I think he likes you," Sharon said as soon as Jackson left.

Tessa blushed again. "You're imagining things. I'm invisible to guys like him."

Sharon snorted. "He saw you all right. He didn't look at anyone else."

Eva cast a quick glance at Jackson, expecting to see a satisfied smirk on his handsome face. Instead, she found a scowl. The boy looked annoyed. Was it because of Sharon's taunting?

"Enough of that, kids." Eva lifted the menus and handed them out. "Hurry up and choose what you want to eat so we can order. I'm hungry."

It was almost seven when they were done eating, and most of the café's clientele had left. Jackson turned the sign to 'closed' and joined them.

"Do you guys have plans for tonight?" he asked.

"We've just got here, dude," Nick said. "First time in Los Angeles for all of us, except for Eva."

Jackson grinned. "Then you need someone to show you around."

"You volunteer?" Sharon asked with a quick glance at Tessa who was very busy looking into her cup.

"I sure do. My friends and I are performing at a club that's not too far from here. Good music, good drinks, you're gonna love it."

Nick regarded Jackson with respect. "You play?"

"I play the guitar. My friend Gordon is on the drums, and Vlad is the bass player and the other lead singer."

Sharon laughed. "Vlad? Is it a nickname?"

"Unfortunately, no. His mother has a weird sense of humor."

"Unless it's short for Vladimir, that's cruel." Sharon crossed her arms under her chest, making her B-cup-sized cleavage look voluptuous.

"Just Vlad."

"Cool," Nick said. "When is your gig?"

"Eight. You guys can hitch a ride with me."

Tessa glanced at Eva. "Do you want to come?"

Right, as if a bunch of teenagers playing hard rock or metal was something she would enjoy listening to. "No. You kids go and have fun. I'm going home."

"You're sure? It sounds like fun."

Eva patted Tessa's slim shoulder. "I'm sure."

"Won't you get lonely?"

"I won't."

Because she wasn't going to be alone.

All those covert looks Jackson and Tessa had been exchanging had gotten Eva thinking about a certain hunk of a man who would jump at the opportunity to pleasure her.

It had been almost two months since her last hookup, and Eva was getting antsy. The problem was that ever since Bhathian walked into her life again, he had been starring in all her fantasies, and the thought of hooking up with some random stranger was as appealing as using her vibrator.

Frankly, Bhathian had been her favorite go-to imaginary lover for years. Despite the deep resentment she felt for the man who'd rejected her over thirty years ago, she'd spent most of her lonely nights with him.

Eva had thought it harmless.

After all, the real Bhathian was supposed to be old and flabby, and the imaginary one was supposed to no longer exist.

But he did, and she wanted him. Not as a partner, he could never be one for her, but as a lover. She could use that incredible body of his without getting emotionally involved.

Eva had love in her heart for only one person in the entire world, and that was Nathalie. The only one she was willing to add to that exclusive club was her granddaughter.

Bhathian had blown his chances with her a long time ago.

A glass of water clutched in her hands, Eva sat at the same bar she'd invited Bhathian to accompany her to a month ago and waited. Why hadn't she asked Bhathian for his phone number, or address, or even his last name? What were the chances that he would come back to this place?

Probably none.

Nevertheless, Eva had gone there each time she'd landed in Los Angeles, twice a week for the past two weeks, hoping he would walk in.

Bhathian deserved to know that she was pregnant with his child. Anxiety squeezed her insides, and she felt like throwing up. What would he do once he found out?

In Eva's more hopeful fantasies, Bhathian was happy, excited, and asked her to marry him so they could give the child a home. In the less hopeful ones, he walked away.

Even if he did, though, Eva expected Bhathian to at least agree to put his name on the birth certificate. Growing up without a father was bad enough, not knowing who he was, was worse. Bhathian seemed like an honorable man. He would do the right thing. Unless he was married...

No, there had been no ring on his finger, and she'd even checked for an impression left by one.

Nevertheless, the news would doubtless come as a shock to him. She had a miniature bottle of whiskey in her purse to soften the impact.

This time he would come, Eva felt it in her gut.

Two hours later, she was ready to give up. With her coworkers long gone, she was left alone to fend off unwanted advances from guys who thought she was waiting just for them.

Her breath caught in her throat when Bhathian walked in. So handsome, so sexy, that for a moment she could think of nothing other than the two of them naked in bed.

He grinned when he saw her and came over. "Trish, what a nice surprise. I was hoping to find you here."

"You were? So was I."

"Great. Do you want to stay a little longer or are you ready to go?" He offered her his hand as if sure of her response.

"I'm definitely ready to go. I've been waiting here for hours." She took his hand and let him help her to her feet.

"I'm sorry I didn't get here earlier."

"You couldn't have known that I was waiting."

Her hotel was five minutes' drive away, and just as before they couldn't keep their hands off each other, touching and kissing on the way up to her room.

She opened the way and walked in with Bhathian close on her heels, then pulled out the miniature whiskey bottle from her purse to remind herself that she was there on a mission and not to have crazy monkey sex with this gorgeous guy.

Her cheeks heated as she handed it to Bhathian.

He arched a brow.

"You'll need it," she told him.

Bhathian twisted the top off and finished the thing in one gulp.

"I'm pregnant."

His frown was a foreboding sign. *"And you think it's mine?"*

She couldn't fault Bhathian for questioning his paternity. After all, they'd been together just once.

"I know it is, I've been with no one else for months." Working undercover didn't lend itself to dating, and she wasn't the type who could do one-night stands.

Except that once.

Eva was so glad she'd broken her own rules. For years she'd been convinced she was infertile. There had been several boyfriends, and she hadn't always been as careful as she should've, and yet she'd never gotten pregnant.

Eva wanted this baby with everything she had.

"I want you to abort it. I'll pay whatever expenses and loss of income you'll incur, but there is nothing more I can offer you. I'm sorry."

He could not have hurt her more if he'd kicked her. She'd been afraid of him not wanting anything to do with her or the baby, but she hadn't expected him to be so cruel. So callous.

"I'm not going to abort my child," she whispered.

"Trish, be reasonable. I am not what you need. I can't be. A beautiful woman like you should have no trouble finding a good man. One that will make you happy, be a proper father to your children."

She fought hard to hold back the tears. "You don't understand, this is a miracle. I'm forty-five, and I haven't been on contraceptives for years because I couldn't get pregnant. And here I am, with a child growing inside me..." She lost the battle and tears began sliding down her cheeks.

"Oh, hell, Trish..." He took her in his arms. "I didn't know..."

"It's okay. I didn't come here expecting anything from you, just thought you'd be happy to know that you've created a child... and maybe... maybe put your name on the birth certificate when the time comes..."

"I'm sorry, I can't do that."

This was the worst scenario she'd run. "Oh my God, you're married, aren't you?"

"No, I didn't lie about that. It's just that I have some legal issues. But I can give you money, enough so you and your child will never lack anything."

Right. As if money would make everything okay. She didn't need his guilt money. He could take it and shove it up his ass.

Hot anger melted away the sweet fantasies she'd allowed herself to indulge in. Putting on her practiced fake smile, she said, "Thank you, that's very generous of you."

Those were the last words that man would ever hear from her.

Bhathian

"Yes?" Bhathian frowned at the unknown caller.

"It's me," Eva said. "I got your number from Nathalie."

Bhathian was shocked speechless.

Eva was calling him.

He needed to sit down.

"Hello, are you there?"

Bhathian shook his head. "Yes, I'm here. Just a little surprised. I didn't expect to get a call from you." Damn, now she'd think he was upset about her calling him. "I'm very happy that you did. That you are..." *Way to sound like a fumbling idiot.*

"Good. Would you like to come over?"

Eva was inviting him? No way. She probably wanted him to bring Nathalie.

"I can ask Nathalie if she's up for a visit, but she might be too tired this late in the day."

Eva chuckled. "I'm inviting you, Bhathian, not Nathalie. My crew went to see Jackson perform at a club. I have the house to myself."

Bhathian's throat felt dry. Was he dreaming? Had he fallen asleep on the couch? Because it sounded a lot like Eva was inviting him for a hookup.

"I'll be there in twenty minutes."

She chuckled again. "Drive safely, Bhathian. I don't want you to arrive all banged up."

Thank you, sweet Fates. His prayers had been answered.

Twenty minutes was what it would take to get to Eva's, and Bhathian still needed to shower and shave. In his rush to scrub every inch of his body clean, Bhathian almost tripped on the soap that slipped out of his hand, and the quick shave to get rid of his five o'clock shadow resulted in two cuts. Fortunately, not a big deal for his immortal body to heal.

He was in the car in under five minutes and driving like a bat out of hell to compensate for the time lost. As he pulled up to Eva's house, he saw her leaning against the railing of her third-floor balcony. She was wearing a long white dress, the wispy fabric billowing in the breeze and wrapping around her shapely legs only to be lifted by another gust and billow out again.

She was a vision of unattainable beauty.

He wasn't a fool. Her invitation wasn't meant to start a conversation that could in turn lead to a relationship. She would've chosen a more neutral ground for that. There had been nothing ambiguous about her summons.

It was a booty call, nothing more.

Eva had changed in the years since he'd first met her. She'd hardened. Not that she'd been soft then. Part of the incredible draw he'd felt toward her had been the effect of her confidence and a sense of purpose. And yet, as many young humans were, she'd been hopeful then, more open with her emotions.

Over the years Eva had lost this naïveté, the one only young humans were capable of. She'd become more like him and his clan members.

Jaded. Disillusioned. Closed off emotionally.

A side effect of living such long lives and witnessing too much shit.

The only time Bhathian had seen Eva's eyes soften was when looking at Nathalie, and sometimes at her young employees, but not at him.

Except for that one kiss.

She'd melted into him, letting her guard down for a moment.

It gave him hope. Where there was passion, feelings would follow. But only if she allowed it. Bhathian wasn't expecting it to happen anytime soon. He was anticipating a long and difficult fight.

"Hello, handsome." She opened the door for him with a seductive smile on her lips.

"I brought beer." He always kept a few in the fridge, saving him from arriving empty-handed.

She smirked as she opened the door wide, motioning for him to step inside. "You don't need to get me drunk to have your wicked way with me."

He didn't remember her being so forward. "Wicked? Is that how you remember me?"

The teasing expression slipped from her beautiful face, and for a split second he glimpsed sadness in her amber eyes. But she recovered quickly. "Wicked good in bed. That's how I remember you."

Bhathian put the beers down on the coffee table and sat on the couch. "Come here, beautiful." He patted the spot next to him.

She hesitated, some of her bravado melting away. "Don't you need a bottle opener?"

He shook his head and patted the couch again. "Quit stalling. I'm not going to bite. Not yet." He winked.

Sitting down, close but not as close as he would've liked her to, Eva chuckled nervously. "From what Nathalie tells me, I'm supposed to be excited about it. But I'm not sure I'm going to like it."

His eyes zeroed in on her neck, and the hard-on he'd been sporting ever since her call punched painfully against his zipper. "Only one way to find out," he hissed through elongated fangs.

Eva's eyes widened. "Oh, dear Lord, look at those teeth." She leaned closer to get a better look. "How come you didn't bite me when we made Nathalie?"

"I couldn't. You were resistant to thralling."

"Thralling?"

There was so much Eva still didn't know. "We can manipulate human minds. Make them forget what we don't want them to remember, like getting bitten during sex. It would've been impossible to keep our existence secret if women remembered it."

Eva frowned. "But you can refrain, right? Like you did with me. You can't go around turning random women."

He chuckled. "Life would have been much simpler for us if that was the case. The need to bite is part of the sexual urge. It's as difficult to refrain from biting as it is from ejaculating. We always bite. But Dormants are extremely rare, so the chance of turning one accidentally is negligible."

She pointed at herself. "I'm proof that it's possible."

"You're an anomaly. Some humans are resistant to thralling, especially those who are highly intelligent. I thought you were one of those. I couldn't erase the memory of the bite from your mind so I couldn't allow myself to do it."

Eva shifted, putting a little more space between them, and looked away. "It must've been hard."

"Extremely."

"So you didn't enjoy yourself as much as you could with someone else." Eva tried to sound casual, but he detected a hint of hurt in her tone.

Bhathian reached for her hand and lifted it to his lips for a gentle kiss. "Even without the bite, you blew my mind. You were, are, and will always be the best. You're incomparable."

She narrowed her eyes, her brows dipping low. "Don't lie to me, Bhathian, not even to spare my feelings. There is nothing I hate more than liars."

"I'm not. You still don't know me, but when you do, you'll see that I'm just too simple of a guy to complicate things with stories. For better or worse, what you see is what you get."

She chuckled. "I'm sorry. I shouldn't have accused you of deliberate deception. I guess I see others through the prism of my own experience. My whole life is one big lie."

"Don't. There is a big difference between lying to survive and lying to take advantage of others."

She sighed. "Thank you for giving me an honorable out."

"It's the truth."

"Mostly it is. But once lying becomes second nature, the distinction between necessity and convenience blurs."

Somehow things had gotten too serious and ruined Eva's flirtatious mood.

Bhathian cupped her cheek and leaned closer, waiting for her to lift her head and look at him. "From now on there is no place for untruths between us. Agreed?"

Eva nodded, but there was a shadow of doubt in her eyes. The question was who she was doubting, him or herself.

Eva

The truth.

Eva demanded it from Bhathian, but did she even know what it meant anymore?

Deception had become a way of life for her, and the only trouble she had with it was keeping her stories straight. Not an easy feat, given her shitty memory. A few rules simplified the elaborate net. One set of lies for her crew, another for her clients, and several sets she used and reused on missions.

Would she concoct a new one for Bhathian?

Or could she for once in her life discard the stories and stick with the truth? Lies had kept her safe. Lies had protected her from getting hurt. The truth might be seductively liberating, but it was also potentially dangerous.

Eva wasn't ready to lift her defenses and let Bhathian in.

He had to prove himself worthy of her trust first.

For now, she could traverse the narrow path between truth and deception—avoiding the latter but keeping the former to the bare minimum. Omitting the truth was still dishonest, but it wasn't at the same level as telling outright lies.

She pushed to her feet and extended her hand to Bhathian. "In the spirit of honesty, talking wasn't what I had in mind when I invited you. Let's go up to my bedroom."

Bhathian's beautiful gray eyes lit up like two flashlights, and when he smiled, the sight of his elongated fangs sent a shiver of apprehension up her spine.

No, that wasn't true.

Eva shook her head. Lying to herself was cowardly, and she was no coward. It must've been a natural instinct for an immortal female to respond with a shiver of lust to something that would've terrified any sane human.

Between one thought and the next, Bhathian took her hand and stood up. "Works for me. I'm not much for talking. Lead the way."

The touch was electrifying. Glancing at their entwined hands, she noted the difference in their sizes. Eva wasn't a small woman by anyone's standards, but Bhathian was such a large male that in comparison she felt dainty. Her hand was completely engulfed in his.

Their first and only time together, he'd picked her up and carried her to bed, and she was kind of hoping he would do the same now. If it were up to her, she would've reenacted every moment exactly. It had been perfect between them, and there was no reason to mess with perfection.

Hopefully, this time wouldn't disappoint.

It probably would, though. She wasn't even sure that the other time had been as amazing as she remembered it. Perhaps she'd built it up in her head to such an unattainable level that nothing would ever compare. None of the many lovers she'd had over the years had come close. The best sex since Bhathian happened between her ears, thinking of him while pleasuring herself.

She lifted her gaze from his hand to his handsome face and gasped. His eyes were smoldering with heat and shining with an eerie inner light. How come she hadn't noticed it then? Had she been too consumed by passion to realize that the man taking her to bed wasn't human?

He touched his thumb to her lips, running it along the seam. "I remembered your beauty quite vividly, but the memory didn't do you justice."

She chuckled nervously before admitting in a near whisper, "I forgot how big you were, but not how handsome, or how perfect it was between us."

His other hand wrapped around the back of her neck, holding her in place as he dipped his head and kissed her. It was nothing like the gentle, hesitant kiss next to her car, this was how he'd kissed her over thirty years ago.

Dominant, demanding, all male.

He let go of her hand to wrap his muscular arm around her, holding her close, the fingers of his other hand digging into the soft skin of her neck almost painfully, his tongue plundering her mouth as if he owned it.

Her muscles going lax and her knees buckling, Eva moaned, relying on Bhathian to hold her up in his steely grip.

She could let go with him.

That's how she wanted sex with a man to be. But it wasn't something she could've indulged in with any of her other lovers. Even if she could've trusted them enough to lower her guard, none had been strong enough to merit her submission, not even in pretense. She'd always been the strong one, the one in control, the one dominating the situation. None of her hookups had had what it took to dominate a woman like her, nor had merited her lowering her shields.

But, oh boy, how she'd craved it.

Was that the reason Bhathian had starred in most of her sexual fantasies? Because he was the only one she could imagine submitting to?

Not that he deserved it. Not after rejecting her. But at least she could pretend with him. The idea of submitting to Bhathian wasn't as ludicrous as choosing some random human to fulfill her darkest fantasies. He was so manly. A pillar of strength that unfortunately hadn't been there for her when she'd needed him most.

Still, it wasn't only his masculinity that affected her. But what else could it be? What else could she even know about him after only one night of passion?

His child, that's what.

Eva had often wondered how much of her real father Nathalie had inherited. She was an amazing young woman, and God knew she didn't get it all from Eva. Even Fernando had been a better influence on the girl than her own mother. All his other faults aside, Fernando had been an outstanding parent to Nathalie.

Bhathian let go of her mouth, a frown riding his forehead as he loosened the grip on her neck. "What's wrong? Did I hurt you?"

Eva shook her head. "No. It was perfect."

"Was it?" He bent and swung her up in his arms. "In that case, there are plenty more where that one came from."

Yes! She wrapped her arms around his neck and rested her cheek against his hard chest.

Taking the stairs two at a time, Bhathian didn't even breathe hard as he reached her third-floor bedroom. Kicking the door shut behind him, he walked over to her bed and lowered her carefully on top of the white coverlet.

For a long moment, his gaze roved over her body as if he was trying to memorize every inch of her. Would he undress her? Or did he expect her to do so herself?

If he were any other man, she would've commanded him to strip first, but Bhathian was different, and she was at a loss as to what to do next.

The skirt of her long, loose dress was hiked up over her knees, but nothing other than her legs was showing. They were tanned, the shade more bronze than her natural olive. Her legs were one of her best features, long and toned, their deep color contrasting with the white fabric of her dress.

Bhathian smiled as he sat beside her. "I remember these mile-long legs." His huge palm encircled one of her ankles, the warmth spreading as he ran it up over her calf and kept going under the bunched up fabric of her dress.

He stopped an inch away from her panties, his palm resting on the fleshy part of her inner thigh, then repeated the same on her other leg. The result of his ministrations was that her dress was hiked up almost all the way to exposing her, but not quite there.

It seemed that his intention was to torture her slowly. She could've ended it with one word, Bhathian would've done whatever she told him to, but Eva didn't want to. She wasn't bold enough to tell him what she needed, but hoped a man as experienced as Bhathian could read her body language right.

She hadn't asked him how old he was, but suspected Bhathian counted his age in centuries, not years. After that much practice, the man should be a master of sexual prowess.

For a second or two, his eyes remained glued to where the fabric of her dress ended and her thighs began. He seemed to be fighting an inner battle for whether to continue the trajectory and bare her, or rather expose her underwear.

She wished he would. There was a surprise waiting for him there.

Her panties were white cotton, but there was nothing modest about them. A small triangle covered her mound, and a slightly larger one covered a tiny portion of her butt cheeks. The two were held together by three elastic strings on each side. The bra was of similar design. A little thing that had nothing to do with providing shape, as her breasts didn't need uplifting and were large enough to forgo padding. Two small triangles covered little more than her nipples, and a small clasp at the front and an assortment of strings at the back comprised the rest.

Eva had a weakness for expensive lingerie, and this French label was one of her favorites. Their interesting designs were done in soft, comfortable fabrics, steering away from skin-irritating lace and fake gems like some of the more well-known brands.

Instead of continuing to expose her panties, Bhathian leaned forward and slipped the shoulders straps of her dress down her arms.

A giggle escaped her throat. He had her dress all bunched up in the middle, hiding all her sexy bits while exposing everything else.

"What's so funny?" he asked.

"I bet you unwrap your chocolate the same way. Remove everything and stop when you get to the tinfoil."

"Are you in a hurry?" He pretended to look behind his shoulder. "Are the kids due to arrive anytime soon?"

"No. We still have a lot of time. Besides, it's none of their business who I invite into my bed."

Bhathian

A growl bubbled up from somewhere deep in Bhathian's gut. "Do you bring men home often?" It wasn't that he thought Eva had abstained for all those years. As long as her hookups had been just that, one-night stands never to be seen again, it didn't bother him. But inviting a guy to her home was different. He didn't want any men hanging around Eva's private space and interacting with the people close to her.

It was difficult enough to think of her with Fernando, whom she'd been married to. How the hell could she have gone to bed with someone as unattractive? One day he would ask her about it, but not today. He hadn't earned the right to ask her personal questions like that yet.

Eva shook her head. "No, I never do. You're the first."

"Except for Fernando."

She averted her eyes. "He was my husband. But I really don't want to talk about him now. Way to spoil the mood."

"My bad." He should've known better than bring up her ex during an intimate moment like that. What the hell had compelled him to open his big mouth?

Jealousy.

Up until that moment, Bhathian hadn't acknowledged the jealousy he'd felt toward Fernando, not even to the therapist with her endless questions, but it had been lurking just beneath the surface. The guy had had years with Eva and Nathalie, years that should've been Bhathian's. It was wrong and unjustified to feel that way about the guy on so many levels, and most of the time Bhathian managed to subdue his jealousy with feelings of gratitude. After all, Fernando had stepped in and raised Nathalie to the best of his abilities. Besides, who in his right mind could be jealous of a guy suffering from a horrible disease that was eating away at his brain.

Eva sighed and reached for his hand. "Let's start over. So where were we? Candy wrappers and delayed gratification, right?"

He smiled. "Yes. I'm a master of self-denial. Most of the time it's just my nasty attitude and self-loathing, but sometimes it's about the pleasure. It's more intense after a prolonged wait."

Eva narrowed her eyes. "Self-loathing? Why?"

Damn. At the rate he was flapping his big mouth and spouting shit, they would never get to the sex.

Bhathian hung his head. "I've never been an upbeat kind of guy. I don't understand those cheerful sorts. What the hell is there to be so happy about? The world we live in is shit, humans are shitty, and so are most of the immortals. But it got worse after I lost you."

Rubbing his palm over his chest, he admitted, "It always felt as if something vital was missing from my life, from my soul. I was going on autopilot, doing my duty but not really living."

Baring his soul to Eva was a mistake of monumental proportions, and yet he couldn't stop the self-destructive streak. Once he allowed a small crack in the wall he'd built around himself, more struggled to push through.

"I'm not good with words, and I can't explain the feeling. The best description I can think of is a gaping hole in my gut. It's like a hunger for something I had and lost but needed to survive. Nathalie soothed some of that ache, but I believe that only you can heal it."

Eva's stunned expression confirmed his fears. She wasn't ready for his confession. The compassion in her eyes lasted no longer than a split second. He watched as her shields snapped back into place, turning her into the emotionless operative she'd become.

"Darling," she husked and pushed to her knees.

Her dress fell around her hips, exposing her bra-covered breasts. "The only ache I can help soothe for you is the one down here." She reached for his belt, unbuckling it with deft fingers. "As I said before, the time for talking is over." She popped his jeans button and pulled down the zipper.

He hissed as she freed him and her hand closed around his throbbing shaft.

With a seductive smirk, she leaned toward Bhathian and caught his lower lip between her teeth, nipping and sucking on it while her hand caressed him in a slow up and down motion.

Dear Fates, if she didn't stop, he was going to explode like a horny teenager touched by a girl for the very first time.

"Stop." He took her hand off his dick.

"Why?"

"Because you're still wearing too much." He reached for her dress and yanked it over her head. Not very romantic, but then what did he know about romance? Nothing. He did know, however, a thing or two about fucking, and since it seemed that it was all Eva was interested in, he didn't need to fumble like a fool trying to be something he wasn't.

Her bra was next. Popping the front clasp, he bared her firm breasts. From her kneeling position, Eva's pebbled dark nipples were level with his mouth and he took one between his lips.

Eva moaned, and her head dropped back on her neck. Bhathian wrapped his arm around her and brought her closer, holding her in place as he teased one peak and then the other, sucking and nipping then laving the little hurt away. When he was done, her nipples were so distended that they pointed out like two slim knobs.

Lifting her head to look at him with hooded eyes, Eva smiled like a satisfied cat, then hooked her thumbs in the strings holding the two parts of her panties together and pushed down. After shimmying out of them, she tossed them over his head and lay back, propped on a big stack of white pillows, her dark wavy hair spilling like silk to frame her beautiful face.

"You're wearing too many clothes," she threw his words back at him.

Yes, he was.

His light blue button-down was tailored for him like the few other dress shirts he owned. None of the store-bought stuff fit his muscular body. His everyday attire was comprised of T-shirts, which stretched to accommodate his bulk, but he wanted to look good tonight —show Eva that he cared.

Far from graceful, he attacked the buttons and shrugged the dress shirt off, then kicked off his boots and got rid of his jeans and socks.

During the entire fifteen seconds or so that it had taken him to get naked, Eva watched him like a hungry tigress, her amber eyes glowing from the inside and betraying her arousal. Not that he needed additional confirmation. The air in Eva's bedroom was saturated with the combined scents of their mutual desire.

"You must work out a lot," she said as her eyes roved over his body.

"You like?" Most females found him attractive, but some were not into big bulging muscles and preferred the slimmer types. He wondered which camp Eva belong to.

"You're magnificent. But then you probably know it and are fishing for compliments."

True, but he wasn't going to admit it. Instead, he climbed on the bed and lay sideways, propping his head on his arm to admire the beauty before him.

She looked at him questioningly, probably wondering what he had in mind. "You're the one who's magnificent." He wrapped an arm around her and pulled her on top of him. At nearly three hundred pounds he was too heavy for her.

Or maybe not.

As an immortal female, Eva could probably take his weight, no problem. But he wasn't sure.

She smiled and kissed him, then nuzzled his neck. "You're overthinking this."

Damn, the woman was perceptive. "I don't know what's okay and what's not with an immortal woman. I don't want to hurt you."

She seemed frustrated as she shook her head. "Don't worry about it. I'm very resilient."

He had a feeling he wasn't reading her right. Hell, he was sure of it. Normally it wouldn't have bothered him, Bhathian didn't need to prove anything to the random females he picked up in bars, but he wanted to do it right for Eva.

Problem was, he was no good at reading people, women in particular. Unless she told him what she needed, he would not have a clue.

Eva

Disappointing.

Eva had expected to be blown away. Having sex with the man she'd dreamed about for so long should've been passionate, combustive, a perfect coming together. Instead, they were both fumbling like a couple of greenhorns.

Maybe it was time for that honesty they'd talked about. Except, what would she say? *I dreamt about sex with you for three decades, but it was nothing like this?*

That would kill the mood completely.

Or worse, he could ask her about those sexual fantasies, and she would rather die than tell him.

It seemed she would have to resign herself to experiencing her fantasies only inside her head. Where was the confident and dominant man she remembered?

Had she embellished the reality of their lovemaking? Transforming what had been good sex into phenomenal?

Or perhaps it was Bhathian who had changed.

It was obvious that guilt sat heavily on his shoulders, as it should, and it made him over-cautious. Bhathian was so desperate to do everything right this time around that he was overthinking every move.

She wished he cared less.

Heck, she wished he was only interested in sex with her and nothing more. Then he'd feel free to be who he was and not the diluted version he was presenting her with.

Maybe she should call it off.

But then what? Go to some club and pick up a lousy human?

She was so sick of those once-a-month hookups. Maybe she could do without for longer, like once every three months. And then once every six months, and then none at all.

But that was just sad.

His arms closed around her, caging her as effectively as iron chains. "You need to tell me," he said softly.

"Tell you what?" Playing dumb was not her style, but she wasn't herself with this man. All the rules she'd lived by for the past thirty years didn't apply to him—to them—two immortals who barely knew each other and yet were connected by the life they had created together.

Who was she kidding, the connection was there from the first moment she'd laid eyes on Bhathian, and it had most likely been the same for him.

"Tell me what you need," he reiterated.

Eva lifted her head and stared into his gray eyes. "I want you to stop worrying, to stop thinking, and just take me like you did the first time." This was as far as she was willing to go with the truth. Hopefully it would be enough. If not, then so be it. It wouldn't be the first dream of hers to go up in smoke. Unfortunately, disappointment was a familiar foe.

Under her, Bhathian's shaft twitched and got even harder. Looking into his eyes, she saw the uncertainty bleed out, that had dogged him ever since their reunion over a month ago, replaced by the steely determination she'd remembered from before. The change was quite startling.

Moving faster than she thought possible, Bhathian flipped them around, pinning her underneath his huge body. God, he was heavy, and if not for the hard stuff immortal bodies were made of, he would've squashed all the air from her lungs. A split second later he grabbed her wrists, pulling her arms over her head, then caged them with one hand.

The predatory smile on his face dared her to try to get free, and the wild thing inside her accepted the challenge. If Bhathian couldn't hold her down, he wasn't worthy of her.

Animalistic thinking, no doubt about it, and for a moment Eva felt ashamed for letting her humanity slip. But then women did it all the time, just not physically. That's why the nicest gals were sometimes absolutely bitchy to their boyfriends, challenging them to see whether they would fold under the verbal aggression or refuse to take it.

Eva tried to pull her hands free, but even though he was holding her wrists loosely, she could move them only as far as the slack he allowed.

She sighed and stopped struggling, a languid contentment overtaking the irritation and discomfort of a few moments ago.

Finally.

That's what she wanted, what she needed, to be at the mercy of a man who she could trust to take care of her sexually. As far as life outside of bed, she had no such illusions. And frankly, no need. She didn't need a man to take care of her financially or even emotionally. She was perfectly satisfied with her life as it was. Especially now that she had Nathalie and shortly a granddaughter to love.

Bhathian didn't let go of her wrists as he dipped his head and took her mouth with bruising passion. The moment he asserted his dominance, Eva was flooded with wetness. Moaning into his mouth, she wished he would enter her and relieve the ache between her legs.

But he was in no hurry, and as his tongue pillaged her mouth, his fingers found her moist center and delved inside.

One, and then two.

She spread her legs wider, inviting more.

He fucked her with his fingers, while his thumb pressed against her clit, until she was writhing under him as much as his weight on top of her allowed.

"I need more," she heard herself beg.

A soft whimper of protest left her mouth as his fingers abandoned her sheath, but a moment later, as he pushed inside her with one forceful shove, her groan of pleasure was laced with pain.

She'd forgotten how large Bhathian was. Their first time together he'd been more careful with her, wringing a couple of orgasms with his tongue before entering her one slow inch at a time and letting her get used to his girth.

But she wasn't complaining. This was exactly what she'd asked for, what she'd wanted.

The pain was welcome, and it was not nearly enough. Regrettably, Bhathian wasn't the kind of man who'd hurt a woman even if she asked him to.

He didn't move, watching her face as he remained poised above her. "Okay?" he asked.

With a tight smile, she nodded.

He dipped his head and kissed her. A tender lover's kiss that made her ache in a completely different way. A yearning for what could've been.

A lone tear slid down her cheek.

Bhathian lapped at the tear and kissed her again, pulling out almost completely. When he pushed back, he was gentle, going slow and shallow until the last of the discomfort was gone.

She wanted to wrap her arms around him and hold him close, to pretend there was love between them, but he was still holding on to her wrists. His tempo increased, and soon he was pounding into her with the power and vigor she remembered so well even after all those years.

Thank heavens.

Eva closed her eyes and just felt—the physical sensations bombarding every nerve ending in her body and chasing away feelings she didn't want. Immobilized by Bhathian's bulk and his iron grip, she was content to be no more than a vessel, a receptacle for his lust and his seed.

It was perfect.

Bhathian

Startled, Bhathian watched a tear slide down Eva's cheek.

He'd been remiss, emboldened by her spurring and the novelty of bedding a resilient, immortal woman. He should've refused to rush and brought her to a climax with his fingers and his tongue first. Then she would've been ready to accept him within her, experiencing only pleasure.

A mistake he wouldn't repeat no matter how much Eva protested.

Why the hell was she in such a hurry?

Was his memory faulty or had Eva's attitude toward sex changed drastically?

The woman he remembered had been playful, adventurous, and overconfident as only a stunning beauty like Eva could be. She'd been assertive, demanding—a tigress who'd fought her male for dominance and only submitted when he'd proven himself worthy by pleasuring her into oblivion.

It had been the best sex of his life.

The one trapped under him now seemed almost docile, like all the fight had been knocked out of her.

She was an immortal, and thirty-one years were supposedly a blink of an eye in her lifespan, but apparently they had taken their toll. The thing was, it hadn't been easy for him either. The pain of guilt and the sorrow of regret had a way of souring one's existence and stretching the hours of wakefulness into infinity until some relief could be found in sleep. And even then, the torment sometimes continued in his dreams.

It was time for the misery to end. Deep in his gut, Bhathian believed that Eva and he were each other's salvation. The healing process would start the moment they reconnected, and the kick off was now, in this bed, where he knew he could give her what she needed.

Bhathian licked the tear off, then kissed her tenderly, pouring his soul into that kiss, communicating with his lips and his tongue what Eva wasn't ready to hear him say. He started to move only when she went soft under him, her muscles losing the rigidity his careless invasion had caused.

He was able to keep up the gentle rhythm of shallow thrusts for about thirty seconds. Maintaining control and going slow when he was starved for her was becoming an impossible task.

His fangs started dripping with venom the moment he started to move. His body was a well-oiled machine, readying for the climax that was bearing upon him like a freight train loaded with granite slabs. There was no stopping it, not even delaying the explosion for a moment or two so Eva could catch up.

With a roar, he jetted into her, his fangs sinking into her neck at the same time.

Eva orgasmed immediately, and he kept pumping her full of his seed and his venom, prolonging her climax until they were both spent.

Bhathian pulled out his fangs and licked the two points of entry closed. He was still hard, but Eva wasn't with him anymore, and it didn't feel right to keep going while she wasn't aware of what he was doing to her.

Holding himself on his forearms, he gave her room to breathe while watching her peaceful face, her beautiful yet harsh features softened by the euphoria she'd experienced moments ago.

He'd seen plenty of women soar on the clouds of post-venom euphoria; the difference was that this time he wouldn't have to erase the memory.

For some reason, it always felt wrong to him. More than the act of biting an unsuspecting female, Bhathian hated taking away the memory of what had to be their best orgasm. Or at least the venom-induced part. The aphrodisiac and euphoric effect of an immortal male's venom was incomparable to any sexual experience a female could ever have. It was a shame to rob her of the memory.

Would it affect an immortal female more than a human?

Or less?

If he were a more outgoing guy, like Anandur, he could've asked Kri. She was a fellow Guardian and more approachable than Syssi or Amanda, the only two other immortal females who had immortal mates. But then Kri and Amanda had always had sex as immortals and wouldn't know the difference. That left only Syssi, who'd experienced a venom bite as a human and as an immortal. But asking the regent's wife a personal question like that was even beyond Anandur's chutzpah.

Eva's lids opened a crack, and a lazy smile spread across her face. With her features more relaxed than he'd ever seen them, she was even more beautiful than before.

Lifting a sluggish hand, she touched her neck where he'd bitten her. "That was amazing. I've never done drugs, but that's what a good trip must feel like."

He kissed her cheek. "It's better. And there are no nasty side effects, only benefits."

Her lids lifted a few more millimeters. "If we make love one more time, would you bite me again?"

"If you want me to. After the first time, I can control the urge better. I will also last longer than a couple of minutes." He chuckled nervously.

With a dazzling smile, Eva wrapped her arms around his torso and swiveled her hips. "You're still deliciously hard, my Bhathian. I think you've got several more in you."

"I certainly do." He retreated a little then pushed all the way in, pulling a throaty moan out of her throat. "How about you?"

"I can go for hours." She lifted her hips and got him to sink even deeper. "I wonder who will give up first."

A grin splitting his face, Bhathian retreated once more and rammed all the way back in. "Challenge accepted, female."

Thank you, dear Fates.

His Eva was back.

Tessa

"It's so freaking noisy in here," Tessa said to no one in particular.

Nick was up on the stage, jamming with Vlad, the loudspeakers blasting the sounds from their guitars at a painful level.

Sharon was all over a cute guy, a soloist for one of the bands that had performed tonight. He wasn't much of a singer, and was probably a few years younger than Sharon, but he was good-looking in a boyish sort of way, and seemed like a nice guy.

Sharon had a sixth sense about stuff like that and could tell right away if a guy was a jerk who only pretended to be nice. She was just as good at sniffing out bitchy girls, but that was easy. Even Tessa could do that. One look was usually enough. The condescending way they regarded others and their body language betrayed their true nature. You couldn't be nice and look down at everyone.

Very few people were genuinely nice. Tessa had experienced the worst and the best in humanity. The thing was, she'd met a lot of demons and only one angel. Eva. The person who'd helped her escape the nightmare she'd lived through. Tessa owed the woman her life.

"Would you like to step outside for some fresh air?" Jackson said as he neared their table. With her friends scattered to do their own thing, she was the only one left.

"You read my mind." She smiled and took the coke he handed her.

"I heard you say it's too loud in here."

He couldn't have. He'd been all the way over at the bar when she'd spoken. "Do you read lips?"

Jackson nodded, looking as if she'd caught him doing something bad. "A little."

Tessa got to her feet and grabbed her purse. "Let's go."

Feeling the chilly air all the way down to her bones, she pulled out the thin cardigan she'd stuffed in there before going out. One of the things she loved about Tampa was the constant heat. The temperature differences between night and day were much more extreme in Los Angeles, and Tessa hated being cold. With her nonexistent fat layer, she had no defense against the chill.

"Here, let me hold your coke." Jackson took the can out of her hand so she could get her sweater on.

"Thanks."

It was dark, the few street lamps leaving a lot of shadows in the spaces between them. If not for Jackson's company, Tessa would've never ventured outside the club even if it was located in a better area. According to Jackson, North Hollywood was not the best of neighborhoods. But for some reason the eighteen-year-old boy made her feel safe.

It wasn't his size, though, but the inner strength and kindness she sensed in him. That being said, she was sure he could hold his own in a fight. Jackson was not only powerfully built, but graceful as a gymnast. Tall and wide shouldered, he carried his body with confidence. His posture was perfect and his limbs so well coordinated that his movements seemed fluid.

She'd expected a guy as handsome as him to be full of himself, arrogant, and he was, but somehow he managed to be charming nonetheless. Perhaps the difference was that Jackson didn't put anyone down to make himself look better. He didn't need to. In fact, he was incredibly generous with his praise.

People liked him.

Hell, she liked him. A lot.

Bhathian, Nathalie's cousin on her father's side, was impressive, but he couldn't hold a candle to Jackson. Not in the looks department. In a fight, it was doubtless the other way around.

Bhathian was a warrior.

Jackson was a lover.

As heat spread over her cheeks, Tessa was thankful for the cover of darkness. It was so embarrassing to lust after a boy who was barely legal.

Lust?

What's that?

Tessa had never felt it before. Her innocence had been brutally stripped away before she'd had a chance to feel anything like that. There were some movie stars and rock stars she'd daydreamed about, but not flesh-and-blood boys. What she'd experienced at the hands of the opposite sex had been so awful she never wanted anything to do with any of them again. If she were a religious person, she could've joined a convent and never looked back.

Until Eva had dragged her along to Los Angeles.

Something had shifted inside Tessa when she'd met Bhathian and then Jackson. Good men. Men a woman could trust.

"There is a bench over there." Jackson pointed to a shadowy enclave.

If he were any other guy, she would've run inside as fast as her short legs could carry her. A dark, isolated spot was what her nightmares were made of.

Jackson must've sensed her sudden flare of panic. "Unless it's too cold for you. We can get back inside."

She forced a smile. "It's a bit chilly, but I like the quiet and the fresh air." If she were ever to get over her fears, this was the perfect opportunity. If she couldn't feel safe with Jackson, she was probably a lost cause.

Tessa refused to accept that there was no hope for her. One day she'd heal. One day she'd be able to suffer a man's touch and not cringe in fear. But for that to happen, she needed to take the first step.

Tiny, baby steps. That was all she could promise herself.

He chuckled. "I wouldn't call this air fresh, but it's better than what's in there." He pointed back at the club.

"Yeah, definitely." She followed him over to the bench and sat down beside him. There was at least a foot between them, but it was the closest she could get.

For now.

Tessa took a sip from her coke and slanted a glance at Jackson. "It must be a bummer to perform in a club and not be able to get a drink."

He shrugged. "I have a fake driver's license. I just don't like the stuff."

"Oh, yeah? How come?" She didn't drink either, but most of the people she knew wouldn't enjoy an outing without a couple of drinks.

"I like being sharp. I don't get what's fun about dulling your brain and diminishing your senses."

Interesting. Very atypical for a guy his age. Not that she'd had much contact with teenagers, but the impression she'd gotten from watching sitcoms and movies was that they all wanted to grow up as fast as they could and considered alcohol consumption as an important milestone and sign of maturity. So stupid. Mainly the rush to grow up. Tessa would've given anything to go back in time and have a normal childhood. Those kids didn't know how good they had it. A home, loving parents, a world that didn't seem bound on devouring them. Innocence was bliss.

"So you never had a drink? Not even once?"

He grimaced. "Let's say that the one time I did was a lesson I will never forget."

Jackson had such a pleasant voice she just wanted to keep him talking. Besides, as long as he talked she didn't have to. The truth was that she didn't have much to tell. The agency's business was confidential, and her private life was boring.

Thank God for that. Tessa would take boring over horrific any day.

"Tell me about it," she prompted.

He smiled. "It was at my cousin's wedding. My friends and I snuck out a few bottles—"

Eva

The house was still quiet when Eva shook off the stupor that had engulfed her like a thick blanket of fluffy pink clouds. The post-coital euphoria had been out of this world.

Eva hadn't felt so refreshed and so calm in ages, not even after a full night's sleep. Not that she'd gotten many of those. Most nights she would toss and turn as a barrage of unwanted thoughts bombarded her mind, keeping her awake. Her immortal body didn't need much downtime, but an hour or two wasn't enough even for her.

Turning on her side, Eva propped herself on her elbow and regarded the male sleeping next to her, letting her eyes roam over his magnificent body. Normally she wasn't into the bodybuilder types, but on Bhathian it looked good. His muscles weren't for decoration. The guy was a fighter—a Guardian.

Their occupations were something they had in common other than contributing to Nathalie's genes. Except, Bhathian was still in the business of law enforcement. Even though his job was the policing of his clan, he wasn't breaking any of the laws governing the rest of American society. Eva, on the other hand, was skirting on its edges.

In the eyes of the law she was a criminal, a murderer, but in absolute terms she was a deliverer of justice. The problem was that a man like Bhathian would never understand it. Three decades ago, neither had she. As a Federal agent, she had not only followed the rules but believed in them. If everyone took matters into their own hands, society would unravel and chaos would rule.

She still believed that, believed in the necessity of following the law, but the law didn't do enough to protect and save the victims suffering at the hands of evil.

So yeah, she was putting herself above the law and answering to no one other than God. The thing was, God had never spoken to her, and her belief that she'd been given her special abilities to deliver His justice was just that—a belief.

The cost of her actions might be the damnation of her soul.

It was a risk she'd considered and accepted.

But that was before.

Now that she'd gotten her Nathalie back and had discovered the fantastic circumstances that had made her, Eva's conviction was starting to waver. It was tempting to leave the meting out of justice to others and go back to being a mother and soon a grandmother.

Life would be so much simpler.

Could she, though?

Probably not. And if she was honest with herself, it wasn't only the concern for the victims. She got a rush out of ridding the world of the worst of its maggots.

It was an addiction of sorts.

The last thing she needed was a man like Bhathian around. He was basically a cop, suspicious and trained to sniff out criminal activity. She doubted he would involve the human authorities if he found anything, but there was no way he could turn a blind eye to her illegal activities.

The best course of action was to limit their interaction to the bedroom and send him home as soon as they were done. The less time they spent talking, the better.

His eyelids popped open the moment she touched his arm.

"Hi," he said with a lazy smile.

She couldn't help but smile back. He deserved at least that after giving her God knew how many orgasms. "Hi to you too. You must be hungry after all the activity. Want to go down to the kitchen?" She couldn't tell him to get dressed and beat it, but going downstairs was a step closer to the front door.

He gathered her into him and kissed her softly. "No, I would much rather stay in bed with you."

So much for polite hints. Men just didn't get them.

Eva closed her eyes and let herself enjoy the moment. Bhathian was so warm, and his arms around her felt as safe as a Kevlar vest. Besides, she needed to think of a way to send him home that wouldn't sound rude or make him feel like a gigolo. It wasn't something she'd done before and had a procedure in place for. The men she hooked up with never came home with her—it was either their place or a hotel.

Easy.

As soon as the guy fell asleep, she snuck out. Once in a while she'd left a note, mostly she'd left nothing behind other than a memory of great sex.

Come to think of it, that thralling thing Bhathian had talked about could come in handy. She needed him to show her how to do it.

She pushed on his chest to get some space. "Could you teach me how to thrall? I can use a trick like that in my line of work."

He chuckled. "My performance must've left a lot to be desired if the first thing you do after is think about work."

"I've been awake for a while."

"Ouch, even worse. I dosed you with so much venom I was sure you'd be out for the night."

She tapped his nose. "You forget I'm an immortal like you. The venom doesn't affect me as it does the human females you sleep with."

For some reason he found her remark funny, the corners of his lips twitching with a smile. "I love how old-fashioned you are. You're still mindful of the language you use. It's sweet."

True, she'd been raised in the Fifties, when using crude language had been considered unladylike. Her parents had been very strict about it, and it stuck with her. Out loud, Eva often used darn instead of damn, and shoot instead of shit.

Yeah, as if foul language was more unladylike than killing.

"Trust me, I'm not sweet. So can you teach me or not?"

"I can try."

"Wonderful. Let's clean up, and you can show me how it's done over a cup of coffee in the kitchen."

Bhathian frowned, the hints finally making it through his thick man-skull. "Mind if I take a shower?"

She waved a hand. "Go ahead. There are clean towels in the basket by the bathtub. I'll use one of the other bathrooms."

His frown deepened, and his eyes darkened. He was definitely getting the gist of it now and not liking it one bit.

Well, tough.

"Aren't the kids back yet?" he asked, although he must've been as aware as she was that there was no one but them in the house.

"No, I hope that means that they are having a good time and not that they ran into some kind of trouble."

"In that case, I hope you don't mind if I don't pull on my pants." Bhathian swung his legs over the side of the bed and sauntered to the bathroom in his birthday suit.

She didn't mind at all.

Watching this finest of asses was a nice treat.

Nathalie

Watching Onidu operate the cappuccino machine, Nathalie said, "I wish we knew how to make more of them." His second day on the job and he was already a pro at it. His machine learning was so enviably fast. Onidu remembered every word and every instruction perfectly. There was no need to repeat anything.

Which meant that instead of working in the café, Nathalie and Carol were enjoying it as guests, chitchatting with Bridget and Syssi who'd joined them for coffee.

"I know, right?" Syssi leaned back in her chair and crossed her arms over her chest. "Imagine a world full of Odus. Other than artists and scientists and the like, no one will need to work."

Bridget snorted. "It'll be the end of the world as we know it. Wars will start out of pure boredom."

"I don't know about that," Carol said. "I have no problem with unemployment. On the contrary, as long as I have the money to pay the bills, I enjoy leisure." She sighed dramatically. "I thought apprenticing with Gerard would be fun. But it's going to be slave work."

Nathalie shook her head. Carol was something else. "You didn't even start yet, and you're already complaining?"

Carol's face twisted in a grimace. "I saw Gerard yesterday."

Nathalie had met Gerard. The guy was nice but a bit of a prima donna. But then most chefs were, even those who weren't as talented and successful as the owner of By Invitation Only. "What did he do?"

"In so many words, he told me that he never takes in amateurs, and that he is doing it for me only because of what I've gone through. I'm to watch and do as I'm told and not ask any questions. Basically, I'm starting as a fetch girl. He said he wouldn't even trust me to cut vegetables, only to peel them."

"Ouch, that's harsh," Syssi said.

Carol sighed. "I'm rethinking the whole idea. I told Gerard I would start in a week, after Onidu took over for me, but I think I should wait for at least a month after the baby gets here and help you. I just can't leave you here with only Onidu. And what are you going to do when you're out of commission? Leave Onidu to do everything by himself? It's not going to work. You'll need to close the café."

Nathalie had been thinking along the same lines. Standing for more than an hour was becoming difficult, and pretty soon she wouldn't be able to do even that. Then after the baby arrived, she wanted some peaceful time with her child and her husband without having to worry about the café. Onidu was a great help, but he couldn't be left alone to handle everything. Someone needed to tell him what to do. The only thing that had stopped Nathalie from begging Carol to stay was that she didn't want to stand in the way of her fulfilling her dream.

"Are you sure? You're not exaggerating Gerard's mean attitude to ease my conscience for keeping you here?"

With a snort, Carol crossed her arms over her chest. "I'm sure. And believe me, I'm not exaggerating. If anything, I downplayed it. He was snotty and looked at me down his nose as if I was a nuisance he was being forced to tolerate. The only reason I didn't tell him to forget it right away was Kian. After I'd pleaded with him to arrange for an interview with Gerard, I would've looked like a flake if I refused the offer."

"Smart. I'm not sure I could've kept my mouth shut. If it were me, I would've probably told Gerard what I thought of his attitude and where he could shove it." Nathalie hated pompous jerks, but Carol had done the right thing. With the girl's reputation, everyone would've assumed that she hadn't been serious and had chosen the easy way out.

Carol unfolded her arms and pointed at her head. "I might look like a bimbo, but I'm not brainless. Can I ask you a favor, though?"

"Sure. Anything."

"I need you to back me up and say that you asked me to stay."

"No problem. And so it wouldn't be a lie, I'm asking you now. Can you please stay and take over the café so I can take a maternity leave?"

Carol dipped her head in a slight bow. "It would be my pleasure."

"If you want, I can make it even better," Bridget said. "I can write a note saying Nathalie needs to stop working four weeks before the delivery. Doctor's orders."

Syssi shook her head. "I don't think it will be needed. If it were up to Kian, he would've ordered you to stop a month ago. He keeps saying that you shouldn't be working with that enormous belly of yours."

Nathalie pouted. "Thanks a lot, Syssi. I already feel like a whale."

Syssi lifted both hands in the air. "It wasn't me, it was Kian who said it. And just so you know, I would trade

255

places with you in a heartbeat. Humongous belly and all."

Everyone's eyes turned to Syssi, but it was Bridget who spoke first. "You want a baby? Already?"

With a sad expression on her delicate face, Syssi nodded, but then forced a smile. "It must be Nathalie's pregnancy hormones. I don't know what came over me. I'm only twenty-six and newly married. There is plenty of time for babies."

It seemed Syssi was trying to convince herself. The truth was that her chances of getting pregnant were so dismal that it would probably take centuries until she conceived. Babies were a rarity in the immortal world.

"I spend most of my days with Nathalie, and I don't want a baby," Carol said.

Nathalie kicked her under the table. "Carol is a special case. It must be the hormones. Right, Bridget?" She rolled her eyes, urging the doctor to agree.

"It's possible."

Good enough. Time to change the subject. "I have a piece of juicy gossip." She tried to lean forward for emphasis, but her belly prevented it. "Bhathian went over to Eva's yesterday, and I know for a fact that they were alone because Jackson told me Eva's crew came to hear him play at the club his band was performing at."

Syssi's smile was back. "Did he tell you that he was going to see her?"

"Not exactly. Anandur saw him leaving. He told me that Bhathian was wearing a button-down, which he wears only on special occasions, and he had enough cologne on him to make the entire parking level smell like a gay brothel. Anandur's words, not mine."

Bridget arched a brow. "It's a lot to assume just by that. Bhathian might have gone out, you know, to prowl the clubs."

Nathalie shook her head. Apparently, in the short time she'd known him, she'd learned more about Bhathian than the people who'd known him for decades or even centuries. "He wears T-shirts to clubs and uses a simple aftershave. I think it's called Tabac. Anandur said this scent was of one of those fancy department store colognes. He'd been surprised that Bhathian even owned something like that."

"Are you excited?" Syssi asked.

The truth was that Nathalie was conflicted. On the one hand, Eva and Bhathian were her biological parents and if they found a way to reconnect it would be wonderful, especially for their granddaughter. But what about Fernando? How long could they hide Eva from him?

One day they would have to face the music and let him see her. How would he react to her? To Bhathian and Eva being together?

Poor Papi. He would probably think his wife was back. It would break his heart.

She needed to confront her mother and find out what the hell had happened between Eva and Fernando. Had the divorce been part of Eva's attempt to hide who she was? But it happened years before her disappearance.

"I'm not sure how I feel about it. I need to have a chat with my mother."

Jackson

"We're going to stay open late again," Gordon murmured as he passed by Jackson, holding a tray with two freshly made sandwiches.

Jackson eyed the booths with a frown. It was nearly closing time, but the café was still packed, people taking their sweet time to finish their fucking coffees and sandwiches.

Maybe he should let Vlad out of the kitchen and have him start cleaning tables. One look at the guy and there would be a stampede to the door. Jackson didn't get it. Vlad was the nicest guy. So what if he looked like a vampire wannabe. A lot of kids were rocking the Goth look. Vlad wasn't that unusual.

Humans were strange.

As if Vlad with his spindly limbs and hunched back posed a threat to anyone. Naturally, that wasn't true. He only looked weak. Vlad was strong even by immortal standards. Jackson and Gordon had both seen him lift a car one-handed. It had been parked over two spots, and he moved it to make room for his Civic.

Vlad scared people for the simple reason that he looked different. A teenager who was over six and a half feet tall, weighed about one hundred pounds, had mismatched eyes, and canines that looked like fangs. Jackson wondered whether Vlad's fangs were defective and didn't retract all the way, or were they just longer than any other immortal male's. Not that he was ever going to ask. The guy felt awkward about it as it was, even among other immortals.

The only place Vlad fit in was on stage. He was one hell of a guitarist, and besides, a strange-looking rocker was the norm rather than the exception. At the clubs they'd performed, hardly anyone commented on Vlad's appearance except to say his costume was cool. Still, it didn't mean that anyone cozied up to him, or that any girls paid him any attention.

Except for Tessa.

Jackson had been surprised at the casual ease with which Tessa had interacted with Vlad. The girl appeared to be scared of her own shadow and yet she'd been sweet to him.

Like everyone else, Vlad assumed Tessa was a kid, so he hadn't flipped out when she'd complimented his performance. If he had known Tessa was a twenty-one-year-old woman, the dude would've been still blushing and stammering today.

The big question was whether Tessa would be okay with dating a guy three years younger than her. Jackson had been with plenty of older girls, but that hadn't been dating. They were fine fucking him but not showing him to their friends. It wasn't about his looks, he was one hell of a good-looking guy, even if he said so himself, but a college girl wouldn't be caught dead dating a high-school student.

Except, Jackson wasn't in high school anymore. He was managing a business and doing well. Hell, he was doing fucking amazing. With the new arrangement he had with Nathalie, he was collecting forty percent of the café's net profits.

Not bad for an eighteen-year-old dude.

Perhaps staying open a little later was not a bad idea. One more hour could potentially add ten percent to his bottom line. A quick check of the day's gross receipts showed that an additional one-tenth of that could've been sweet even after paying Vlad and Gordon and the new human waitress overtime.

Nah, not doable. He and the guys couldn't work late because of the band—most of the clubs they performed at wanted them there by seven—and he was not going to leave the human in charge. She was still new, and he wasn't sure she could be trusted with the register and all the money inside.

Not that he was suspicious by nature, but it was just common sense. The new employee had to prove herself first.

The chimes on the door jingled, announcing yet another customer. Jackson lifted his head and was about to tell whoever it was to come back tomorrow, but then he saw it was Tessa. Now that was a customer he didn't mind serving late.

"Hi, Tessa." He grinned at her.

"Hi," she said, looking uncomfortable. "Is the kitchen closed already? Am I too late?"

"Even if it were, I would've reopened it for you."

She shifted from foot to foot, looking even more uncomfortable. "I don't want to inconvenience you. I would've come earlier, but I had work to finish. I didn't have dinner, and everyone was out, and I didn't feel like making something at home."

Cute. Tessa was nervous like an awkward middle-schooler. Was it because she was into him? He took an inconspicuous sniff. The strong coffee smell that permeated the place overpowered all but the strongest scents, but Tessa was standing only a couple of feet away from him and yet he could detect no scent of arousal, just a faint whiff of nervousness.

Bummer. She wasn't attracted to him. Did she want a friend? Was that the reason she came?

Was she lonely?

He supposed there was a first time for everything. Like a girl that wasn't a relative wanting to be just friends with him.

Embarrassing.

His reputation as a ladies' magnet was at stake. Gordon was going to give him hell once he discovered that the girl was immune to Jackson's charms.

The jealous bastard.

"You came to the right place. Take a seat." He pointed to a barstool. "Cappuccino?"

She smiled shyly. "Yes, please."

"What kind of sandwich would you like? I can have Gordon prepare anything your heart desires."

"Anything?"

He leaned forward and flashed her his most charming smile. "Anything."

Tessa blushed but didn't lose her cool. "Well, my favorite is Camembert on wholegrain bread with walnuts and raisins. The garnish can be whatever." Given her smirk, she thought they didn't have the ingredients.

He typed the order in and sent it to Gordon. "Coming right up."

Her eyes widened. "Seriously? You have the bread and everything?"

"I do. And if I didn't, I would've made a supermarket run just for you."

"That's so nice of you." She sounded genuinely surprised by his flirting.

Did she think she was unattractive?

Who dumped that load of crap on her?

To hide the sudden anger flare, Jackson turned around and got busy with the cappuccino machine. Tessa was tiny and in desperate need of some fattening, but she was beautiful. Big hazel eyes, huge in her small face, and dark brown hair, thick and shiny and cascading in soft waves around her shoulders.

No makeup, no particular hairstyle, jeans, T-shirt, and a pair of white Keds, Tessa looked like a twelve-year-old. But that was just the first impression. The woman had old eyes, and the expression on her face was far from innocent. In fact, she looked much older than her twenty-one years.

"Here is your cappuccino." He waited for her to notice the heart design he made with the foam.

"That's so pretty. But now I can't put in the sugar. It will ruin it."

With a chuckle, Jackson plunged a spoon into the cup and stirred the foam around. "Now you can."

She smiled and reached for a packet of brown sugar. "What other designs can you make?"

"Just that one. It takes a lot of practice, and I hate wasting perfectly good cups of cappuccino."

Tessa took a sip. "It is good. I think it's the best I've had so far. Though I have to admit that the only other cappuccinos I've had were from Starbucks. Not exactly gourmet."

Jackson pretended horror. "Don't even mention that name in here. It's blasphemy. Compared to ours theirs is no better than mud."

Gordon's face lit up when he saw whose order he was delivering. "Hi, Tessa, where is the rest of your gang?" He placed the sandwich in front of her on the counter.

"It's just me today. Everyone is out, doing their own thing."

"If I would've known it was you, I would've made the sandwich extra special and super-sized. Especially since it's the last of the day."

She chuckled. "Are you kidding me? This is huge." She lifted the plate. "I'll eat half here and take the rest to go."

"First take a bite and then we'll talk. You'll be asking for seconds." He turned to Jackson. "Did you put up the Closed sign?"

"Fuck. I forgot." He straightened his arms and pushed up from the counter he'd been leaning on to get closer to Tessa.

Gordon stopped him. "I'll do it, and then I'll start clearing tables so people will get the clue it's time to go. Not you, Tessa. You can stay."

"Thanks," she mumbled with a full mouth.

As the last of the customers had said their goodbyes, Tessa was done with about a quarter of her sandwich. The girl had the appetite of a sparrow.

"What's the matter? You don't like it?" Gordon put his hands on his hips and glared at her.

Tessa wiped her mouth with a napkin. "It's delicious, but I can't eat that much."

Jackson grabbed her plate. "Come on, let's move to a booth. I'll make you a new cappuccino."

She followed him to the front booth. "I don't want to keep you guys after closing. You probably want to go home."

"We are home," Gordon said and pointed a finger at the ceiling. "We live upstairs."

"That's cool. Eva and Sharon and Nick and I live in the same house the office is in too. But we don't have any clients coming in. It's all done online."

"Sweet," Gordon said. "And there is no kitchen to clean, so it's even better. Which reminds me that I need to go help Vlad finish up in there."

"Thanks," Jackson whispered as Gordon passed him by.

"You're welcome." Gordon winked.

A cappuccino cup in each hand, Jackson sat across from Tessa. The poor girl was struggling to put a dent in what was on her plate and looking like she was choking on every bite. "You don't have to finish. Gordon will get over it."

She looked at the little that was left from the half she'd been working on and dropped it on the plate. "Okay. I'm done."

"I'll bring you a box to go." Jackson got up, grabbed a box from under the counter, and was back in seconds.

Tessa put everything that was left on her plate into the box, including the untouched potato salad. "This will be my lunch tomorrow." She reached into her purse and pulled out a wallet. "How much do I owe you?"

"It's on the house." Jackson covered her hand with his to stop her from opening the wallet. "And tomorrow's lunch too. This one will be soggy by then."

Her expression was hard to read but he sensed that he'd annoyed her. Tessa pulled her hands from under his and took out a twenty from her wallet. "I think this covers it."

Jackson ignored the twenty. "Did I offend you? You look pissed."

For a long moment she didn't respond, pretending to focus on finding the right place for her wallet inside her purse. But Jackson wasn't going to let Tessa hide. He was still staring at her as she lifted her head, and she had no choice but to respond.

"You didn't offend me. I just don't like anyone paying for me."

"I'm not paying for you. I'm just not taking your money."

"You know what I mean. It's the same thing. People do things like that and then expect something in return."

"You mean men."

She nodded.

Jackson smirked. "You have no idea how happy I am that you think of me as a man."

"You are a man."

"Thank you." He dipped his head.

Eventually, his teasing pulled a smile out of her. "You're so cocky and such a flirt, Jackson, it's easy to forget you're only eighteen."

False modesty wasn't his thing, and Jackson wanted Tessa to know how different he was from other guys his age, mortal and immortal alike. His different genes had nothing to do with what was between his ears. "I also run a successful café and manage a band. Age is irrelevant. It's what you do and how you do it."

She sighed. "True. But in my case, I'm both a kid and an ancient. I kind of jumped over the entire middle, and I'm straddling the ravine."

As a bitter scent of sadness reached his nostrils, Jackson wanted to ask Tessa what she'd meant by that, but he was interrupted by Gordon and Vlad who chose that moment to leave the kitchen and join Tessa and him in the booth. "Everything is done, and we are heading out. You guys want to come?"

"Where to?" Tessa asked.

"A new metal band is playing tonight at the club. I heard they are good," Vlad said.

Tessa waved a hand. "Ugh, I can't stand metal." She pushed up and grabbed her purse. "You guys have fun. I'm going home."

Jackson wasn't going to let her flee. "I'm not going. Can you stay a little longer and keep me company until the cleaning crew arrives? I need to show them the oven. The bastards didn't clean it in I don't know how long."

Gordon lifted a brow at Jackson's lie, but he wasn't stupid enough to say anything. "That's right. I forgot about the oven. Come on, Vlad, let's go." He slid out of the booth. "See you guys later."

Tessa sat back down, but kept her purse in her lap, ready to make her escape.

"Thank you for staying. Can I make you something to drink?"

She shook her head. "With two cups of cappuccino in me, I'll probably stay awake until God knows when. Maybe a cup of water, or herbal tea."

"Coming right up."

As he reached the counter, Jackson heard her murmur under her breath, "It's not as if I'm looking forward to sleeping."

An uncomfortable sensation settled in Jackson's gut as he started to put together the little snippets Tessa had let loose. Something had happened to her. Something bad. She'd talked about missing childhood, and she obviously had nightmares—the only reason for her to prefer staying awake at night.

Whatever it was, Jackson wanted to fix it. For some reason, he felt more protective of Tessa than he'd felt of other girls. As a big guy who was stronger than any human, he'd always felt like it was his job to protect those who couldn't protect themselves, especially girls, but the need was even stronger with Tessa.

Was it because he was attracted to her? But then he'd been attracted to plenty of other women. In fact, Tessa wasn't even his type. Most guys would've said that she was pretty but far from sexy, and yet he felt an inexplicable pull toward her. Was he suffering from the knight-in-shining-armor syndrome?

Did he want to save Tessa?

The answer was yes. More than that. He felt it was his duty—independent of his chances of ever getting Tessa to trust him and let him get closer. The girl seemed asexual. Which made him think that whatever had happened to her had to do with sex. After all, he was the son of a therapist and not totally clueless about things like that.

Had she been abused as a child? Jackson needed to find out and do away with whoever had hurt her. Or at least beat the perv into a pulp. He wasn't sure he was capable of actually killing someone, even a vile, worthless piece of shit who'd abused a child, but castrating the bastard was a different story.

Jackson wondered if he lacked the killer instinct because he'd grown up sheltered and loved. He was aggressive, sure, like all immortal males, but he wasn't a killer.

When they were younger, Gordon had dreamed of becoming a Guardian. Not Jackson, though. He wasn't a coward and if ever the clan needed him to step up he would, but, if he could help it, the only killing Jackson wanted to do was on the stock market.

One day he would make it big in the business world.

Bhathian

With a frown, Eva glanced around, taking in the opulent decor of By Invitation Only. "This is some fancy place. Are you sure I'm dressed for it? Elegant just doesn't seem to cut it here."

Bhathian felt like a penguin and probably looked like one too, even though the suit he was wearing wasn't a tux. It had been custom made for him for Syssi and Kian's wedding, and the torturous garment had been uncomfortable from day one when it had supposedly fit him perfectly. How did men move in those things? He must've gained muscle over the past year because the seams holding the jacket together were about to give up.

Fucking hell.

As they followed the hostess to their table, Bhathian was stuck doing the penguin walk instead of wrapping his arm around the most stunning woman in the room. Hell, he couldn't even bend down to whisper in her ear. Fortunately, he didn't need to. Eva could hear his whisper even from the other side of the room. "You're the most beautiful woman here, and everybody is looking at you. Do you really think it matters what you have on? Besides, I may not be a big expert on fashion, but I love this dress. In fact, I don't want you to wear it in public ever again."

Eva cast him an indulgent glance and ignored his comment. "When was the last time you wore that jacket? At your bar mitzvah?"

Very funny. Though it did feel like something he'd worn at thirteen.

"Kian and Syssi's wedding."

She gave him another look over. "You must've been working out a lot since."

"You have no idea."

The hostess brought them to the private enclave he'd requested, and pulled out a chair for Eva. Their table occupied the most private spot in the restaurant, the one clan members with memberships requested the most. No one could see inside or overhear a conversation as long as voices were kept low. It was perfect for the intimate dinner he had in mind.

Bhathian took off his suit jacket, stifling a relieved breath as he hung it on the back of his chair. The freedom of movement only whetted his appetite for more. Loosening the tie, he took it off and stuffed it in the jacket's pocket. Next were the gold cufflinks. He took them out, slipped them inside the same pocket, and rolled the sleeves of his dress shirt up.

What were they going to do to him? Throw the owner's cousin out? Not likely. Not after Bhathian paid the bloody membership fee just so he could take Eva there tonight. It had started with the *brilliant* idea that he should work on getting their small family closer by taking his mate and his daughter and her husband to nice places. Bhathian wasn't one to procrastinate, though this time he should have. From idea to execution hadn't taken more than one phone call and a credit card, and with what Gerard charged members, he could've bought the entire restaurant.

Bhathian had never thrown away so much money on something so frivolous. But what was done was done, and now that he had paid for the fucking membership, he should at least be able to enjoy it.

But when the hostess turned to him, her eyes were far from critical. She was looking him up and down and up again as if she were in a trance.

Bhathian wanted to snap his fingers and wake her up from whatever daydream she was having when he heard Eva clear her throat. "Darlene, could you be a doll and bring us something to drink?"

A professional, Darlene plastered an amiable expression on her face and turned to Eva. "Certainly. What would you like?"

"A Moscow Mule. And you, darling?" Eva's smile was all sugar, but hey, he wasn't complaining, she'd called him darling.

Bhathian waved a hand and sat down. "Snake's Venom." Very few places carried the brand, but Gerard should have it. No other beer could give an immortal a buzz.

"Well, that was embarrassing. For her," Eva said as soon as Darlene was out of earshot. "You are probably used to it."

Bhathian shrugged. "Not really. My bushy brows and permanent scowl scare most people off. I don't look friendly."

She frowned. "That's not true. You don't scowl that much."

"Not at you, and not at Nathalie, but everyone else gets the ogre look." He pointed at his face.

Eva laughed. "You're not scary at all."

"I'm glad you think so."

Their drinks were brought by a waiter, not Darlene.

"Thank you," Eva said.

Bhathian palmed the beer before the guy had a chance to pour it into a glass. "That will be all." He shooed the waiter away.

"Now I see what you mean about the angry scowl. You were so grouchy to him. Why?"

Bhathian finished a long gulp and put the bottle down. "I like doing things my way, and I don't care what some snooty waiter thinks is the proper way to drink beer."

Eva raised her glass. "I'll drink to that."

When the food was all eaten, and a flurry of waiters had cleared the table, Bhathian ordered coffee instead of another beer and so did Eva. They hadn't talked much during dinner and now that it was over Bhathian was searching for a topic to start a conversation. Would Eva care to hear about his job?

He should ask her about hers. Then she'd do all the talking, and he could relax. "Any interesting cases you're working on?"

A shadow passed over her eyes, but she was quick about banishing it. If Bhathian weren't so focused on every nuance in her expression, he would've missed it. "I'm working on getting more jobs locally. I want to be here for Nathalie when the baby comes."

"I'm sure she'd appreciate it. She misses you, by the way. You didn't come visit for the past week."

"I've been so incredibly busy. It's not easy moving a business to a new location. So many things needed to be done. But we spoke on the phone." Eva chuckled. "Every time I asked her about you, she said you were in the gym. How many hours a day do you train?"

That was a nice surprise. Nathalie hadn't told him that Eva asked about him. "I teach several self-defense classes and train two groups of wannabe Guardians. My own workouts don't take more than a couple of hours a day."

"That's a lot. Do the other Guardians train as hard? The ones that I met were not as muscular as you."

He shook his head.

"Why do you do it? Is it for looks? I'm just curious."

Eva's bluntness was aggravating but also refreshing. Although he didn't want to expose what motivated him to push himself so hard, Bhathian liked that she was direct and didn't beat around the bush. Besides, by forcing him to talk about himself, Eva was opening the way for him to do the same to her.

Bhathian shifted in his seat and opened another button at the top of his dress shirt. The food and the beer and Eva's questions had made him sweat. Or maybe it was the prospect of answering her truthfully. He'd already told her how losing her had affected him, and her response hadn't been encouraging.

"Ever since I hit puberty, I had this simmering disquiet in my gut. It went away only during training, and the harder I worked, the more I exerted myself, the longer the reprieve lasted. It got worse after I lost you the first time. I had to train even harder, and after I lost your trail in Brazil, I pushed myself to the limit. And still it wasn't enough."

"Why? Was it the guilt?"

"Maybe. Or maybe I'm just a grouch." He'd already said enough. The first time he'd hinted at his feelings for her, she'd retreated into her shell like a scared turtle. Telling her the real reason again would send her running faster than a bomb exploding in the restaurant.

Tessa

"I'm taking my new car out for a spin," Nick said as he headed for the door.

"When are you coming back?" Tessa asked. With Eva gone on a dinner date with Bhathian, Nathalie's cousin, and Sharon out shopping, Tessa and Nick were the only ones left at the house, and now he was leaving too.

Tessa didn't like being left alone in the new place. Frankly, she didn't like being alone anywhere. But admitting that she was scared would've embarrassed her.

"I don't know. A couple of hours. Maybe more. Why? Do you want me to stay home with you?"

Yes.

"No, of course not. Go, have fun."

Relieved, Nick didn't ask again. He was out the door before she had a chance to change her mind.

Tessa sighed as the door banged shut behind him.

They had spent the morning shopping for cars, and all four ended up getting identical Priuses, just in different colors. It had been a no-brainer. The lease was reasonable, and they'd gotten a discount for getting a mini-fleet. In addition, given how big Los Angeles was, the Priuses' incredibly low fuel consumption meant big savings.

Eva was financing everything, including the new fleet, and as the one in charge of accounting, Tessa had warned Nick and Sharon to choose something inexpensive. After the huge splurge on the house in Venice, there wasn't much budget left over for transportation.

Her boss was good at many things, but handling money wasn't one of them. Eva's philosophy was that she could always take on another job to pay for the extra spending.

Not as long as Tessa had a say in it.

Eva was already working long hours and taking on odd jobs she wasn't telling the crew about. God only knew what those were about.

They must've been pro bono because those jobs weren't bringing in any money. Unless Eva had a bank account Tessa wasn't aware of.

Why keep it a secret, though?

Tessa shrugged. Eva was like a vault. As much as their boss loved the three of them, showering them with affection as well as material things, she didn't share much of herself. Probably came with the territory of being a detective.

Today was the first time Tessa had seen Eva going out on a real date, and not one that was part of a job. Eva needed to live a little as herself and not through the prism of her many fake identities.

Tessa rubbed her chest. *What about me? I need to start living too.*

Jackson had invited her for another non-date at the café tonight. This time after the place was closed to customers. Tessa had promised him she would, it would've been impolite to refuse after how nice he'd been to her, but she'd had no intentions of showing up. Her plan had been to call him with an excuse. Something about work.

Except now, alone in the empty house that didn't feel like home yet, she was tempted to go.

With a sigh, Tessa let her head hang low. It wasn't fair to Jackson. If she went, she would be insinuating that she was interested. When she wasn't—not in anything Jackson had in mind. The only thing she could offer him was friendship, and for a little while he might even accept that it was enough. But then it wouldn't be.

Jackson would try something, and she would run screaming.

But she was lonely, and as the adage went, beggars couldn't be choosers.

A little over an hour later, Tessa parked her shiny new red Prius in front of Jackson's café. The good thing about coming after closing time was that there were plenty of parking spaces available and she didn't have to walk far in the heeled sandals she'd strapped on. The bad thing was that Jackson might see her checking her hair and makeup in the rear-view mirror. She'd actually blow dried her shoulder length hair and used a round brush to curl the ends and give it some bounce. As for makeup, all she had on was mascara, and even that felt weird, kind of sticky.

Why the hell am I doing this?

Jackson was the kind of guy any girl would've salivated over, and if not for her phobia, Tessa would have been so into him even though he was too young. At eighteen, he was more of a man than most. A good man, the kind a mother would've been proud to call a son.

The kind a woman would've been proud to call her own.

Unfortunately, Tessa couldn't claim him. She had nothing to offer a sexually active guy like Jackson. If he were sworn to celibacy or gay, they could have been best friends.

But he was neither.

Still, phobias and hang-ups aside, she was a woman, and a woman wanted a hot guy like Jackson to see her as such regardless of her intentions, or rather lack thereof.

Clutching her purse and trotting on a pair of heels she had no business wearing, Tessa went up to the café's front door and knocked.

Jackson opened up the way as if he'd been waiting by the door the entire time. "You're late." He looked her up and down, then whistled softly. "But it was worth the wait. You look hot." Reaching for her hand, he pulled her inside and locked the door.

Trouble! Trouble! Trouble! Taylor Swift's song rang in Tessa's head. She shouldn't be so happy about that whistle and that compliment.

"I got rid of Gordon and Vlad so we could be alone." He dragged her behind him down the aisle between the two rows of booths until he reached the last one.

"My lady?" He offered her a seat.

"Thank you," she murmured.

This was worse than she'd anticipated. Jackson had a white tablecloth spread over the simple Formica top, with two small lighted candles that were housed in clear glass jars, and a small vase with flowers for decoration. The place settings were the usual café fare, as was the large bottle of Perrier and the two tall tumblers.

Jackson, apparently, believed it was a real date.

Hypocrite. So did you. Otherwise why did you bother with the dress up?

Jackson slid into the booth and smiled apologetically. "Don't read too much into the nice setting. I'm still going to serve you a sandwich and coffee. I'm a whiz with the cappuccino machine, but I can't cook worth shit."

The panic squeezing her throat eased. He was right. She'd been reading too much into it. After all, Jackson hadn't tried to get her upstairs into his living quarters, and even though he gave it a slightly romantic twist, he was serving dinner down in the café and joking around as usual.

Still, she needed to make it clear that romance was not on the agenda. "What's the occasion?" She waved her hand over the table. "Did I miss your birthday or something?"

Jackson shrugged. "You agreed to come, and I just felt like doing something nice for you."

Now he made her feel like a jerk.

Shit. She needed to tell Jackson to stop trying. But then he would ask why and she would have to tell him something to make him understand. Maybe she could reveal just one small thing out of the nightmare she'd been through. No one could ever know the whole truth. Not even a therapist.

That's why she'd never gone to see one.

"Thank you." She reached for the bottle of Perrier, but Jackson stopped her. "Allow me." He opened it and poured the bubbly into her glass first and then his. "Cheers." He lifted his glass.

"To friendship." She clinked hers to his.

Jackson nodded.

Good. He didn't look upset.

"There are things you need to know about me," Tessa blurted out fast before she had time to change her mind. "Why I can't be anything other than a friend to you. Not just you. Any guy."

He arched a brow.

"I'm not into girls, if that's what you think." She pointed at his brow.

Jackson lifted his hands. "I didn't say a thing."

"Right. Anyway. I've been through some shit when I was young, and I can't even stand the thought of a guy touching me intimately. I wanted you to know so you wouldn't think it's about you. You're a nice guy. It's just that I can't."

His handsome face darkened, and Tessa had another moment of panic, anticipating his anger to explode and lash out at her.

Instead, he asked in the softest tone, "Are you seeing someone about it?"

She expelled the breath she'd been holding and thanked God that Jackson hadn't pelted her with questions about what had happened to her.

She shook her head. "I can't. For me the best way to deal with it is to push the thoughts away and just go about my day."

"I can see how well it's working for you," he said sarcastically.

That's why she didn't like talking about her past. Without having a clue as to what kind of evil she'd been subjected to, people sought to give her advice on how to deal with it.

Tessa narrowed her eyes. "I know you mean well, Jackson, but please don't try to fix me. You have no idea what you're talking about."

Her anger took him by surprise. "I'm sorry. I should've phrased it better. It's just that my mom is a therapist and she helps people overcome all kinds of traumas. Living with nightmares and pushing people away is not really living. Even for a slim chance of a normal life, I think it's worth talking to someone like my mom. It's not that expensive, and I think medical insurance covers it."

So that was what he thought, that she couldn't afford therapy. "It's not about the money."

"Then what?"

"I want to forget. And talking about it isn't going to help. It will only bring it all back. You want to talk about normal? I barely cling to sanity as it is. Rehashing my past will shatter what little of it I have."

Frustration darkening his features, Jackson opened his mouth to say something, but then decided against it and closed it. Too young to have learned to hide his emotions, he was so easy to read. The boy was suffering from savior syndrome. His inability to save Tessa was eating him up. Jackson wasn't used to encountering problems too big for him to solve.

He raked his fingers through his light blond hair, shoving the long bangs back. "Tell me what to do, Tessa, because I'm sure as hell out of my depth here."

At least he was honest.

She reached for his hand. "Just be my friend. Let's eat, let's talk about movies and music and shoot the breeze. Can it be enough for you? Or do you want me to leave?"

Looking as if she'd offended his mother and spat in his face, Jackson pulled out his hand from her grasp.

"Damn it, Tessa. I didn't invite you here because I wanted to get laid. I like you, as a girl, as a woman, but that doesn't mean I want nothing from you other than sex. So yeah, I'm bummed out that there will be no kiss goodnight, but it's not like it's the end of the world."

Ouch. It seemed like tonight was all about awkward blunders and stepping on each other's toes. "Can we start over? Press replay?"

"Sure." Jackson let out a long breath, his big body deflating back to its normal size.

Dimly, she was aware that even though Jackson was far from mellow and swelled with aggression whenever he got angry or frustrated, she hadn't felt threatened by him.

The big guy was growing on her.

Other than Nick, who was like a brother to her, Jackson was the only man she felt comfortable around.

Eva

Just as things were getting interesting, Bhathian clammed up.

It had been gutsy of him to admit how deeply he'd regretted letting her go. He'd said something to that effect before, but she'd thought he'd been trying to sweet-talk her. This time she'd listened with more than her ears, and her instincts had told her he was sincere.

His honesty had started to melt away her shields, and for a few moments Eva had forgotten to keep up her guard, letting herself feel a connection to Bhathian. But he'd yanked that fragile thread loose before it had a chance to gain substance.

What surprised Eva, though, was that instead of relief she felt anger. After working for so long to keep her walls up, she should be glad they hadn't crumbled just because a man had been honest with her for a few minutes.

Would the world come to an end when men bared their souls to the women in their lives and just laid it all on the table?

Probably.

If a strong warrior like Bhathian had chosen the cowardly route, then there was no hope for the rest of his gender.

"I see that you're uncomfortable talking about your feelings. Would you like to switch to a less sensitive subject?"

Her jibe hadn't gone unnoticed, and Bhathian's scowl deepened. He crossed his massive arms over his chest, the seams of his white dress shirt groaning in protest. She must've offended his male ego.

"As if you're any better."

It was Eva's turn to scowl. Not that Bhathian was wrong necessarily, she was as close-mouthed as a priest with a confession, but he piqued her curiosity. Was Bhathian more perceptive than he seemed?

"What do you mean?"

"Like what's the deal with you and Fernando. You'd left him years before skipping town."

"It's none of your business."

"You may be right, but doesn't Nathalie deserve to know?"

Ouch, that was a sore point. Eva had deflected Nathalie's hints on the subject several times. In fact, she'd been avoiding meeting Nathalie face to face for over a week because she knew it was coming.

"I don't know what to tell her."

"How about the truth?"

"What if the truth hurts her? She's in the last weeks of her pregnancy, and the last thing I want is to upset her."

"Nathalie is made from sturdier stuff."

Oh, hell, what did she have to lose? It wasn't as if any of it would affect her relationship with Bhathian one way or another. Maybe when he heard her story he would help her come up with a modified version for Nathalie.

"I've never loved him," she started.

Bhathian didn't look surprised.

"I was pregnant and alone, and I didn't want my child to be born without a father. I had only one criterion for the kind of man I wanted: a guy who would love my child as if she was his own and be the best possible father to her. Nothing else mattered."

Bhathian didn't try to hide the guilt that was twisting his features, but he said nothing.

"I met Fernando in his café. A friend from the airline dragged me there, saying I had to taste his baking. Sitting there with my coffee and bagel, I watched him interacting with the customers. His cheerfulness and friendliness were genuine. Fernando really loved people and especially the kids. It brought tears to my eyes watching him with them."

"He's been an amazing father to Nathalie," Bhathian said.

Eva nodded. "Right then and there I knew he was the one I wanted, and since he had no ring on his finger and was flirting shamelessly with each and every female customer, I figured he was single. We were married a month later."

"Did he know?"

Eva frowned. What kind of woman did he think she was? "Of course he knew. I told him on our first official date."

"And he didn't mind?"

"Fernando loved children, and he wanted me so much he would've agreed to anything. He proposed on our second date. Turned out he'd made the right choice. I wanted to give him more children, but it didn't work out. For obvious reasons I refused to go for a check-up and told him to go."

Bhathian reached for her hand. "Let me guess. There was nothing wrong with Fernando."

Eva frowned. "Why would you assume that it was me when in fact the doctors confirmed it was him?"

"A coincidence. Immortal females have such low conception rates that I'm surprised you got pregnant with Nathalie."

True. Eva had suspected she was infertile for years, but when she'd conceived at an age most women entered the early signs of menopause, she'd figured she was good for another baby or two.

"It was a miracle."

Bhathian squeezed her hand. "One of many. You seem to contradict every statistic law in the universe, being the only woman in history who has been accidentally turned by a random immortal male."

"I was wondering about it. Could it have been one of your clansmen?" Maybe they had a database she could look through.

"No. I investigated the possibility. I even emailed your picture to every male of my clan, asking if they recognized you, but no one remembered ever being with you."

"Whoever it was might have forgotten a girl he'd slept with only once over fifty years ago."

"No man would've forgotten you, Eva. You're unforgettable."

That was the nicest compliment anyone had ever given her, and what's more, it had been sincere. "Thank you." Suddenly embarrassed, she looked away for a moment. "But then who? Are there any immortals other than your clan and your enemies? What do you call them? Dumbers?" Nathalie had told her a little about the secret war going on between the two immortal factions.

He laughed. "Doomers. Though Dumbers fits too. Doom is the acronym for the Devout Order of Mortdh. It might have been one of them, but I doubt it. At the time they had no presence in the area."

"It happened in Rhode Island, not here."

"I meant the United States. There might have been some who came on short reconnaissance or acquisition missions, but I doubt any of them went looking for young women to seduce. It wasn't that easy then. Most girls wanted to get married first."

"Then who was it?"

"That's the mystery. It was either a Doomer deserter or an unaccounted for immortal. The first is in the realm of possibility; the second would be another miracle. We've spent endless years searching for other immortals and never finding any."

Eva leaned back in her chair and closed her eyes for a moment, recalling the one she suspected was the culprit. The guy had taken her virginity and must've thralled the memory away, but he hadn't been very good at it because she remembered him, just not the sex.

"It happened in college. The guy took my virginity and then made me forget he did. For years, I thought he did it while I was drunk, and that's why I couldn't remember anything about that night. But now that I know about the thralling business I realize that it wasn't the alcohol."

A growl escaped Bhathian's throat, and his eyes shone from the inside. "If we ever find the motherfucker, I'm going to kill him."

Eva smiled. His bloodthirsty response made her happy. "Don't be so hasty. If not for him, I would've aged as any other human woman, and you wouldn't have hit on me on that flight."

"I would've found you attractive even with a few wrinkles."

It was on the tip of her tongue to ask him if he'd ever bedded an older woman, but she put a cork in it. "That's nice. But back to that alleged immortal, I remember him well. I met him at a college party. He said he was a student, and I had no reason to doubt him. Back then the girls had a separate building within Brown, Pembroke College, and we didn't hang out with the boys much. He was handsome, and I was a little tipsy, and we necked."

"Son of a bitch," Bhathian growled again.

Eva ignored him and kept going. "The next morning I woke up with what I thought was the flu, but there was no soreness, nothing to indicate that I was no longer a virgin. I thought that I must've passed out from drinking too much and that the nice fellow had brought me back to my room. I couldn't remember his name, which was embarrassing considering all the kissing and touching we'd done, but I blamed everything on the alcohol. The high fever kept me in bed for several days, and when I came back to school, I didn't look for him because I was so embarrassed about what I'd done. Two years later, when I finally had sex for what I believed was the first time, and there was no blood and no pain, I started to suspect that the nice fellow hadn't been so nice."

"Do you remember what he looked like?"

"Six feet tall give or take an inch, athletic build, brown hair, and smiling blue eyes. I know the description fits countless guys, but I would recognize him if I saw him."

"Andrew has a friend who is a forensic artist. He can draw the guy from your description. He drew your picture for me, and it came up very accurate."

"I would love to see it."

"I framed it, and it's hanging on the wall in my bedroom. If you want to see it, you'll have to come over."

Sneaky Bhathian.

She ignored his hint. "But what will we do with his portrait? Start looking for the guy? To what end? So you can beat the shit out of him?"

"That too. But no. If there are immortals out there, we want to find them and see whose side they are on."

"What if he's a lone wolf?"

"Then we find him. I would love to hear his story. After I beat the crap out of him."

Bhathian

Son of a bitch. Bhathian wouldn't be surprised if the creep was a Doomer. Taking a woman's virginity without her knowledge was nothing a Doomer would've felt conflicted about. They had no respect for human life let alone a woman's right to say no. On the contrary, their entire hateful philosophy was about denying women their rights.

Eva took a sip from her second Moscow Mule, then put it down. "Ever since I figured out who and what he was, I keep thinking that it might have not been as bad as it looks. The necking had gotten steamy with my full blessing. I might've even initiated the sex. He could've assumed I was more experienced than I really was, and upon discovering my virginity decided to thrall more than the memory of the bite away."

"Are you trying to excuse the scumbag?"

"Not if he did it on purpose, or thralled me to have sex with him. But I don't want to put the blame on someone for something I did willingly or even encouraged. I want to give him the benefit of the doubt. Don't get me wrong. I think most people are deceitful and selfish and would take whatever they wanted if they could get away with it. But I also believe in taking responsibility. If I initiated or even just agreed to the sex, then he did nothing wrong."

"You were drunk. So even if you agreed he still took advantage of you."

Eva tilted her head. "Bhathian. Do you really believe people would do things they absolutely didn't want to just because they were drunk? Inebriation lowers inhibitions; it doesn't make you do things you really don't want to."

True. He'd been drunk plenty of times, but he'd never done something completely out of character or that he regretted later.

Bhathian chuckled. "As I said before, you're a magnet for the impossible. Not only did you hook up with an immortal who turned you, but he was your first one. Then years later you hook up with another immortal, me, miraculously at the right time of the month to conceive a child, and *boom*, Nathalie is created. If I were a believer, I would've said that all of it was fated." He shook his head. "You know what? That must actually turn me into one. One miracle can be coincidental.

But one after the other happening to the same person? Must be the work of a higher power."

Eva nodded solemnly. "God works in mysterious ways." She took another long sip from her drink, finishing what was there.

"Do you want another one?"

"No, I think I've had enough." She snorted and winked. "With my luck, I'll go home with you, and you'll knock me up again."

"Would it be so terrible? Another child would be a blessing."

She shook her head. "I'm happy where I am, with my agency and my crew. Besides, I'm about to become a grandma. I'll get my baby fix babysitting my granddaughter."

"Don't you want more?"

Eva looked down inside her copper mug and fished out a slice of lime. "I used to. It didn't work out for me."

The hurt in her tone squeezed at Bhathian's heart. "You still didn't tell me what happened with Fernando. Not loving him didn't stop you from marrying him and even trying for another kid. What changed?"

She leveled her amber eyes at him. "Can you believe he was unfaithful? I, who supposedly didn't love him, stayed faithful to him. I believed in the sanctity of marriage. But the man who'd claimed to worship the ground I walked on cheated on me." She pointed at her chest.

Not what Bhathian had expected to hear. Rotund, bald Fernando didn't strike him as much of a Casanova. "How did you find out?"

"Pffft, he made plans for a rendezvous right in front of me in the café." Eva waved her hand in the air, her eyes blazing with pent-up anger. "I never told him about my super senses, so he didn't know I could hear their hushed whispers."

"That must've hurt."

"You bet it did."

"Did you confront him about it?"

She nodded.

"What did he say?"

"At first he tried to deny it, and then when I told him what I had heard, he blabbered the most absurd of excuses." She rolled her eyes and waved her hand in the air again. "That he needed to reaffirm his manhood because I made him feel insecure. That he didn't feel appreciated or loved and had to seek it from others. Blah, blah, blah. It was all about him not being able to keep his dick in his pants." Eva's chest was heaving and her cheeks were red.

So much anger after all those years. Maybe in her own way she'd loved Fernando. Otherwise her rage didn't make sense.

"If you didn't love him, why does it still upset you so much?"

Eva slumped in her chair. "Because he shattered my dream of a happy family. I might have not loved him, but I liked him and appreciated him despite what he thought. Fernando was charming and funny and a great dad to Nathalie. I was content with that. He wasn't."

He understood Eva better now. No wonder she'd put up defenses and preferred to stay detached emotionally. Men had been jerks to her, present company included. Why would she trust anything he said?

Her initiator had taken her virginity without her knowledge, Bhathian had knocked her up and abandoned her, and her husband, the guy who she'd believed would always stay true to her, cheated.

What would it take to convince her that she could trust again? That Bhathian would gladly dedicate his long life to her?

Should he tell her she was his fated mate and it had taken his stupid brain over thirty years to realize that?

Eva would think it was nothing more than sweet talk. He had to convince her with deeds, not words.

"I'm sorry," he said.

"What for? You didn't promise me anything, and you didn't cheat on me. Just knocked me up. But I'm not sorry for that. You gave me my Nathalie."

Okay, that was good to hear. She wasn't as angry at him as she was at Fernando. "I'm glad that you don't hold a grudge against me."

Her lips twisted in a wicked smile. "I didn't say that. You rejected me, and at the time it hurt. A lot. But you can make it up to me."

"Tell me how."

She raked her eyes over his body. "Take me to bed."

In the span of a blink, Bhathian was out of his chair with his jacket draped over his arm. "Yours or mine?"

"Mine."

He offered Eva a hand up. "Let's go."

She let him pull her up. "What about the bill?"

"Gerard has my credit card."

"Then what are we waiting for?"

Eva

It had been an emotionally charged evening, and the best antidote to the turmoil in her head was rough, no-holds-barred sex that would go on for hours.

Only two weeks had passed since the last time Eva had indulged with Bhathian, and she was already antsy and needy as if she'd gone without for a couple of months. Never mind that she'd pleasured herself nightly, sometimes more than once.

For some reason what had sustained her for years wasn't cutting it now.

As Eva reached over the center console and put her hand on Bhathian's thigh, he sucked in a breath. Encouraged, she continued up until her hand rested on the bulge in his slacks. Through the thin fabric, his shaft pulsed and swelled in response to her touch, but she wanted to feel skin.

"Don't." Bhathian stayed her hand as she reached for his belt buckle.

"Why? Don't you like my hands on you?" she teased.

"I fucking love it, but I'm driving and what you're doing is distracting."

The guy was a cop down to his soul. What was he worried about? That they would get arrested for indecent exposure? She was willing to risk it.

"No one can see what I'm doing to you."

"It's not safe."

"We're immortal, for crying out loud, what could happen to us?"

Bhathian cast her a sidelong glance. "Nothing, but we are not alone on the road. You wouldn't want to cause an accident and kill someone? Would you?"

No, she wouldn't. That was the last thing she needed to add to her guilty conscience. "Fine."

"Ten more minutes," he said with a smirk and stepped on the gas. Evidently, there were some laws Bhathian didn't mind breaking.

They got to her place in less.

As soon as the front door closed behind them, Bhathian grabbed her and pinned her to the wall. "You're driving me crazy, Eva." His lips smashed over hers, and he pushed his knee between her legs. She let herself rub over it for a few seconds then pushed him away. "My bedroom."

They climbed the stairs to the third floor as fast as only two immortals could.

"Why are you making me so horny?" She pulled her dress over her head and dropped it on the floor.

He kicked off his shoes and chuckled. "Is it a bad thing?"

"Yes. Usually once a month with a man is enough for me. The rest of the time it's a solo performance." Eva unhooked her bra and let it fall.

Bhathian was on her in a heartbeat. Dropping to his knees, he took one nipple between his lips while cupping her other breast and thrumming her other nipple with his thumb.

Freezing in place, her thumbs hooked in the elastic band of her panties, she moaned with pleasure. He was so good at this. Either that or the sight of his enormous body kneeling before her was a turn on. Or maybe it was his intoxicating scent, the one that intermingled with the expensive cologne he'd used. Or maybe it was the whole package. If there was ever a man who deserved to be called sex on a stick, it was Bhathian.

God. Those muscles.

Her hands itched to reach down and tear the shirt off his shoulders.

He distracted her by pulling her panties down and lifting her up so his mouth was aligned with her slit. She nearly orgasmed when his tongue found her clit.

After a few teasing seconds he put her down. "I had to have a little taste first. An appetizer."

Naughty boy. "Why don't you take me to bed and have a full course?"

In a show of incredible strength, Bhathian lifted her up by her thighs and pushed to his feet at the same time. "How about a five-course meal?" He walked over to the bed and lowered her gently.

"Be my guest. But first take off your clothes. A body like yours shouldn't be covered."

With a satisfied grin, Bhathian freed two more buttons and pulled the shirt over his head.

Her intake of breath was audible. "If only I had any talent for sculpting."

Bhathian shucked his pants off. "I'd rather have your hands on me."

"Then come over here."

No man had ever gotten rid of his briefs and socks faster, or sported a more massive erection. It was good she wasn't small or fragile.

Eva lifted up from the pile of cushions she'd been propped on and reached for the hard length. Before Bhathian got to devour her, she could give him a blow job that would blow his mind. "Come closer." She pulled him toward her and lowered her mouth over the tip.

He groaned the moment her lips touched his velvety skin. Eva was willing to bet that not many women could handle that thing, but she knew she could. Taking him a little deeper, she cupped his sack and massaged it gently.

His knees buckled, and he braced them against the mattress.

Men were such simple creatures. Even a mighty warrior like Bhathian could be toppled by a woman with a skillful mouth.

He surprised her by caressing her cheek and pulling out. "The appetizer whetted my appetite for more, and I'm ready to go to work on those five courses."

Such an unselfish move, putting her pleasure before his own. Eva leaned back and pulled her knees up, then spread her legs a little and ran a finger down her wet slit. "I wouldn't want to keep you away from your feast."

Bhathian's gray eyes, which had been normal a moment ago, lit up like a pair of headlights as he dove between her legs. Spreading them wide with his hands, he speared her with his tongue. For several long moments, he fucked her with it, groaning like a beast, cupping her butt cheeks and lifting her up to his hungry mouth.

It was almost enough to push her over the cliff.

With his strong fingers digging painfully into the flesh of her ass, he moved his tongue up to the throbbing center of her desire, giving her the first climax of the night.

The next four came in quick succession, leaving her boneless and sated. "That's five," Eva mumbled, lifting her head a few inches off the pillow to glance at her lover.

Bhathian looked up from between her legs, his lips glistening with her juices. "I didn't have dessert yet."

"Oh, God. You're going to kill me." Her head hit the pillow.

"With pleasure, I hope."

"Yeah, with pleasure. But I'll be dead nonetheless." She lifted a limp hand. "Tell Nathalie I love her."

He chuckled and went back to work, wringing one more climax out of her tired body.

"Now I'm done." Bhathian moved up, kissing her with her own juices still on his lips and sending pulses of desire to her center.

She spread her legs even wider to make room for him. "I think you've earned the right to enter."

"I did." He surged into her, filling her so completely she sighed with the pleasure of it.

Bhathian wasn't too big. He was perfect as if he'd been custom made for her.

Syssi

Syssi walked into Amanda's office and closed the door behind her, signaling to the postdocs not to disturb them. Unless a private conversation was going on, Amanda's door was always open. "I've been thinking." She took a seat.

"About?"

"Ever since our talk about the Fates and finding Dormants, I've been mulling over it and realized that there is a big problem with our hypotheses."

Amanda closed the notebook she'd been scribbling in, giving Syssi her full attention. "I'm all ears."

"William's game only tests precognition, and all we test in the lab is the same thing and telepathy. That's a very narrow slice of all the possible paranormal talents."

Amanda leaned back. "We talked about it already. We have no way of testing the other more esoteric phenomena without administration shutting us down and recommending psychiatric evaluations."

"That's just one problem. We have a bigger one. I think most Dormants don't have any paranormal abilities at all. Think about it. I'm not aware of Anandur having any special talent aside from making people laugh. Neither does Brundar. All the immortals I know have varying levels of thralling ability, but very few exhibit something extra. Arwel and Michael are telepaths, Andrew is a lie detector, Sylvia controls technology, Nathalie communicates with ghosts, or at least she used to before her pregnancy, and I see glimpses of the future. Did I miss anyone?"

"I can exert influence without resorting to thralling and so does Kri, but it's a questionable talent and not very strong. Annani can sometimes remote view, but again, it's not always reliable."

"You see? If there are so few immortals with special abilities, why would we expect Dormants to have them?"

Amanda crossed her arms over her chest and tapped her fingers on her biceps. "I found you and Michael, and it only took one year of testing that was sporadic and limited. Before I hired you, I was conducting the tests myself and couldn't devote much time to it. Maybe we just expect too much too soon as you said before."

"I wish it were true. But I really think we are wasting our time."

Amanda shook her head. "I agree, but I would hate to think that it's all in the hands of fate and there is nothing we can do."

"There is one other thing, but I don't see how we can use it. I think Dormants feel an affinity to other Dormants and to immortals. When I met you, we hit it off immediately even though we are nothing alike. Same with Michael. I liked him and felt comfortable with him despite his constant flirting. There is a connection, an attraction, and I'm not talking about sexual pull. It's like recognizing like. An immortal and a Dormant just need to be in close proximity, and they'll gravitate toward each other. Same for two Dormants."

Amanda uncrossed her arms and started doodling in her notebook. Her way of thinking things through was either writing down bullet points or drawing squiggles that made sense only to her. Syssi waited patiently for her sister-in-law to gather her thoughts.

"I think I know what you mean. When I first met Andrew, I immediately felt it, but I thought it was sexual." She smirked. "You know me. That's where my mind always goes, and Andrew is an impressive man."

Syssi rolled her eyes. "I thought that now that you're with Dalhu you'd mellowed out."

"I did. Naturally, I still think about sex—a lot—but only with my mate."

"Any thoughts as to what we can do about identifying Dormants?"

Amanda doodled a little more. "Even if we assume that immortals really feel a special affinity to Dormants, basing our findings on such a subjective test would be irresponsible. Especially given what Dormants have to go through for the final test."

True. The final test was whether they turned or not, and the catalyst was sex for the females and fighting for the males. In both cases prior consent was needed, which meant divulging the immortal secret. If they failed, and most probably would, their memories of the whole thing would have to be erased.

"What if we have the potential Dormant exposed to several immortals, and let's say three report feeling it? Would that be enough?"

Amanda dropped the pen and leaned back in her chair. "Three would definitely be better than one but still not conclusive. Besides, how do you propose we do it? Bring potential Dormants to hang out in Nathalie's café at the keep?"

"Kian would never allow it. But we can bring the immortals here on a volunteer basis. Once a month they will come and spend a day in the lab, or even just a few hours, administering tests. We will have each subject tested by three different immortals. Actually, make it four, because we need both sexes to test each one, so two and two."

Amanda grinned. "Did I already tell you that you're brilliant? That will also solve our problem of finding an assistant. Who needs employees when we can have volunteers?"

"Right. But do you think they will agree? Most have jobs."

"It all depends on how we sell the idea. They would jump through hoops for a chance of finding their destined mates."

"Yeah... no. Even desperate people will not buy the odds."

"Hah, but throw in the Fates, and suddenly the odds look better."

Syssi still wasn't convinced anyone would agree to volunteer their time based on those odds. On the other hand, as unscientific as it was, the Fates needed to be factored in. She still remembered the day she'd met Kian.

So many things had had to happen to bring that about.

And their reaction to each other...

From the first moment their eyes met, they'd both known on a visceral level that they were meant for each other, fighting the inevitable because logic had dictated that things like that just didn't happen. Neither had believed in destiny and yet had no choice but to surrender to it.

But convincing a bunch of skeptical immortals to put their trust in fate wouldn't be easy. "We need to sweeten the deal."

"How?"

"Arranging for get-togethers. Throw the testers in with the Dormants in an informal setting and let nature take its course. It can be in the guise of a lecture about paranormal phenomena with a reception following. We just need to find a place to hold those meetings."

Amanda looked optimistic for the first time in months. "That's not a problem. Kian can give us access to one of the large conference rooms in one of the office buildings we own."

"Then it's settled. The only problem now is to find someone to manage that. Neither you nor I can take on more work."

"Right."

Losham

Drink in hand, Losham sat at the bar and observed his clientele. Two weeks since opening and the club was doing great.

He'd aptly named it Allure.

Allure Los Angeles was the first in the chain, with Allure San Francisco opening next month. New York was the largest and fanciest of the three and would take two more months to complete. After that Losham planned on expanding the chain to Europe. Paris, London, Monte Carlo, and maybe Hamburg. He wasn't sure about that one. When those in Europe were up, he planned to open one in Tokyo and one in Singapore. Not that he expected to find any immortals there. Those were purely for profit.

Naturally, no one here knew Losham was the owner. He came under the guise of a prospective member with only Rami, his trusty assistant, to accompany him. Losham's bodyguards stayed behind in Las Vegas.

By now Navuh must've suspected him of having a gambling problem, and Losham played the part. It was the perfect excuse for the trips he was making to various spots around the globe. Wherever there was a fancy casino nearby, he was good.

Navuh was convinced that Losham hopped from one casino to the next to avoid suspicion since he always won. It was partially true. With his eidetic memory and quick mind, Losham couldn't lose in a card game. Sometimes he lost on purpose. He had to if he wanted to keep coming back.

"It's even better than I imagined," Rami said.

"I agree. I'm sure you can't wait to check out the third floor."

Rami blushed. "I don't know if I should." He leaned closer. "Because of the special security feed."

Losham clapped his assistant's back. "Don't worry. The third floor is not included in the special surveillance."

Rami's eyes lit up. "Thank you, sir."

"You're most welcome."

The third floor had been inspired by Rami. It was dedicated to gay males and was a huge hit. The second floor was dedicated to gay females, but for some reason none had bought a membership yet. But then the club was new, and there were many memberships still to be sold. Besides, if it proved not as successful, Losham could always find a new purpose for the space.

The beauty of the operation was that it was all run by unsuspecting humans. The only immortals on the premises occupied a separate room in the administrative section and monitored the special feed. If someone flashed a pair of fangs in one of the private rooms, the two would be on him in seconds.

"Mr. Domingues, are you ready for your tour, sir?" A young man wearing a club uniform offered his hand. "My name is Logan, and I'm going to be your guide."

Losham shook what he was offered while scrutinizing the guy's appearance. One of his requirements was that the uniforms should be professionally dry cleaned, ironed, and delivered daily. He wanted the club's staff to look meticulous.

In addition to the big name tag every club employee had pinned to the pocket of his or her button-down shirt, they also wore a uniform to indicate their function and make them clearly identifiable to the clientele. All except security wore black pants and black ties, but the color of their satin dress shirts varied. Red for the guides, electric blue for the bartenders, purple for servers, yellow for the valets, and so on.

Security wore all black accented by a red tie and a red belt.

After his many visits to Las Vegas, Losham decided on identical uniforms for male and female employees. The revealing costumes Vegas casinos had their female workers wear were cheesy and distasteful.

Losham's clubs were all about elegance and style. The debauchery happened behind the closed doors of the various sections dedicated to the different kinks his clients wished to engage in.

There was no reason to expose the general vanilla crowd who comprised the majority of the members to things of that nature.

As he'd suspected, there was a need for a sex club catering to the non-kink crowd. People with money who wanted anonymous, casual sex in a safe and supervised environment. No one was going to be victimized in Losham's clubs unless they wished to be—in writing, and with a club employee witnessing the signing of the agreement.

Obviously, the signing of the contract was also video recorded.

Not a moral call on his part, Losham couldn't have cared less, it was just good business. People were getting what they paid for and that included safety.

"Follow me, sir," the guide said.

Leaving Rami behind for his own tour of the third floor, Losham pushed to his feet and smiled at the guide. "Lead the way."

Eva

Eva looked at the address her snitch had provided, then glanced again at the building the club was housed in. Not bad. For the most part, sex clubs hid behind façades posing as warehouses, or private gates leading to mansions with long driveways. She'd followed a few suspected cheaters to those.

This one had a big neon sign. A single word—Allure.

Maybe her snitch had been pulling her leg, and this was a regular club. The only thing special about it was that it seemed to be geared toward those with money. Parked across the street, Eva watched as a Mercedes S-class Cabriolet pulled up to the valet station. The uniformed valet opened the driver's door and helped out a woman in an elegant cocktail dress.

Shit. She'd been misinformed. Her slutty costume, overdone makeup, and fake big boobs didn't belong in there. She looked like a hooker.

Eva waited until another car pulled up, a Ferrari this time. A man in a suit got out. This was a high-class joint, and she was dressed all wrong. The best she could do was to remove the bra with the fake boobs in it, but then she would have to go braless. Every contour of her nipples was going to be outlined by the stretchy fabric of her short dress. The makeup had to stay on. It was part of her disguise.

Are you sure it's a sex club? she texted her snitch.

Sure. It's new and costly. Did you call to reserve a tour?

No.

So how do you expect to get in?

Like she always did, by charming the bouncer. Young, attractive women were seldom turned away from places like that. This one should be no different.

Hopefully.

Why hadn't she checked it out on the Internet before getting dressed?

The answer was simple. Eva had been eager to be done with it. Seduce the piece of shit; take him to some hotel and dispose of him in a way that would look like he dropped dead from natural causes.

It had taken her over a month to track that particular scumbag. Not only was he a key player in a slave operation that dealt in trafficking women for sex, this one in particular went after underage girls. The worm was personally responsible for destroying God knew how many Tessas.

The question was, what was a lowlife like him doing in a fancy sex club?

Wasn't sampling his merchandise enough for him?

Maybe he was looking for potential clients. Yeah, that made sense. The scum was trying to make some deals on the side.

Eva lifted the phone off her lap and typed the club's name into her Internet browser.

A singles' club. A place to meet interesting, quality people. An unforgettable experience, it said.

I bet.

It didn't mention sex anywhere.

Maybe that was what the appointment was for.

Oh, well. She was already here, wearing a disguise her own daughter wouldn't have recognized her in, and her mark was inside. It was up to the powers that be whether the owner or manager would let her in without an appointment.

Luckily, the car rental company had been out of everything other than luxury class. Showing up with a decent car would modify the effect of her slutty outfit. That combined with a show of condescending attitude should do the trick. Just another nouveau riche with bad fashion taste.

She pulled up to the valet, and took the hand he offered to help her out of the car. With her four-inch heels, she was taller than him and could look down her nose at him. It wasn't that she wanted to impress the valet, but there were cameras at the front entrance, and someone was monitoring the new arrivals.

"Thank you," she said quietly with her back turned to the camera.

The guy cast her a puzzled glance, and she winked at him before sauntering inside.

As the doorman opened the way for her, Eva stepped in, entering an elegant vestibule where a young woman wearing the club's uniform sat behind a desk.

The snitch must have been high on something. No way a female receptionist in a sex club was dressed in a pair of slacks, a dress shirt that was buttoned all the way up, and a tie. A glance at her footwear revealed more of the same. A pair of conservative pumps with two-inch, chunky heels.

"Welcome to Allure, madam, please take a seat." The girl pointed to one of the armchairs facing her desk.

"Can I have your name?" She opened a leather-bound appointment book.

Eva waved a dismissive hand at the book. "I don't have an appointment. I didn't realize I needed one. Can you just pencil me in?"

The girl smiled like the professional she was. "We are fully booked for tonight, but I can check with my manager. If he is free, I'm sure he would love to give you a tour."

Eva lifted her face to the camera mounted in the corner behind the receptionist and flashed it one of her sexy come-hither smiles.

"A client walked in without an appointment. She didn't know one was needed. Is there any way we can accommodate her?"

Eva crossed her legs and pushed out her enhanced cleavage. It couldn't hurt to flaunt her assets.

"Have her fill out the confidentiality agreement and then the questionnaire. I'll come down when she's done." Eva heard the guy on the other side.

"Yes, of course, sir." The receptionist put down the receiver and smiled at Eva. "My manager would love to take you on a tour. But first you need to sign a confidentiality agreement, and after that there is a lengthy questionnaire that usually takes about half an hour to fill out."

"That's fine. I'm not in a hurry." Not true, her mark might leave before she was done with all that nonsense. On the positive side, the tour would give her the perfect excuse to look for the scumbag all over the place. The picture she had of him was five years old. Hopefully, he hadn't changed much.

When she signed the confidentiality agreement without really reading it, the receptionist asked for her driver's license and authenticated her signature. She then pulled out a thick folder and wrote Eva's fake name on the label.

"I couldn't help notice that you only skimmed the document you've just signed, so I'll sum it up to prevent future misunderstandings. From now on everything you read or see in this club is confidential, including this questionnaire." She tapped the folder. "Breaching the agreement may result in a lawsuit and significant monetary loss. Do you still want to proceed?"

Eva waved a hand. "Yes, of course I want to proceed. Give me that thing and a pen so I can get it done as quickly as I can. I wasn't expecting paperwork when I came here tonight."

The woman nodded with a polite smile. "Naturally." She pushed out from her chair and walked over to one of the doors lining the walls of the reception room. Opening the way for Eva, she ushered her into a small office. "You'll have complete privacy here, and you're welcome to use the beverage bar." She walked over to the cabinet and opened the door, showing Eva a fully stocked fridge.

"When you're done with the questionnaire, please press this button." She pointed to a box with an intercom. "And I'll inform my manager that you're ready."

"Thank you, darling." Eva sauntered over to the chair.

"My pleasure." The receptionist backed out from the room and closed the door quietly as if it was a medical clinic and not a club.

Eva made herself comfortable in the roomy wing chair, picked up a clipboard from the side table and opened the file. She wasn't fooled by the promise of complete privacy. Somewhere up on the ceiling or on the walls was a camera. Probably more than one. Her facial expressions while reading the questionnaire should reflect the person she was pretending to be.

Fortunately, Eva was a superb actress.

Jackson

"Is Tessa coming over tonight?" Gordon asked.

Jackson nodded.

"So I guess it's just Vlad and me. Again." His friend walked out, the chimes on the door jingling long after he was gone.

They should remove them. The chimes had been necessary when Nathalie and her father had worked in the café and lived in the apartment upstairs. She'd put them up because of her father's dementia. They'd alerted her whenever he'd tried to sneak out. The old man had gotten lost a few times.

Terrible thing to have a brain that's not working right and nothing can be done about it.

Jackson sat on the edge of one of the bar stools, watching the darkened street through the café's big front window. Tessa should be arriving any moment.

For the past week, she'd been coming to the café every evening. Sometimes she would also come during lunch to pick up a to-go order for her coworkers. A couple of evenings she'd come a little before closing and hung out with Jackson and his friends. The rest of the time Jackson had invited her to come over later and spend time with him alone.

Tessa was getting more comfortable, but he was making no progress uncovering what had happened to her. She'd deflected every time he steered the topic of conversation to something she'd suspected would lead to questions she didn't want to answer.

Damn it.

He should just thrall her. Get the information straight out of her head so he could find the bastard who'd ruined her life and end him. What Jackson imagined happened to Tessa kept mushrooming in his head, until he started rethinking his inability to kill.

But as tempting as it was, Jackson couldn't thrall her. Getting into Tessa's head and going through her memories without her permission was like raping her brain. It had already happened to her body. He wasn't going to do it to her mind.

The more he thought about it, the more certain he became of that. Otherwise, her aversion to men wouldn't have been justified.

Yesterday had been the first time Jackson had managed to convince her to come up to his room and watch a movie. They'd sat on opposite sides of the couch with a cushion between them like a couple of second graders.

Just as she'd asked, Jackson was doing his best to treat Tessa the same as he treated his guy friends, save for the crude jokes and farting competitions.

Not an easy feat since Tessa was beautiful and smart and fun, and he was attracted to her. The situation was made even worse by his unexplained self-imposed celibacy. Jackson just couldn't bring himself to have sex with another girl, and not for lack of trying. But none appealed to him anymore, even those he'd hooked up with before and enjoyed.

Thank the merciful Fates, Jackson was so far removed from the original gods that his sex drive was more controllable than that of immortal males whose blood was purer. Or at least that was what he believed.

The thing was, he and Tessa weren't in a relationship. Jackson didn't owe her anything, certainly not some misguided fidelity. He should've felt free to do as he pleased.

But he didn't.

Damn it.

As he saw Tessa's Prius slide into a parking spot one storefront over, Jackson opened the door and walked out to greet her.

"You don't have to do that," she said as he opened the door for her.

"I'm trying to be a gentleman. Just say thank you." He offered her his hand.

Tessa rolled her eyes, but took it. "Thank you," she said and then did something that shocked him. Stretching up on her toes, she kissed his cheek.

Fuck, it made him hard. That was the thing about abstinence. A kiss on the cheek would've done nothing for him a couple of weeks ago. Now it was making him hard.

Good thing Tessa seemed embarrassed by what she'd done and hurried ahead of him without looking back. Unable to take his eyes off her ass as he followed behind her, he knew that the situation in his pants didn't improve. Unaware of the light swing of her hips, Tessa had a sexy walk.

Jackson hurried ahead of her and opened the door. "I hope you're hungry," he said as he closed it behind her.

"A little. What did you make for me?"

"Take a seat, get comfortable, and I'll be right back."

As Tessa sat down on one of the bar stools, Jackson ducked into the kitchen. He pulled out from the fridge the two sandwiches he'd prepared ahead of time, placed each on a plate and added coleslaw. There was no more potato salad left. Two glasses of orange juice joined the rest of the stuff on the tray.

"Your favorite." He put the plate in front of her and then added the orange juice.

"Thank you," she said in a tone that sounded a little choked up, and lifted her fork. But instead of taking a scoop from the coleslaw, she started pushing it around on her plate.

Jackson paused with his sandwich midair, waiting for her to take the first bite. "Eat. I waited to have dinner with you, and I'm hungry as hell."

She cast him a sidelong glance, then lifted a minuscule amount of the salad and put it in her mouth.

If he weren't as hungry, Jackson would've argued that it didn't count. Instead, he attacked his triple-decker three kinds of meat sandwich, devouring it in record time. When he was done, Tessa was still pushing the coleslaw around on her plate.

Jackson wiped his mouth with a napkin and took a long gulp from his orange juice. "Why aren't you eating?"

Without looking up, Tessa shrugged her narrow shoulders.

Jackson smelled tears.

Swiveling the bar stool she was sitting on, he forced her to face him. "What's wrong?"

"I shouldn't be doing this."

"What? Eating?" He tried to go for humor.

She shook her head. "Coming here every day. Kissing you, turning you on. I shouldn't have done it. It's not fair to you."

Damn it. She'd noticed his reaction and was back to that crap again. "Stop it. I have no expectations from you. That kiss was nice, and you're an attractive girl. I couldn't help my reaction. But I will never make a move on you, and I don't expect you to make one on me. I'll be happy if you do, and I won't say no, but it's entirely up to you."

"I didn't know guys like you existed," she whispered.

"I'm nothing special, trust me. If it were Vlad or Gordon instead of me, they would've done the same. Most men are not monsters."

She nodded. "I know. But very few are really nice, like you, and some are real monsters. The middle is made up of those who don't care and are looking out only for themselves."

He reached for her hands, and she let him clasp them. "Tell me about the monsters, Tessa."

"Why would you want to hear that? What good would it do to you? You're better off not knowing."

"No, I'm not. My imagination is supplying me with one hell of a horror movie. What you're going to tell me can't be worse than that."

She lifted her head and pinned him with the saddest eyes he'd ever seen. "It's going to be way worse than anything you could've ever imagined."

"Tell me."

She shook her head. "I don't want you to feel sorry for me. I like it that you look at me and see an attractive girl and not a miserable wreck. I don't want you to look at me with pity in your eyes."

"I don't, and I will not. I've known for a while now that something awful has happened to you. Did you catch me pitying you even once?"

She dropped her eyes again. "No. But you will if I tell you."

He hooked a finger under her chin. "The only strong emotion I will feel is a murderous rage toward the monsters who harmed you. And if I ever find them, I'll make them pay."

Damn. Getting all angry and aggressive in front of a human was a really stupid move. Jackson's glands pulsated as they filled with venom and his fangs elongated. Doubtless his eyes were blazing too. He let go of Tessa's chin and looked away, trying to get himself under control.

"I grew up in foster homes," she started in barely a whisper. "Some were better than others, but the last one was bad. I was fifteen when I ran away, thinking there was something better out there. I should've stayed. The stuff that made me miserable in that foster home was nothing. They were strict and ran a household full of troubled kids like a military base. I shared a room with three other girls, but I had my own bed and my own box under it to store my things. Not that I had much. Just a few changes of hand-me-down clothes and my school books. I got into a fight with another girl and got punished even though it was her fault."

Tessa shook her bowed head, her wavy hair hiding her face. "I was stupid. I still believed in the concept of fairness and felt wronged. So I packed a few things in my backpack and ran. I got as far as the train station. The monsters got me that same night. I think they lurk in places like train stations and central bus hubs, lying in wait for stupid runaway girls like me."

Jackson wanted to just let Tessa talk, but he couldn't help himself and growled, "Stop calling yourself stupid, please."

She lifted her sad eyes. "If I were smart, I would've stayed. I should've been grateful to my foster parents for providing a roof over my head, food on the table, and a relatively safe place to come home to. So what if they had no love to give me? If I stayed, none of that would've happened to me."

Jackson cupped her cheeks with his hands and thumbed her tears away. "You were a kid. Give yourself a break."

She nodded, but he knew nothing had changed in her warped perception. Tessa still thought it had been her fault. "There were other girls in the place I woke up at. They drugged us and beat us. Obedience was rewarded with drugs, anything perceived as disobedience was punished with severe beatings. The monsters were masters at inflicting maximum pain without leaving any permanent marks or damages. After all, they still needed to sell us. Whoever bought us could do whatever he pleased to us. Including killing. We were presumed dead anyway."

With a shaky hand, Tessa reached for the orange juice and took a long sip, then continued in the same monotone, flat voice. "The other girls warned me to obey everything immediately, but I didn't listen. I tried to fight. The first time they only beat me up. The second time I didn't do what I was told they broke each one of my fingers. One at a time over twenty-four hours. They gave me nothing for the pain, but put my broken fingers in splints. I passed out a few times, but they revived me. I was supposed to learn my lesson, and I did. After that, I obeyed every command without thinking. No matter how degrading and how awful, I did it. The only thing I was grateful for was my virginity. They didn't rape me because they could sell a virgin for more money. Some of the other girls weren't as lucky. But it wasn't as if they left me alone, they just used me in other ways."

It was good that Tessa was still looking at the floor and not at him, because Jackson's whole body shook with rage. Impotent rage was the worst kind. Neither he nor anyone else could change the past. Pressing his lips tightly together, he hid his fangs, which had by now elongated to their full size and were dripping venom into his throat.

"After three months, they deemed me fully trained. I was sold at an auction and raped before he even got me to his home. I say it was rape, but I didn't fight. All the fight had been beat out of me, and I was drugged. So I just lay there and let him do whatever he wanted. I was his slave for over a year."

"What's his name?" Jackson hissed.

"It doesn't matter. He's dead."

"Who killed him?"

"That doesn't matter either. I escaped that night."

"Where did you go?"

"Eva found me and took me in. She and Nick and Sharon took turns helping me detox because I couldn't go to rehab. I was sixteen and on the run. The dead guy's family thought I was the one who killed him."

"Did you?"

She chuckled and lifted her head, searching his face to see his reaction. "You sound like you hope I did."

"Because I do."

"I wish. But someone else did."

"Who?"

Tessa shrugged. "It doesn't matter. What's done is done and he deserved to die."

She was protecting someone, but that was fine. Whoever had freed her had Jackson's everlasting gratitude, and so had Eva and her crew for taking Tessa in and helping her.

"True. If I knew who did it, I would shake that person's hand and thank him."

Taking in a deep breath through her mouth, Tessa released it slowly through her nose. "You were right. I feel better now. Thank you for listening."

Jackson placed his hand over his beating heart. "Always and forever. I'm here for you."

Tilting her head, Tessa looked into his eyes. "That sounded like a pledge."

"It is."

Eva

"**D**o you have any questions?" the manager asked after introducing himself. A pleasant fellow, Peter was cut from the same cloth as the receptionist. Courteous and pleasant. Someone had done a fabulous job training the club employees. If not for the questionnaire, Eva would've doubted again her snitch's information.

"I'm good for now." Frankly, the thing had been so extensive and explicit that she was still recovering from the shock of going over it.

"Very well. Feel free to ask me anything during the tour, and if anything makes you uncomfortable, please tell me. This club caters to all sorts of tastes. You may wish to remain in the main area, or venture into the more exotic zones. It's up to you."

"I understand."

The nice part was that not all of it was about kink, and nothing explicitly sexual was allowed in the main area, which was comprised of a large room with a full bar in the center, a cigar lounge in a covered patio outside, and plenty of love seats and intimate little enclaves for conversation and other things.

"Members are allowed to bring guests, for business or pleasure, with business conducted in the main room or out on the patio, and pleasure in one of the many places dedicated to it," Peter explained.

There were private rooms, communal rooms for those who liked to watch or be watched or both, and of course various levels of kink areas. Private rooms could be used for whatever. They all came equipped with a large variety of sex toys and torture instruments.

"I think that's as far as I go." Eva had stopped the manager at the second level of public kink.

"Of course." Peter led her outside the room and closed the doors behind him.

For the humans, the soundproofing would've been enough to block the disturbing sounds that had sent her running, but Eva wasn't that lucky. The thuds and the screams that followed trailed her until she and Peter stepped back inside the main room. She'd read a little about it, even had a few fantasies, but to witness it done was too much. Anything that left red marks on the flesh or pulled screams of pain out of the victims repulsed her, and bondage was not something she could ever tolerate either.

So even though she marked BDSM as an interest on the questionnaire, Eva didn't want to see any more. Luckily, she'd already spotted her mark at the beginning of the tour, sitting on the patio and wheeling and dealing with other scumbags while sucking on a thick cigar.

"Is it your first time in a club like this?" the manager asked.

"Is it that obvious? I thought I was ready for some of the stuff that's going on in the other rooms, but I guess I'm more vanilla than spice."

"No problem. As you can see, most of our members share your preferences. A beautiful woman like you will have no shortage of partners here."

"How soon do I need to give you an answer?" The price of membership was staggering, but Eva had pretended it was nothing for her. The story she'd told the manager while touring was that she was recently divorced, had a large settlement from her rich ex, and was eager to party after years of unsatisfactory sex.

"You can enjoy the rest of the evening here, look around, get acquainted with the staff and the other patrons, and then decide if Allure is for you. If you need one more evening to look around it can be arranged. However, after these two complimentary visits, you'll have to either purchase a membership or come as a guest of one of the members."

"Of course. Thank you for your time." She offered him her hand.

Instead of shaking it, he pulled out a white rubber bracelet from his pocket and slipped it on her wrist. "This is to identify you as a potential member and grants you free access to the bar. The drinks are on the house."

"Much appreciated. You created a really classy establishment here." Eva meant it. Doubtless, other sex clubs were nothing like this.

"Thank you. Have fun." He waved his hand toward the bar.

"Oh, I will."

As soon as the manager departed, Eva made her way to the bar and ordered a drink. Waiting, she sat with her back to the counter and looked across the room to the patio, checking her target was still there.

Confirming that he was, she let herself relax a little and look around.

"Here you go, ma'am." The bartender put her Moscow Mule on the counter and added a small plate of nuts.

"Thank you." Eva palmed the drink and went back to scanning the room out of sheer curiosity. The one thing common to everyone in there was wealth. From the designer clothes they were wearing to the perfectly done hairstyles, everything about them screamed money.

Eva's eyes landed on a gorgeous woman in a blue dress and her much older companion. They were heading for the door which she and Peter had come back through, as another guide escorting a guest opened it from the other side.

For a moment, her heart skipped a beat—the guest looked a lot like the immortal who'd taken her virginity—eerily so. Similar height and body shape, even the coloring was identical, except for the eyes. Whereas her immortal's eyes had been blue and smiling, this man's eyes were so dark they were almost black. There was sharp intelligence in those eyes. And menace. A deadly combination if ever she'd seen one.

Cold dread slithering up her exposed back, Eva shivered.

That man was dangerous, and her instincts urged her to distance herself from him as soon and as far as possible.

She was about to hoof it out of there as the man and his guide passed her by and continued to the exit door. The man shook the guide's offered hand, then turned around and looked straight at her.

Eva froze.

He must've felt her eyes on him.

Please don't come near me, please don't come near me... she prayed as he looked her over and smiled.

God must've heard her prayer. As the guide opened the door, the man thanked him again and stepped out. Eva collapsed back on her bar stool and emptied what was left of her drink. Her reaction didn't make any sense. For nearly her entire adult life she'd been dealing with dangerous people, but she'd never felt anything like the fear that had gripped her because of one man's dark, menacing eyes.

Come on, Eva. You act as if you've seen the devil. Shake it off. You have a job to do.

A quick glance confirmed that her mark was still sitting outside on the patio, chewing on his cigar.

Maybe she should buy a cigar to justify going out to the lounge. "Can you recommend a cigar for beginners?" she asked the bartender. "I love the smell but never tried one. And I would like another one of these." She pointed at her empty glass.

He pulled a couple of boxes from the huge humidor behind him. "Both aren't strong but have a nice flavor."

She chose the smaller one and paid for it. "Thank you," she told the bartender and took her new drink and the cigar.

"Wait, don't you want matches?"

"No thank you." Asking the scumbag to light her cigar was the perfect excuse to start her seduction.

She sauntered to where the mark and his friend were sitting. "Hello, gentlemen, mind if I join you?"

"Please," the friend said, pointing at the third armchair next to the round table.

"Thank you." She put her drink down and crossed her legs. "Hi, I'm Veronica." Eva offered her hand to the friend first.

"Ricardo, a pleasure to make your acquaintance, Veronica."

The name was as fake as hers. No one here gave their real ones. Eva tossed a few red locks behind her as she offered her hand to the scumbag. The red wig was top quality, and there was no chance she could accidentally dislodge it. A hurricane couldn't snatch that thing. "And you are?"

"I'm James."

"Nice to meet you, James." She pulled the cigar from her purse. "I've never tried one of these before. Can either of you show me how it's done?"

The one calling himself Ricardo cut the cigar for her and showed her how to light it.

She took a puff and choked.

"Gently," Ricardo admonished. "Don't inhale, just hold it in your mouth."

She did, sucking on the cigar as if it was an entirely different thing and giving both *gentlemen* visible hard-ons.

There was a green rubber band around James's wrist, indicating that he was a guest, not a member. Ricardo had none, which meant that he was. Eva wondered why someone like him would invite a scumbag like her mark to a club like this. The one calling himself James was a lowlife. Ricardo was sophisticated and obviously rich, but doubtless a scumbag as well. Otherwise, he wouldn't have been hanging out with James.

What was his deal? Drugs? Was he in the market for a personal slave?

She lifted her wrist and dangled the white bracelet. "I want to ask you something, Ricardo. I'm new, so I don't know what's okay to ask and what's not. You'll need to tell me if I'm overstepping the boundaries."

Ricardo waved his cigar in a magnanimous manner. "I'll be happy to satisfy your curiosity."

The obvious double entendre wasn't lost on her. Eva took another puff of her cigar and pretended to concentrate on her question. "Is it too personal to ask someone about their preferred type of kink?"

Ricardo seemed unfazed by her question. "The protocol is that you ask to be introduced to people who are interested in the same thing as you are. The guides do the introductions. But there is no law against asking."

"What's yours?"

Ricardo snorted. "I like bluntness. I'm a dominant, if you're familiar with the term."

"Like BDSM?"

"Exactly."

"My guide told me there are many levels. Do you prefer a sexual submissive or a twenty-four-seven slave?" If they were anywhere else that type of question would've gotten her in trouble, but not in here.

Ricardo tapped his cigar on the ashtray, then took another puff. "Slaves take too much effort. A woman who desires that kind of a relationship wants her master to decide everything for her. What to wear and what not, what to eat, what to drink. I don't have the time or the patience for that. So to answer your question, I prefer a submissive who wants to play and go her separate way once it's done."

From the corner of her eye Eva observed James's reactions to Ricardo's answer, and the guy wasn't happy.

Eva raised her drink. "Smart man. I couldn't agree more."

Ricardo smiled and lifted his martini. "And what do you like, Veronica? Are you into domination or submission?"

"I haven't decided yet. I plan to try both and see how it works. Something very mild to start with."

"You could be a switch and enjoy both."

"That would be awesome. So many variations of play."

Ricardo seemed more interested by the moment, and if he were her target, it would've been great. But Eva sensed he was too big of a fish for her. She needed to focus on the other one and get him to take her to his hotel room.

"How about you, James, what do you like?"

"Everything, as long as it has a pussy, that is. I'm not into guys."

Ricardo's mouth twisted in distaste. Apparently he didn't approve of vulgarity any more than she did.

Eva laughed and put a hand on James's thigh. "Are you as undiscriminating about food too?"

He shrugged. "I eat just about anything. None of that French stuff, though. No frogs, and no snails."

She laughed again. "I hear you. I'm getting a little hungry. Is there anywhere I can grab a bite?"

"The club has a restaurant," Ricardo said.

Damn it. She needed James to suggest they go somewhere else. "Do they serve tuna melt sandwiches?

Because that's what I'm craving." Hopefully the club's restaurant was too fancy for something like that.

This time, the disdain in Ricardo's expression was directed at her. "I'm afraid they do not."

"Figures. They probably serve frogs and snails, isn't that right, James?" *Come on, get a clue.*

"Yeah." James extinguished what was left of his cigar. "What do you say we go find ourselves some decent food?"

"I would love to. How about you, Ricardo, want to come? Sample some common folks' fare?" *Please say no.*

"I'm afraid I can't. As I was telling James right before you joined us, I have a session scheduled in"—he glanced at his watch—"ten minutes. Just enough time to finish my drink and cigar. Give me a call when you're in the mood for really good food." He winked as he handed her a business card.

Score!

If she ever learned how to thrall she would go after this one. After she did a background check on him, of course. Eva didn't go killing people who she wasn't absolutely sure deserved it.

"Thank you." She dropped the card into her purse then hooked her arm through James's. "Let's go, handsome."

Bhathian

"Can you come over?" Eva said as soon as he answered his phone. No hello, no how've-you-been. She sounded on edge.

"Sure. When?"

"How about right now?"

"Did something happen?"

"No. It's just that I've been working on several assignments at once and I need to unwind."

Obviously, Eva wanted him for one thing only—sex.

More than fine by him. "No problem. I'm just going to grab a quick shower."

"Great. See you here." She disconnected.

Eva had been busy with work the entire week. Or so she claimed.

At first, Bhathian had thought she was avoiding him, but she hadn't come over to see Nathalie either. Mother and daughter talked on the phone daily, sometimes more than once, but given that Nathalie's due date was approaching rapidly, Eva should've made an effort to see her.

Was she avoiding Nathalie as well?

Maybe she was afraid of the questions Nathalie would ask. It wasn't easy to tell a daughter that the father she adored had been cheating on her mother.

Bhathian didn't envy Eva her predicament.

An hour later, when he knocked on her door, he was surprised to see all three of her crew members there. Nick was watching a show on television, while Tessa and Sharon huddled over some fashion magazine.

"Come." She took his hand and led him to the staircase.

Bhathian barely managed to say a quick hello before she was urging him up the stairs.

"Someone's horny," he whispered even though he wasn't detecting any scent of arousal. Aggression seemed to be overpowering all of Eva's gentler emotions.

Strange.

Bhathian associated that particular scent with his fellow Guardians, and then only when they had a good reason to get pumped up. Kri almost never emitted it even though she was a warrior through and through.

Eva was a detective, not a soldier. Something must've gone wrong on one of her assignments.

She turned her head and flashed him a chilling smile that would've made babies cry and little children hide behind their mama's legs.

He smiled back.

Without a word, she just kept climbing, her beautiful ass sashaying in front of him. When Bhathian entered her bedroom, the first thing he noticed was that there were beers and several bottles of liquor on top of the coffee table in the sitting area. The vodka had a third missing from it but it didn't mean that Eva had drunk all of that while waiting for him. The bottle could've been opened before.

"Care for a beer?" She pointed at the assortment. "I've got your favorite."

Bhathian felt encouraged. She'd remembered. "Don't mind if I do." He grabbed a bottle of Snake's Venom.

Eva poured vodka into one of the tumblers, then added lime juice and ginger beer. Homemade Moscow Mule.

"Salute!" She lifted her glass.

"What are we celebrating?"

"A successful mission."

"Oh." He'd been hoping it had something to do with the two of them.

"Yep. I'm really good at what I do. A true professional." She grimaced, took a long sip from her drink, and grimaced again. "I made it too strong, and it tastes awful, but anything less has no effect on me."

"What's wrong, Eva?"

She closed her eyes and shook her head. "Work stuff. Confidential."

He chuckled. "Who am I going to tell?"

"I don't want to talk about it."

Respecting her commitment to her clients' confidentiality, Bhathian wasn't going to pry. Even if he and Eva were a committed couple, she could not have told him secrets that weren't hers to disclose. Andrew and Nathalie were married and he couldn't share work-related stuff with her either. As a private eye, Eva's secrets weren't on the same level as Andrew's, it wasn't about national security, but the principle was the same.

Bhathian put his beer down then moved behind Eva and wrapped his arms around her. "I have just the thing to make you feel better." He pushed her hair aside and trailed his lips down her neck, his fangs scraping lightly over her taut skin.

Eva slumped against him, tilting her head to give him better access. His hand slid beneath the shoulder straps of her long dress, pulling them down her arms. The loose dress cascaded to the floor, pooling at Eva's slender feet. What was left were a tiny thong and a bra that didn't cover much. Each time he undressed Eva, she was wearing one of those exquisite numbers he'd never seen on a woman before. The best part of the designs was how easy they were for a man to take off.

In a rush of jealous haze, he cupped her breasts and squeezed not too gently. Eva belonged to him. No other man would ever touch her again.

"Oh God." She moaned and arched her back, pushing into his hands.

Careful not to nick her with his fangs, he caught the fleshy part of her ear between his front teeth and bit down, gently, thumbing her pebbled nipples over the fabric of her bra at the same time.

She whimpered, and he released her ear. "You're mine," he whispered without thinking. If that would make her run, he would just have to chase her. "You'd better not let another man touch you, not if you want him to stay alive."

Turning her head to look up at him, Eva surprised the hell out of him. Bhathian expected his unjustified possessiveness to bring out indignation, even ridicule, but there was none of that.

She smiled. "You say the sweetest things. Would you really do it? Kill any man who touched me?"

He wasn't sure if she was asking jokingly or not, but his answer would've been the same in both cases. "You better believe it."

She closed her eyes and let her head rest on his chest. "Am I a terrible person if that turns me on?"

It wasn't a lie or a tease. The scent of her arousal had doubled in potency.

He nuzzled her neck. "You're an immortal female, Eva, not a human. We are more savage, more intense, especially when it comes to our mates."

Again, he expected denial, a rebuttal, a vehement I'm-not-your-mate. Instead, Eva almost purred with satisfaction. "Same goes for you, lover. From now on you don't go near any other woman."

"Since you came back into my life, I haven't been with anyone else."

Her head snapped around, anger flashing in her amber eyes. "Don't lie to me, Bhathian."

The woman's responses were never what he expected.

"I'm not. I can't even think about being with another woman. I started drinking with my son-in-law to numb the cravings."

Eva pushed out of his arms and turned, looking so fuckable it hurt. "Andrew drinks? Nathalie didn't tell me."

Damn it. Bhathian didn't want to talk about this now. He wanted to divest Eva of the rest of what covered her, bend her over the arm of the armchair and fuck her senseless.

"For the same reason I started to. He can't have sex with Nathalie until the baby is born because his bite will induce Nathalie's transformation. He numbs his sex drive with shitloads of alcohol."

Eva nodded. "I suspected there was something going on between them that Nathalie wasn't telling me. No wonder Andrew is almost never around when I come over."

Bhathian grabbed his T-shirt and yanked it over his head. "The time for talking is over."

Eva's eyes raked over his muscular torso, and the scent of her arousal flared again. She put her hands on his chest and lifted her face to him. "Kiss me, lover boy."

Eva

Standing on tiptoes and offering Bhathian her mouth, Eva wondered if he'd been telling the truth. But when he smashed his mouth over hers, fisting her hair and holding her head in place so he could devour her, it no longer mattered.

The only thing that mattered was how soon he could be inside her. Eva wasn't in the mood for loving and gentle. Maybe later, after the hunger that had been gnawing at her for days eased. Right now she just wanted to get fucked. Hard.

"I need you inside me," she said the moment he let go of her mouth to come up for a breath. The kiss had been hot, but Eva needed that sexual ferocity directed where she ached.

His gray eyes bored into hers for a split second, then between one blink of an eye to the next, she found herself bent face down over the thick armrest of the overstuffed chair.

Hot!

Her butt up in the air and her legs dangling over the armrest, with only the tips of her toes barely reaching the carpet, she felt vulnerable, exposed. But it was only her flesh that was on display. Letting Bhathian see it was easy. Her outer shell was pretty. Showing him the ugliness that was inside was another thing altogether.

With a strong pull, Bhathian yanked her thong down her thighs and left it there, effectively binding her legs together. As his finger slid along her wet slit, she heard him pop the button on his jeans, and as he pushed two into her hungry core, she heard them fall on the floor.

A moment later his fingers were replaced by the tip of his shaft, and she braced for the invasion that never came. Bhathian teased her entrance, pushing in no more than an inch and retreating.

When she lifted her butt up, trying to get more of him inside her, he rewarded her with a loud slap on her ass. She didn't mind the sting, on the contrary, but the sound was another thing. Even with normal human ears and an entire floor in between, her crew must've heard that.

"Don't," she hissed.

Bhathian bent over her, covering her back with his torso. "Then don't move and don't try to take over."

His words pulled a ragged moan out of her.

Eva needed this. Needed him to dominate her. Bhathian was probably the only male she could let herself submit to. Her gut insisted that she could trust him, that it was okay to let go because he would never let anything bad happen to her. For the next couple of hours, she could let instinct take over and not let her logical mind stand in the way of her pleasure.

She didn't move when he lifted off her, even though she missed the feel of his warm, smooth skin, and she didn't move when he teased her entrance again, rubbing her stinging butt cheek with his warm hand. And yet he delivered another smack to the other cheek, just as hard as the first one.

"Shh." He stopped her protest before it could leave her mouth, and pushed in, letting her have more of his length but not all. "It was for the sake of symmetry. Now both sides are pink."

A thought crossed her mind that later Bhathian could thrall her crew to forget what they'd heard. It wasn't that she owed them an explanation, and if they weren't her employees she wouldn't have even been embarrassed, but she could do without the snickering and the comments about their boss and spanking. Not unless she was the one administering it.

Her reputation as a hard-as-nails detective was on the line.

All was forgotten a moment later when Bhathian moved. With a gentle push, he slid all the way in, then bent over her and wrapped his arms around her. Snapping the front opening of her bra like a pro, he peeled the cups away and palmed her breasts.

Eva was on fire. Bhathian's fingers were pinching and tugging on her nipples as his shaft drove in and out of her in shallow thrusts. It was all too much and not enough at the same time.

"More," she groaned.

As Bhathian moved one hand over to her most sensitive spot and rubbed, the pleasure got so intense that she dug her nails into the chair cushion, tearing into the fabric.

"More?" Bhathian asked.

"Yes."

With his other hand, he grabbed her chin, twisting her head around, and kissed her long and hard. But it was impossible to maintain contact as he lost the battle with his self-restraint and started pounding into her.

Gripping Eva around her waist to hold her in place, he went harder and faster. With his pelvis slapping into her butt with each forward surge, and his fingers circling her swollen clit, the coil inside was winding up tighter and tighter until it sprung free with the power of an exploding grenade.

Eva bit her own arm to stifle the scream. The sharp pain of Bhathian's fangs sinking into the flesh of her neck eclipsed that small sting, and then there was no pain at all.

The euphoria washing over her wasn't instantaneous, though. With Bhathian's roar keeping her tethered to this world, she was still aware when his own climax exploded into her, the warm jets coating her welcoming sheath and then dripping down her thighs. A moment later the tether snapped, and she soared up and away into the land of bliss.

When she came to, Eva found herself sprawled on the bed, her legs flopping lewdly to the sides, and Bhathian lying on his front between them with his tongue buried deep inside her.

She reached to caress his short hair and chuckled. "I didn't know you were so kinky."

He lifted his head with a comically puzzled expression on his handsome face. "You call this kinky?"

She cupped his cheek. "The cunnilingus in itself isn't, but combined with necrophilia it is. I was passed out, lover boy."

His smile was wickedly sexy. "You're awake now." He dove his head between her legs and went back to licking and sucking, bringing her to another shuddering climax in no time at all.

The man loved eating her up, and she loved him doing so, especially when it culminated with a deliciously wicked bite on her inner thigh and another trip to the clouds.

Bhathian

Holding Eva in his arms as she slept felt so good that Bhathian dreaded the moment she'd open her eyes and start pushing him away. It always went like that. The sex was phenomenal, and he would let himself hope that they were getting closer, that she was lowering her shields and letting him in, only to have his illusions shattered the moment the sex was over.

Fates, he sounded like a chick.

Bhathian wanted to laugh. What a role reversal. He looked like a guy who could lift up a truck, which he could, while Eva looked like the personification of everything that was soft and feminine. Her hair was long and always styled in soft big curls, and she rarely wore pants, preferring long, light-colored dresses. On the inside, though, she was hardened steel. Strong and unbendable.

Was he fighting a losing battle?

Maybe this was all she had to give?

It wasn't enough, but he could live with it, provided she promised him exclusivity. Not only because he couldn't tolerate the mere thought of her having another man in her bed, but because being her lover could open the way for more. Eventually, she would grow fond of him. He would make sure of that. Once that was achieved, crossing the distance all the way to love shouldn't be too difficult.

Eva shifted in his arms and yawned. "How long was I asleep?"

He kissed her forehead. "Not long. A couple of hours."

"It's quiet here. Did the kids go to sleep?"

"Yeah. Except for Nick. He's in his room, watching porn."

"You can hear that?"

"Yeah."

She pouted. "Your hearing is better than mine."

"Not all immortals are the same. We all have varying degrees of skills and enhanced senses."

As Eva closed her eyes and snuggled closer, Bhathian offered silent thanks to the Fates. This was progress. Maybe she would let him stay the night.

"Are you hungry?" she asked, and his heart sank.

That was how it always started. She'd ask him if he was hungry, and regardless of his answer, she would have him get dressed and go downstairs for a snack. Twenty minutes later, tops, he was out the door.

"Trying to get rid of me already?"

She had the decency to blush. "Do you want to stay the night?"

"You know I do." He smoothed his hand over her silky hair.

"Okay. But I really want to grab a bite." She extended her tongue and licked his nipple, pulling a hiss from his lips and a twitch from his cock which was still erect despite their marathon lovemaking. "Rigorous exercise always makes me hungry."

After that tease, Bhathian would've skipped food and gone back to lovemaking, but if his mate was really hungry, he needed to feed her first.

"How hungry?"

She laughed. "I need to refuel. After we eat, I'll see if I have enough energy for another round."

"Deal."

They ended up having that additional round in the shower.

After he dried her with a soft towel and carried her back to the bedroom, despite her protests, Eva put on a long nightgown with a matching robe over it.

Always so feminine... if one didn't know her. Eva was proof that looks can be deceptive.

Down in the kitchen, Bhathian sat on the same wooden chair next to the same wooden table as every other time, but his mood was much different. Eva letting him stay overnight was a huge step. They were making progress.

And just as all the other times, she pulled out boxes of leftover takeout food and put them in the microwave to warm up. That was another thing they had in common, neither knew how to cook.

Eva had told him that when she was married to Fernando, he'd done all the cooking, so she'd never bothered to learn, and Bhathian just didn't. He wasn't finicky and ate anything as long as someone else prepared it.

"I hope you like Thai food."

"Love it."

Eva tilted her head and smiled. "You love everything. I've never heard you say you didn't like something."

He shrugged. "That's true."

Eva pulled out a bottle of wine from the fridge. "Sharon opened it for lunch. We need to finish it." She brought it to the table and went back for two wine glasses.

Bhathian held his up for Eva to fill up, then waited for her to fill hers before taking a sip.

"Tell me something," she asked. "Are you as undiscriminating with women as you are with food?"

A loaded question if he'd ever heard one. "Not at all. There is only one woman I want, and she's sitting in front of me."

"I meant before."

Bhathian stretched his head and smiled sheepishly. "You can say that I had a type."

She lifted a brow. "You did?"

"Yeah, still do. I like brunettes, about five feet seven inches tall, with amber eyes and cupid-bow lips that are begging to be kissed."

She rolled her eyes. "I'm serious."

The microwave beeped, and Bhathian got up to bring the boxes over. Eva pulled out a couple of paper plates and plastic forks. Another thing they had in common. Neither liked washing dishes.

"Me too," he said. "There have been a lot of lookalikes, but none came even close. There is only one female in the world that matches that description perfectly. You know who she is."

Eva scooped some rice from one of the boxes and chicken pieces from another, then poured the sauce from the box over everything. "I've never met anyone like you," she admitted. "You're one of a kind."

That was the best compliment Bhathian had ever got, even though he wasn't sure it was one. "I hope you mean it in a good way."

She laughed. "Of course, you dummy. Has no one ever told you how handsome you are?"

"The term I hear most often is ogre."

Lifting her fork like it was a weapon, she mock-frowned. "Tell me who it was and I'll beat them up."

He put his hand over his heart. "I'm touched that you'd defend my honor like that."

For the next few minutes they got busy eating. Bhathian liked watching Eva eat. She did it in such an elegant and refined way.

"Why are you staring at me?"

"I'm admiring your table manners. You're such a lady."

She snorted in a very unladylike fashion. "Right..."

"You are. Tell me one thing that you do that is not ladylike. Except for that snort, that is."

For some reason his innocent compliment seemed to bother her. "What I do for a living. A private eye does a lot of things that are neither gentlemanly nor ladylike."

"I thought you liked doing what you do."

She shook her head. "I'm good at it. Doesn't mean I like doing it. I get to witness humanity's ugly underbelly. I'd rather not. Ignorance is bliss."

He couldn't argue with that. That was the downside of being a law enforcer or a fighter. Even though their services were crucial and appreciated, job satisfaction wasn't part of the rewards. Bhathian often envied those who had other talents. Like Dalhu. The guy had transformed himself from a killer into an artist, from a destroyer into a creator.

The thing was, someone had to do the policing and the fighting. And those people needed to be good at what they did.

Like him and Eva.

Eva

In the silence that followed, Bhathian seemed lost in thought. Was he thinking about his own job as a Guardian, or was he trying to imagine what her work was like? What bothered her about it?

The detective part was okay, though she hadn't lied about seeing the ugliness that she would rather not see. But it was small potatoes compared to her "hobby." Eva felt dirty and evil. And it wasn't only because of the killing. Worse than that was getting exposed to the atrocities the scum she eliminated had committed.

"You shouldn't feel bad about what you do." Bhathian pulled her out of the morbid place her mind had taken her. "I would've loved to have some other ability besides fighting. But that is what I'm good at, while others are not. It's my responsibility to defend those who can't do it for themselves, the same way the creative types create things for me that I cannot. Those are the gifts we were born with. Not much we can do about them. Besides, it's better than having no gifts at all. Imagine if you couldn't do detective work."

"I don't need to imagine. For years I was stuck at Fernando's café waiting tables because I couldn't bake or cook if my life depended on it, and then after the divorce I was stuck selling clothes at Nordstrom. I hated every freaking moment of every freaking day."

It had been such a stressful time in her life. Eva had divorced Fernando but couldn't leave Nathalie yet. She had to hang on until her daughter became an adult, going through her days terrified that someone would see through the heavy makeup and the baggy clothes and realize that the sixty-year-old woman she needed to look like had the body and face of a twenty-something-year-old.

"Why did you stay there? You could've found another job."

"Not really. I was a woman in her sixties, and my work experience was good for nothing. As a retired DEA agent and a waitress, I didn't have much to offer. Nordstrom paid commission and I was good at telling men what to wear. The pay was decent, and together with the government pension, I saved up enough to later open my agency. I needed to buy a new identity, I needed to get a license, and I needed some money to live on until my business took off."

Bhathian looked impressed. "You'd been planning this for years."

"Yes."

"Good for you. You rose like the Phoenix from the ashes of the old Eva and made a new life for yourself."

She sighed. "I had no choice. At some point, the pension checks were going to stop coming, and I needed to find a way to support myself for years to come while keeping my identity secret. The detective agency seemed like a perfect solution."

"And it was the kind of work you've been trained for."

"Exactly."

It felt good to talk about herself without resorting to the necessary lies and omissions. Not only that, Bhathian understood her and the hard choices she'd had to make. He didn't blame her for abandoning her family, didn't look at her as if she was some kind of monster. Sharing her story with him lifted some of the heavy guilt that had been her companion for so long.

Bhathian refilled their glasses, emptying the rest of the bottle. "I think doing a job that you're good at is satisfying no matter what it is. I'm sure there are days doctors hate their jobs, especially if someone they were trying to save dies. And yet most wouldn't want to do anything else. It's a calling. Not everyone can be a doctor, just as not everyone can be a cop or a soldier or a detective."

She nodded. "God has a purpose for each of us. I was given the powers I have so I could use them to make the world a better place."

Bhathian reached for her hand and gave it a gentle squeeze. "I wouldn't go so far as divine intervention. People put too much stock in fate."

Bhathian

Eva's eyes blazed as she lifted her head and pulled her hand away. "Really? So explain to me how I came about. I'm a Dormant, a rarity, who encounters not one but two immortal lovers who are even rarer. One activates my dormant immortal genes, and the other knocks me up, even though I'm practically infertile. Coincidence? I don't think so."

He couldn't argue with that. But seeing divine purpose in corporate espionage and gathering evidence on cheating spouses was taking the fate thing too far.

"I don't want to belittle what you do, I'm sure catching cheating husbands or wives and dishonest business partners is very important to the people who hire you, but it's not the kind of stuff that will change the world for the better or worse."

As Eva frowned and reached for her wine glass, then took a long sip, Bhathian wanted to bang his head against the wall. What a dumb-ass move for a guy who was trying to win over a woman. Like questioning her beliefs and making her lifework seem insignificant would get him anything other than a kick out the door.

She put her wine glass down. "That's not the only thing I do."

"I apologize for what I said. That was stupid of me. What you do is important."

Eva shook her head. "Don't. I want you to always be honest with me. And you were right. But as I said, there are other things I do that I can't talk about."

"Do they have anything to do with the mood you were in when I got here?"

She nodded but didn't elaborate.

Whatever was troubling her, she needed to get it off her chest and not keep it there where it festered like a rotten egg.

"I know that you can't tell me your clients' secrets, but you can talk about it without mentioning names. It would help you deal with whatever it is that's bothering you."

"You wouldn't understand." She lifted the wine glass to her lips and took a tiny sip.

Funny how Eva didn't realize her own hypocrisy, expecting him to lay it all on the table and at the same time keeping everything close to her chest. And it wasn't only about her clients. She didn't share much about herself either. Tonight had been the first time she'd let him have a glimpse into her past. For obvious reasons, she didn't trust him, or anyone else.

Perhaps if he just went ahead and said what was in his heart, she would trust him a little more. Knowing how he felt about her should reassure her that he would never betray that trust. Problem was, it could also backfire big time.

"Try me."

Without looking at him, she shook her head. "I can't." The incredibly sad tone of those two words tipped the scales.

He reached across the small table, took the wine glass from her and put it down, then clasped both of her hands. "Look at me, Eva."

She lifted her head.

"I know you're not ready to hear it, but I love you. I think I've loved you from the first moment I saw you. We are each other's fated mates. And you know how I know it?"

She shook her head.

"Because for the past thirty-one years I was more dead than alive, and nothing other than losing my one and only fated mate could've caused that big hole in here."

He pointed at his heart. "You took a big chunk of my heart with you when you left."

Eva laughed.

Out of all the responses he'd been expecting, Eva's was the opposite. Would he ever get it right with this woman? If she was his destined mate, shouldn't he be better attuned to her?

"You love me? Do you even know who I am? You're in love with an idea of that destined mate thing, not the real me." She leaned forward, all vulnerability gone from her expression as if it had never been there. The hardened steel was back. "I'm not a good person, Bhathian. If you knew the real me, you wouldn't be spouting rainbows and butterflies." She chuckled. "Bats and spider webs are more my thing."

It was his turn to laugh. "Then I'm the right guy for you. Do you think my life is all nice and pretty, or that it ever was? Do you have any idea what I've done? I'm over three hundred years old, Eva, and I'm a fighter. Do the math."

For once, it seemed that he'd said the right thing. Eva's eyes held his as she asked, "How many?"

He didn't need to question her meaning. "I stopped counting after the tenth."

"Was it in wars?"

"Some of it. A lot of it was during skirmishes with bands of bandits who wandered too close to our stronghold. At those times it was kill or be killed. We protected our own."

There was respect and approval in her expression. "As you should've."

"We see eye to eye, you and me. We have much more in common than you think, Eva. You can talk to me and your secrets will be safe. Unless what you do or did has anything to do with the safety of the clan, there is no way I'm going to share it with anyone else. Ever."

Eva pulled her hands out of his and leaned back, but her hard calculating gaze didn't waver. Neither did his. He held her eyes.

Another moment of silence passed, as Eva lifted her wine glass and emptied it. "I'm a murderer."

A chill ran down Bhathian's spine. Eva? A murderer?

For a split second, he entertained the disturbing notion that she might be a contract assassin and not the private eye she claimed to be. But then he dismissed it. The only way he could imagine Eva killing anyone was in self-defense. There was another possibility. Unaware of her strength, she might've killed someone accidentally.

"I'm sure it wasn't premeditated. You think I don't know you, but I do. You would've never killed someone in cold blood. It was either in self-defense or an accident."

Eva smiled that chilling smile of hers. "The first one was. The next four were not only premeditated but investigated and planned for a very long time."

"Are you a hit woman?" In his gut, he knew she couldn't be, but he had to cross it out for sure.

"No, I'm not doing it for personal gain. I'm a vigilante."

That was more fitting for the woman Bhathian knew Eva was. He leaned back in his chair and crossed his arms over his chest. "Tell me the whole story."

She walked over to the fridge and pulled out another wine bottle, then refilled their glasses. "Swear to me on whatever you hold dearest that what I tell you stays between the two of us."

He put his hand over his heart. "I swear on the lives of my daughter and granddaughter that unless you give me explicit permission to share what you tell me, I will take it to my grave."

She nodded. "You may also disclose what I tell you in the event of my death. I'm not ashamed of what I do. But I'm breaking the law."

"Agreed."

"The first time the killing was accidental. It was during a corporate stint assignment, but unrelated to it. I seduced the guy I needed to pump for information and stayed the night."

Bhathian heard himself growl. She was using sex to spy on people?

Eva chuckled. "Don't get all puffed up, Bhathian. It wasn't part of the deal, and I'm not in the habit of sleeping with my targets or my clients. That was a one-time thing. The guy was single and decent-looking, and I was due for my monthly hookup."

"What the hell is a monthly hookup?" Was Eva saying that she had sex only once a month?

"It's exactly what it sounds like, but this is a topic for a different conversation."

"Agreed. Please continue."

"I woke up to the sound of a girl pleading for her life. The situation sounded critical. If I called the cops, by the time they arrived the girl would've been dead or mutilated. The only thing I had that was of any use was a canister of pepper spray. I grabbed a heavy candleholder, the pepper spray, my handy burglar kit, and ran to where the pleading was coming from. Long story short, I got the pervert away from the girl—a sixteen-year-old who looked even younger. All I wanted was to knock him out for long enough to allow her to escape and get a good head start. I knew I was strong, but not that strong. The adrenaline rush must've added to my strength, and when I hit him with the candleholder, I fractured his skull. More like smashed it. I verified that he was dead and took the girl."

"What did you do with her?"

"I took her in. She had nowhere to go, and the pervert's family and business partners would've assumed she'd been the one who killed him. She needed a new identity and a safe place to stay. He'd kept her as a slave, making her obey and cooperate using drugs as rewards and beatings as punishments. It took her weeks to detox. But she's a fighter. A survivor."

A light flipped on in Bhathian's head. "Tessa."

"Yes."

Rage, hot and bubbling, painted Bhathian's vision red. Tessa, that tiny, fragile girl. "You did a good thing, Eva. If the scum weren't dead already, I would've gone after him and made sure that he was, but not before beating him to a pulp."

She smiled. "You say the sweetest things."

Bhathian got up and started pacing, trying to shake off the haze of fury. "This makes me so angry I can't breathe."

Eva's eyes followed him as he paced. "We really are a lot alike, you and me," she said. "That's exactly how I felt."

A moment later Bhathian forced himself to sit back down. "Okay, I'm ready for the rest."

Eva

It was such a tremendous relief to talk to someone about it. Someone who understood. Bhathian's positive response, if one could call rage positive, made her feel less of a monster.

She took a deep breath. "The thing was, I didn't feel bad for taking that life, not at all. On the contrary, it was like everything that had happened to me and had made me what I was suddenly clicked into place. The super-senses, the strength, the youthful appearance that was mine to keep—it all had a purpose. And as you said before, cheating spouses and crooked business types didn't seem important enough. But taking out the kind of filth that preyed on the young and the innocent and the helpless was. This was my purpose, that's why God had given me my special gifts. It even made the sacrifices I had to make more tolerable. I had to leave my daughter behind and let her think I was dead, but I was going to help others keep their children safe from predators."

Bhathian was listening raptly, and judging by his expression it seemed he agreed with everything she'd said. Nevertheless, Eva's throat felt dry and scratchy. Letting her secrets out felt like spitting out shrapnel. She drank more wine, swallowing the liquid with difficulty.

"I'm just one person, so there isn't much I can do. I can't go after the big fish because they are always surrounded by bodyguards. So I choose the scum in the middle, and each one takes months of research because I don't want to go after the wrong person and I don't want my crew involved. I do it all myself."

"When was that first one?"

"Five years ago."

Bhathian nodded. "One a year, then."

"More or less. It's not like I have a schedule. Whenever information falls into my lap, I investigate it. I have several snitches who sniff out things like that for me. I let them think I was hired by parents to look for their missing kids."

"It's a great cover. Maybe you should take on real jobs like that."

"I thought about it, but no. I don't want my crew involved and I'm afraid things will get too tangled up. I prefer to keep the two completely separate."

"Are you sure that everyone you took out needed to die?"

"Yes."

"So why the guilt? Why do you call yourself a bad person? You're an avenging angel."

"Taking a life is bad. It's even worse not to feel any remorse."

"It seems to me that you do."

"I don't. I just feel tainted by evil. You can't deal with that ugly sludge without it infecting your soul. I feel like mine is dark and getting darker, especially after the last one."

Bhathian frowned. "That's what you were upset about earlier?"

She nodded, not really wanting to talk about it. Out of the five that one had been the worst.

"What happened? Did something go wrong?"

Maybe talking about it would make her feel better. Though the only thing that could do that for sure was erasing the memory. Which reminded her. "Can you thrall me to forget it?"

"I wish I could, but thralls don't work on other immortals. The only one who can do it is Annani."

Eva felt a smidgen of hope. "Do you think she would agree to do it for me?"

"Is it that bad?"

"Worse."

"Just tell me before I start imagining shit."

"Okay."

Bhathian let out a breath. "Thank you."

"I had the target take me to his hotel room and told him I had Ecstasy pills. The story I fed him was that watching porn while high would make the sex amazing. It always works. I have them log into their laptop or even a smartphone so I have access to it, and I give them a strong sleeping pill instead of what they think is Ecstasy. It's the last verification I make before taking them out. So the guy drops five minutes into the porn flick, and I go into his laptop to double check that I have the right one. I find what I need as far as the sex-slave trade, but then I find something even worse: Child pornography in which he stars."

Bhathian growled, his fangs elongating so fast they punched over his lower lip and were already dripping venom. He looked terrifying, but it warmed her heart to see him like that. That's how good people responded to the horror that she'd witnessed.

"I wanted to wake him up and beat him to death, but I couldn't. The whole thing was hinged on it looking like he died from natural causes because people had seen me with him. There were hidden cameras all over the club I picked him up from. I injected him with a drug that interacted with the sleeping pill, granting him a merciful death he didn't deserve."

She waited for Bhathian to say something, but he seemed too worked up to do anything other than growl.

"I wish I could forget what I saw on that laptop, but that wasn't the end of it. I was so upset that I knocked over his wallet and a picture fell out. I didn't see it when I checked for his identification. It must've been hidden in the money compartment that I hadn't touched. The pervert had a family, a wife and three kids. I don't know how he managed to keep them so well hidden that they didn't come up in all my background checks. I know he deserved to die a thousand deaths, but I can't stop thinking about those kids. Who will provide for them now that I killed their father?"

Eva broke down, sobbing, as all the stress and the horror burst out through the opening she'd provided for it. In a split second, Bhathian was at her side, pulling her into his arms and rocking her like a baby.

"Shh, it's okay. I got you." He lifted her and carried her to the living room, where he sat down and rocked her until she had no more tears to shed.

"I'm sorry." She buried her face in his hard chest.

"What for?"

"Crying like a little girl. I'm stronger than that."

"You are strong. Incredibly so. But you no longer need to be strong all of the time. When it becomes too much, you can lean on me and let me be strong for you. We all need someone to catch us when we fall."

Bhathian

Eva had spent the night curled up in Bhathian's arms. After she'd fallen asleep in the living room, he'd carried her up to her bedroom and got them in bed while still holding her.

For so many years she'd carried such a heavy burden on her slender shoulders. All alone, with no one to lend a hand or an ear. In comparison, his life had been easy, and he'd had no right to his bad moods and nasty attitude. He had a whole clan at his back, people who cared about him despite his scowls and his frowns. But instead of gratitude for what he had, he'd allowed himself to be angry. A classic case of someone who always saw the glass half-empty instead of half-full.

His loneliness had been all in his head.

He kissed Eva's forehead. Courageous woman. Eva would've made one hell of a Guardian, but he doubted she was the type who could take orders. Being her own boss and making her own decisions suited her much better. She could've used a partner though. Someone to shoulder some of the responsibilities, to share her doubts and worries with. Unfortunately, Bhathian couldn't leave the Guardian force. There weren't enough of them as it was, and none of the trainees other than Michael had what it took.

It seemed he was stuck in his job forever.

"What are you thinking about?" Eva murmured.

"I thought you were sleeping."

"I was. All the heavy thinking next to me must've woken me up."

It was good to hear her teasing. "I was thinking that you need a partner. And I would've loved to offer myself, but I can't resign from the Guardian force. There are so few of us and no new blood is coming in. My trainees suck."

She snuggled closer and kissed his pec. "You could've been a great partner. With your help, I could've done so much more."

Eva never failed to surprise him. Whenever he anticipated her response to be negative it was positive, and the other way around. He'd been certain she'd dismiss the idea completely. Except, she might've not been so accepting if he'd been available for the position. One way to find out.

"Maybe I can still help. Not full time, but when you need me."

There was a hopeful smile on her face when she looked up at him. "That would be great. Having no backup was always the thing that stressed me out the most. That's one of the first things they drill into the heads of new agents. Never go solo. But I had no choice. My guys are civilians, they couldn't help even if I could confide in them about this."

Victory.

Bhathian had just won the second battle for Eva's heart. The first one had been her inviting him into her bed, and now she was inviting him into her secret world.

All that was left was for her to invite him into her heart.

More than ever before, he now believed it would happen sooner than later.

Eva's cellphone rang somewhere in the room, but she let it go to voicemail. A moment later his phone rang, but he was loath to leave the bed to go get it. Having Eva in his arms felt too good. Whoever that was would leave a message.

But the moment his phone stopped ringing, hers started again.

They exchanged worried looks, and a moment later both were out of bed.

Eva leaped over to the dresser where her phone was docked for charging and snapped it. "What's going on?"

"Nathalie's water broke." Bhathian heard Andrew on the other side. "We are down at Bridget's clinic. I thought you guys would want to be here."

"On our way." Eva closed the phone and turned to Bhathian. "Oh, my, God. It's happening. We are about to become grandparents!"

"We need to hurry." Bhathian forced a smile. It should've been one of the happiest moments in his life, but so much could still go wrong.

Eva wrapped her arms around his neck and stretched to plant a quick kiss on his lips. "Erase that frown, Bhathian. Everything is going to be alright. I promise."

He closed his eyes and prayed. *Please, dear Fates, make it so.*

Eva & Bhathian's story continues
Book 12 in The Children of the Gods Series
DARK GUARDIAN CRAVED
Turn the page to read the excerpt.

DARK GUARDIAN CRAVED

Cautious after a lifetime of disappointments, Eva is mistrustful of Bhathian's professed feelings of love. She accepts him as a lover and a confidant but not as a life partner.

Jackson suspects that Tessa is his true love mate, but unless she overcomes her fears, he might never find out.

Carol gets an offer she can't refuse—a chance to prove that there is more to her than meets the eye. Robert believes she's about to commit a deadly mistake, but when he tries to dissuade her, she tells him to leave.

William

As he scrolled through the day's mediocre gaming results, William lifted his glasses over his head and pinched his eyebrows between two fingers. Admitting failure was difficult, but to keep hoping for a pleasant surprise every time he opened the portal was irrational. The idea that had seemed so promising was good for producing profits but not for discovering Dormants.

At first he thought he'd made the game too difficult, but he was starting to realize that precognition, the only thing his game was designed to test, was just too rare of a talent.

With a sigh, William powered down his desktop. It was after midnight, and staring at the screen wasn't going to change the numbers. It was time to call it a day.

The sound of a phone ringing in his quiet apartment startled him. Who could be calling now? It wasn't as if people had tech emergencies that couldn't wait for normal business hours. Unless it was Kian. On occasion, when the guy was on the phone with someone in a different time zone, a tech question would come up.

But when William looked at the screen, it was Anandur's smiling face that stared back at him and not Kian's.

"Is everything all right?"

"Could you do me a favor and come stay with Fernando tonight? Nathalie's water just broke, and Andrew took her to Bridget's. I can't stay, and Bhathian will want to be with his daughter."

"Sure. I'll be there in a couple of minutes." William disconnected the call.

What exciting news.

With most of the clan's expectant mothers traveling to Annani's retreat to deliver their babies, Nathalie and Andrew's would be the first baby born in the keep.

Laptop tucked under his arm, William headed out and almost tripped over the wires strewn over the living room floor. Carefully, he maneuvered around them to reach the door. One of these days he'd have to organize his equipment better so he could vacuum the floor. The dust bunnies coating the wires were getting bigger by the day.

When he got to Andrew and Nathalie's place, Anandur was waiting for him with the door open. "Thanks, man. I really appreciate it." He clapped William on the shoulder and headed out. "I'm late for my rounds."

"No problem." William didn't mind helping out with the old man. Fernando was good company. Loony at times, but that was entertaining as well. Certainly beat spending entire days alone.

Making himself comfortable on the couch, William flipped open his laptop. But he wasn't in the mood for looking over more uninspiring reports.

Instead, he leaned his back against the couch's soft pillows and closed his eyes. Nathalie's mother was probably on her way as well. They would need to be careful about keeping Fernando from bumping into her in the morning.

To see his ex-wife after so long, looking even younger than when he'd met her over thirty years ago, would freak him out. Dementia made Fernando forget many things, but not Eva. He still talked about her as if they were together.

Fascinating story. Statistically, Eva's activation by an unknown immortal was impossible. As was the probability of there being unknown immortals at all. If only there were a way to find them.

But if there was, he couldn't think of one. Embarrassing for a guy who was supposed to be a genius and have a solution for every problem.

With a shrug, William picked up one of the throw pillows and put it on his thighs, then put the laptop on top of it. Better ergonomics. Navigating to one of his favorite news apps, he started scrolling through the articles in search of something new and interesting to read.

One piece caught his attention. It was about a new information-sharing agreement the US was trying to broker with other countries. Specifically their facial recognition databases.

If that happened, it could prove problematic. Clan members' fake documents had to be redone every fifteen years or so. If countries started running passports through facial recognition software and looking for matching pictures on documents belonging to different people, it would make travel abroad complicated. After all, if Mr. John Doe's picture from twenty years ago looked exactly like Mr. John Smith's picture today, someone would start asking questions.

Wait a minute, how the hell didn't I think of it?

If Andrew could get him access to that database, William could run it through his own facial recognition program and look for those alleged immortals.

I should start working on it right away.

Snapping his laptop closed, William tucked it under his arm and got up. Only when he was at the door, he remembered why he was there.

Damn.

With a sigh, he went back to the couch. There wasn't much he could accomplish with the help of his laptop, for that he needed the heavy lifting equipment in his lab, but he could start organizing his thoughts.

Eva

Eva put her hand on Bhathian's thigh, taking comfort in the connection as her feelings kept swinging between excitement and apprehension.

This late at night the roads were practically deserted, which was good since he was driving as if his heavy sport-utility vehicle was a race car, speeding and taking sharp turns—screeching tires and all. The way his powerful hands were gripping the steering wheel, it was a wonder the thing hadn't disintegrated under the pressure.

"Slow down, Bhathian, we don't want to get into an accident."

"We won't. My reflexes are fast enough to avoid collision."

"There is no reason to hurry. This is Nathalie's first delivery, and it's not going to happen for a while. We have hours of waiting ahead of us."

Bhathian lifted his foot off the accelerator an infinitesimal fraction. "I worry about her. The baby is big."

Eva patted his shoulder. "Nathalie was big too, eight and a half pounds, and her birth wasn't particularly difficult."

He cast her a sidelong glance. "You were an immortal when you had her. Your body would've fixed any internal bleeding and whatever other possible complications that could've happened before any of the doctors or nurses became aware of them. Nathalie is still a human."

He was right. As her gut did the flip and sink thing, Eva ran a shaky hand through her hair.

No, he wasn't right.

She shouldn't let Bhathian stress her out like that. He was overreacting. Women gave birth to big babies every day, and most of them survived. Especially in a well-equipped hospital with a well-trained staff assisting in the delivery.

Crossing her arms over her chest, Eva turned to Bhathian. "I don't like it that your in-house doctor is taking care of Nathalie. If you're really that concerned about your daughter, you should insist that she be moved to a hospital with a proper labor and delivery department."

Bhathian nodded. "Nathalie is human, and she should be in a human hospital. Bridget is a good doctor, but her experience is mostly with immortals." Finally slowing down, he turned into the entrance of the parking garage. A few moments later they stood in front of the bank of elevators. He pressed the down button.

"The clinic is in the basement?" Eva asked.

"Not exactly. I wouldn't call the underground complex a basement. It's several stories deep and sprawls under several buildings."

"For safety?"

"Yes. There are exit and entry points in several of the neighboring buildings."

As the elevator doors opened at the clinic's level, the sound of multiple voices indicated that they were not the first to arrive. "Who else is down here?"

He shrugged. "Probably half the immortal population of the keep. Everyone loves Nathalie."

The hallway outside the clinic was teeming with immortals. Some were standing and talking, while others were sitting on the carpeted floor and leaning against the concrete-block walls.

Clasping her hand as he strode briskly through the crowd, Bhathian only nodded in greeting to the people as they moved aside to let Eva and him pass.

He knocked on the clinic's entry door and opened the way. The doctor's office was to the right of the reception area, and since her door was open, they walked right in.

"Where is Nathalie?" Bhathian asked.

"Over there." Bridget pointed as she pushed to her feet. "Let me check if she is okay with you coming in." The petite redhead ducked into the adjacent room and closed the door behind her.

"How come we don't hear anything?" Eva still remembered Nathalie's birth, and it hadn't been a quiet and peaceful affair. The grunting, and in the end screaming, could not have been silenced by a wall and a closed door. Especially when those on the other side had immortal hearing.

Was Nathalie sleeping? Not likely if she was having contractions.

"The soundproofing here is done with immortals in mind. Unless the door is open, we won't hear a thing."

Bridget opened the door wide and stepped out. "Go ahead."

"Hi, guys." Nathalie looked lovely and still smiling. The doctor must've given her something for the pain.

"You got here fast." Andrew stood up and offered Eva his seat, then sat down next to Nathalie on the hospital bed.

Eva ignored the offer and walked over to Nathalie's other side. "How are you feeling, sweetie?" She clasped her daughter's hand.

"As well as can be expected." Nathalie grimaced. "The contractions are coming every three minutes. I didn't know they would hurt like that."

Eva glanced at the various wires connecting Nathalie to the monitoring equipment. No wonder her daughter was in pain. She wasn't hooked up to an IV drip yet. "Why no pain medication?"

"Too early. Bridget wants me to walk around a little before she hooks me up. Only after my cervix dilates to four centimeters, she's going to give me an epidural."

Just then another contraction gripped Nathalie. Her pretty face twisting in pain, she rose up and clutched Andrew's hand on one side, and Eva's on the other, breathing in and out until it passed.

"God, I hate this." She collapsed back on the bed.

"About that," Bhathian said, his raspy voice drawing Eva's attention to his face. The poor guy looked green. "I think you should go to a human hospital."

Nathalie arched a brow. "Why?"

"Bridget is only one person. What if you need a cesarean? Who is going to assist her? And what about complications? She has no experience with human mothers."

Bridget entered through the door which had remained open. "I assure you I can handle it. If I couldn't, I would've been the first to suggest moving Nathalie to a hospital."

"And what about a cesarean? You can't do everything yourself."

"I have two nurses to assist me. They are on their way."

A tight squeeze on her hand alerted Eva a moment before another contraction rolled over Nathalie. Stronger and longer than the previous one. A quick glance at the screen confirmed it. The spike was higher.

"I need to check how Nathalie is progressing." Bridget walked over to the sink and washed her hands, then pulled a pair of surgical gloves from a dispenser. "You should leave." She snapped the gloves on.

Eva pushed a strand of sweat-soaked hair off Nathalie's forehead. "We will be right outside if you need us."

Nathalie managed a weak smile. "It's getting worse. I don't think I want anyone other than Andrew to see me like this. After all, it's his fault, so he should suffer along with me."

Andrew paled and swallowed.

"It was a joke, Andrew!" Nathalie slapped his bicep.

Before the next contraction had a chance to roll out, Eva grabbed Bhathian's hand. "Let's go. We're not helping Nathalie by being here."

"One moment." He pulled his hand out of Eva's grip and walked over to Nathalie. "We are here for you. Anything you need. If you decide you want to go to a hospital after all, I'll take you. I'd like to see anyone try to stop me." He smoothed his hand over her hair and bent down, planting a quick kiss on her cheek.

"I'll be fine. Don't worry about me."

He nodded, but the worry lines on his face didn't fade.

"Come on." Eva hooked her arm through his and dragged him out.

"I'm walking. You don't need to pull me." Bhathian pushed the door closed behind them.

"I know. But I didn't want Nathalie to suffer through another contraction with us there. The sooner Bridget checks her, the sooner she is going to give Nathalie pain relief."

Outside the clinic, it looked as if Nathalie's café had been moved to the hallway. Robert was pushing a rolling cart similar to those Eva had used while working for the airline. A big carafe with coffee and another one with tea were on top; wrapped sandwiches and cold drinks were on the bottom. Carol handed out the sandwiches, while Robert served the drinks.

Nice fellow, Eva thought. He was helping Carol despite the dismissive way she treated him. Most guys wouldn't have given her the time of day. Living in such a close-knit community, the odd couple was the main subject of gossip. Even Eva, who was still an outsider and hadn't visited the keep often, had heard the whole story.

It was a shame he couldn't leave the keep. Sharon would've liked him. A quiet, hard-working guy, who also happened to be tall and handsome, was exactly her type.

Andrew

The Demerol drip was doing nothing for Nathalie. She seemed to be in as much pain as before, just lacking the energy to do anything other than whimper.

It was killing him. Every contraction, every grimace, every whimper was tearing him to shreds.

"I'm so sorry, baby." He kissed her hand, which hadn't left his since her ordeal had started. He was dying to take a piss but refused to leave her side even for a moment. It would have to wait. As long as she suffered, so would he.

"Nothing to be sorry about," she whispered. "Not your fault. I was joking before."

"I know. But I can't watch you suffer like this. I wish I could bear the pain for you."

Nathalie closed her eyes. "Can you ask Bridget to come and check if I'm ready?"

The doctor had done it less than twenty minutes ago, and there was little chance Nathalie had dilated enough since, but he was going to ask anyway. He'd do anything so Nathalie didn't have to suffer a moment longer than necessary.

Andrew pressed the button, and a few seconds later Bridget walked in.

"I know." She lifted her hand, forestalling his arguments. "Let's check again. The contractions are getting stronger and closer. You may be ready, Nathalie." She snapped a new pair of gloves on.

As Bridget lifted the thin blanket covering his wife, Andrew pushed to his feet and turned around, giving her a measure of privacy. No one wanted to be watched at moments like that. Not even by their spouse.

"You're good to go," Bridget announced.

Thank God. Both he and Nathalie sighed in relief. Salvation was near.

Bridget opened the door and called for her nurse. "Hildegard, I need you in here." She then turned to Andrew. "You have to leave. I'll call you once the epidural is in."

"Why?"

"It's okay, Andrew. Go grab something to eat and drink. There isn't enough room in here. You'll just be in their way."

The women looked at him impatiently. He hated to leave, but it seemed no one wanted him to be there during the procedure.

"Fine, I'm going." Andrew kissed Nathalie's forehead and made himself scarce, so she could get what she needed as soon as possible.

"What's going on in there?" Bhathian grabbed Andrew's arm.

"Bridget is giving Nathalie an epidural. Let go. I need to take a piss. I've been holding it in for hours."

Bhathian nodded, and his hand dropped away.

When Andrew returned, he was in a better state to notice what was happening in the corridor outside the clinic. Guardians and civilians were everywhere, talking, eating...

"Where did everyone get the food?" he asked Syssi.

"Carol is making rounds. She went to the kitchen to make another batch. I think I hear her cart rolling back." She looked behind his back.

"Okay, gang. I made more!" Carol called out before noticing Andrew.

"Hey. How are things going? Is Nathalie okay?"

"So far so good. She is so brave."

Carol pulled out a sandwich and handed it to him. "Yeah. I never want to be where she is now. I'm going to come play with your baby, but I don't want any of my own."

Andrew unwrapped the napkin and peeled away the top slice to see what was inside. "Lots of meat. Just as I like it."

"Enjoy. Coffee?"

"Yes, please."

Robert poured some into a paper cup. "Milk? Sugar?"

"No, thanks. I take it black."

"Here you go." The guy handed Andrew the cup.

The two continued down the hallway, with Robert pushing the cart and Carol handing out stuff. Nice collaboration. Maybe their lack of compatibility wasn't a forgone conclusion.

Andrew was on his last bite when Bridget came out. "You can come back in."

"Dispose of it for me, will you?" Handing Bhathian the wrapper and empty cup, Andrew rushed in.

Inside, he found a different woman than the one he'd left only moments before.

Nathalie's face was relaxed, and she smiled as soon as he came in. "This is amazing, Andrew. No pain. None at all. The only way I know I'm having a contraction is a slight rolling sensation, or seeing that graph spike." She pointed at the monitor.

The relief was so tremendous Andrew had to sit down. "You have no idea how happy it makes me."

"Oh, yes I do. But not as happy as me."

He chuckled. "True."

Bridget came in and dimmed the lights. "Try and get some sleep while you can, Nathalie. Andrew, do you want me to get you a cot?"

"No, I'm fine on the chair."

"As you wish." Bridget backed out of the room and closed the door.

"I think I'm going to listen to the doctor." Nathalie closed her eyes and a moment later began to snore lightly.

Excellent. She needed as much rest as she could get.

Following Nathalie's example, Andrew let his eyelids drop. The next time he cracked them open was when Bridget came in to check on her patient.

"I'm sorry to wake you guys up, but I have to check Nathalie's progress. Andrew, do you mind?" She started lifting the blanket.

He turned away and looked at the monitors. The big spikes were getting closer. Their daughter was almost ready to come out.

"We have an eight. It won't be long now," Bridget confirmed his uneducated guess.

But an hour later the opening was only eight and a half.

Bridget pulled the surgical gloves off and sighed. "I'm afraid we will have to do a cesarean. The baby is big, and she is stuck in the birth canal. I don't want to wait any longer and risk her going into distress."

Nathalie and Andrew exchanged glances. Bhathian had talked with Nathalie about a cesarean, but she'd dismissed him. For some reason, neither had considered that it might be a real possibility.

"I've always been told that I have childbearing hips. You want to tell me that they are good for nothing except making shopping for clothes a nightmare?"

Bridget smiled. "That's an old wives' tale. How you're shaped on the outside has nothing to do with how you're shaped on the inside. Let me call Gertrude. We need to wheel you out to the operating room."

"I can do it." Andrew stood up.

"Sorry, buddy. Medical staff only."

"Please don't tell me that I'm not allowed in the operating room. I need to be there for Nathalie." And to witness the birth of his daughter. Andrew wasn't going to miss that for the world.

"You can follow behind. Hildegard will give you scrubs to change into and show you how to properly clean up before entering the OR."

Pressing the button that lifted the back of her bed, Nathalie asked, "Are you sure there is no other way?"

"Theoretically, we can wait and see. Maybe a miracle will happen, and you will dilate fully. But I don't advise it. It's safer for the baby if we act now."

"Okay." Nathalie looked deflated.

Bridget patted her hand. "Don't look so glum. The way she is born is not important, only that she's healthy and thriving. Most mothers expect to have a vaginal delivery, and yet around one-third of births end up being cesarean. And if you're worrying about the big, ugly scar, don't. After the transition, there will be no trace of it."

"I know. It's just that I've never considered it, and I wasn't mentally prepared. I was so sure I'd be in the two-thirds that have a normal, vaginal delivery."

Bridget patted Nathalie's hand again, then turned to Gertrude. "Let's get this party moving."

"Yes, Doctor."

Bhathian

When the door opened and Bridget stepped out, Bhathian's gut clenched with worry. The doctor didn't come out unless there was trouble.

"Talk to me," he barked.

"Calm down, Bhathian, everything is alright. You're getting your wish granted. Nathalie is going for a cesarean."

Eva walked up to Bridget. "Why, are there any complications?"

"The baby is stuck in the birth canal."

That didn't sound good. Bhathian didn't remember reading about it. "Is Nathalie or the baby in danger?"

Bridget shook her head. "It's nothing out of the ordinary. A common problem and a common procedure. I'm going back to get ready."

"Wait, can we see her before she goes in?"

"Sorry, but no. By the way, there is a waiting area next to the operating room. It's two doors down. You'll be much more comfortable there."

Eva tugged on his arm. "Let's go. I prefer sitting in a chair to standing or sitting on the floor."

He nodded. "Anyone else want to join us?" he addressed Syssi and Amanda who were standing right next to Eva and him. Not that he really wanted company, but it would've been impolite not to offer.

"Sure. Do you know if there is enough room?"

"How should I know? I've never been there."

The four of them proceeded down the hallway and found the waiting room. The place was utilitarian but cozy. Its six chairs were divided into two rows of three, one on each side of the room. A square wooden coffee table, topped with stacks of old magazines, was part of each row, tucked between the second and third chair, and there was a slim fridge next to the door.

Opening the thing, he was surprised to find it stocked with soft drinks. Bhathian wondered how long they had been there. Probably years, unless the room was a late addition to Bridget's sprawling underground empire. He couldn't remember anyone using or even mentioning this room before. "Anyone want a Coke or a Sprite?"

"Is it Coke or Pepsi?" Eva asked.

"Coke."

"Then I want one."

Bhathian smiled and tossed her a can, then pulled out one for himself. "I don't like Pepsi either." He loved to discover another thing he and Eva had in common.

Syssi clicked on the television that was mounted above the fridge and started flipping channels, then clicked it off. "There is nothing on."

Amanda picked up a magazine then dropped it back on the table and picked up another one. A moment later she dropped it too. "The stress is killing me."

"Where is Kian?" Bhathian asked Syssi, just to start a conversation and lower the stress level in the room.

"In his office."

"This late at night?"

"Sari called. Over there it's the middle of the day. Something about a car manufacturing facility that came up for sale on her side of the Pond."

That piqued Amanda's interest. "Cars? That's new."

"Not just any cars. Flying ones. They think there is a market for them in Alaska."

"What about California?"

Syssi chuckled. "Maybe in rural areas. I can't see flying cars in the city."

"Bummer." Amanda lost interest and picked up another magazine.

Eva shifted in her chair. "Have any of you heard about a club named Allure?"

Amanda shook her head. "I know of a cruise ship by that name. But I'm not up to date on clubs. That chapter of my life is closed. I'm happily mated now."

Syssi cast her a sidelong glance. "Do you miss it? You used to love the club scene."

"Not at all. I'm a home body now. Spending time with Dalhu or with you guys is all I want to do."

Syssi shook her head in mock despair. "How the mighty have fallen."

Amanda lifted a finger. "Not fallen, risen. No one compares to Dalhu."

Eva seemed fascinated by the exchange. "I haven't met your husband yet. And after all that praise I'm curious."

"Dalhu is not my husband. Mated is not the same as married."

"How so?"

"Mated means that he is the one and only for me, and I am for him. We don't need a big party or a piece of paper to sanction our union."

"Are you saying that it's for life?"

"Of course. And a very long life at that."

"So you guys stay together no matter what? What about cheating, or discord?"

"There is none."

"How is it possible?"

Amanda put down her magazine and crossed her legs. "I don't know if Bhathian explained it to you, but we have a concept of fated mates. It doesn't mean that everyone finds one. Even in the old days, when there were plenty of potential mates to choose from, only a few were lucky enough to find their one and only."

Eva frowned. "How do you know, though? How does a fated mate differ from a non-fated one?"

Amanda pinned Eva with her blue stare. "When no other man would do. When being away from him means agony, and being with him is the only thing that feels right even if your mind tells you that it's all wrong."

Next to her Syssi nodded. "Exactly. I couldn't have said it better."

Eva turned to Bhathian and regarded him as if seeing him in a completely different light. "Is it true? Is that how you feel?"

He grabbed her hand and clasped it. "I'm not as eloquent and concise as Amanda, but I told you the same thing once or twice." He lifted her hand and kissed it.

On the other side of Eva, Syssi cleared her throat. "Amanda, are you up for another cup of coffee? Carol said she used the commercial coffee maker in the basement kitchen and made enough to last everyone the entire night."

"Sure, why not?"

"You don't have to go." Eva lifted a hand to stop them. "I promise not to embarrass you guys again."

Amanda's brows lifted, making her expression seem condescending. "I'm not embarrassed. It would take much more than a little love talk to achieve that."

"I don't think an orgy would." Syssi snorted. "Amanda thrives on scandalizing people. Especially me."

"That's because you blush so prettily. You make it far too easy."

"You know I can't help it."

"I know." Amanda leaned over and kissed Syssi's cheek. "I love you just the way you are."

Watching Eva listen to the friendly exchange, Bhathian was surprised to see a look of longing on her face. Was she envious of Amanda and Syssi's close relationship? Did she lack female companionship?

"You seem really close." The tone of her voice more than the words themselves confirmed his assumption.

"We are. As soon as Syssi walked into my lab, I knew she was the one for my brother. I fell in love with her first."

Syssi blushed and leaned her head on Amanda's shoulder. "I love you too."

Eva cast Amanda a curious look. "How did he feel about your matchmaking? From the little I've seen of him, Kian doesn't strike me as a man who would let anyone interfere in his life."

"The old goat fought me every step of the way. But then fate intervened and he had to come to my lab. It was a done deal the moment he laid eyes on her."

"How about you, Syssi, was it a done deal for you too?"

Eva's questions gave Bhathian hope. Perhaps she was finally ready to accept that they were meant for each other.

Syssi nodded. "I wanted Kian like I've never wanted any man before, but I thought it was just an infatuation. Someone as incredibly handsome as Kian would make any woman weak at the knees. I tried to shield my heart and not fall for him because I was sure he was going to chew me up and spit me out. But it was futile. There was no fighting this thing between us. And mind you, I was still human back then, and although Amanda believed I was a Dormant, Kian didn't. We both thought our relationship was doomed, and yet we couldn't help the incredible pull. Luckily for us, I transitioned and the impossible dream became a reality."

There was a suspicious shine in Eva's eyes. Was his tough-as-nails mate a closet romantic?

"Unlike Amanda and her mate, you guys got married, though, right?"

"We did. Since it was the first the clan ever had, Kian wanted a huge wedding. I was terrified. An introvert like me hates big crowds in general, and especially when all the attention is on me. But I did it for Kian and for the clan. The funny thing was that I ended up enjoying our wedding tremendously, which proves that sometimes we need to step outside our comfort zone to find out what makes us happy."

ORDER DARK GUARDIAN CRAVED TODAY!

JOIN THE VIP CLUB
To find out what's included in your free membership,
flip to the last page.

The Children of the Gods Series

Reading Order

THE CHILDREN OF THE GODS ORIGINS

1: Goddess's Choice

When gods and immortals still ruled the ancient world, one young goddess risked everything for love.

2: Goddess's Hope

Hungry for power and infatuated with the beautiful Areana, Navuh plots his father's demise. After all, by getting rid of the insane god he would be doing the world a favor. Except, when gods and immortals conspire against each other, humanity pays the price.

But things are not what they seem, and prophecies should not to be trusted...

THE CHILDREN OF THE GODS

Dark Stranger

1: Dark Stranger The Dream

2: Dark Stranger Revealed

3: Dark Stranger Immortal

Dark Enemy

4: Dark Enemy Taken

5: Dark Enemy Captive

6: Dark Enemy Redeemed

Kri & Michael's Story

6.5: My Dark Amazon

Dark Warrior

7: Dark Warrior Mine

8: Dark Warrior's Promise

9: Dark Warrior's Destiny

10: Dark Warrior's Legacy

Dark Guardian

11: Dark Guardian Found

12: Dark Guardian Craved

13: Dark Guardian's Mate

Prepare for the heart-warming culmination of Eva and Bhathian's story!

Dark Angel

14: Dark Angel's Obsession

The cold and stoic warrior is an enigma even to those closest to him. His secrets are about to unravel.

15: Dark Angel's Seduction

Brundar is fighting a losing battle. Calypso is slowly chipping away his icy armor from the outside, while his need for her is melting it from the inside.

He can't allow it to happen. Calypso is a human with none of the Dormant indicators. There is no way he can keep her for more than a few weeks.

16: Dark Angel's Surrender

Get ready for the heart pounding conclusion to Brundar and Calypso's story.

Callie still couldn't wrap her head around it, nor could she summon even a smidgen of sorrow or regret. After all, she had some memories with him that weren't horrible. She should've felt something. But there was nothing, not even shock. Not even horror at what had transpired over the last couple of hours.

Maybe it was a typical response for survivors--feeling euphoric for the simple reason that they were alive. Especially when that survival was nothing short of miraculous.

Brundar's cold hand closed around hers, reminding her that they weren't out of the woods yet. Her injuries were superficial, and the most she had to worry about was some scarring. But, despite his and Anandur's reassurances, Brundar might never walk again.

If he ended up crippled because of her, she would never forgive herself for getting him involved in her crap.

"Are you okay, sweetling? Are you in pain?" Brundar asked.

Her injuries were nothing compared to his, and yet he was concerned about her. God, she loved this man. The thing was, if she told him that, he would run off, or crawl away as was the case.

Hey, maybe this was the perfect opportunity to spring it on him.

Dark Operative

17: Dark Operative: A Shadow of Death

As a brilliant strategist and the only human entrusted with the secret of immortals' existence, Turner is both an asset and a liability to the clan. His request to attempt transition into immortality as an alternative to cancer treatments cannot be denied without risking the clan's exposure. On the other hand, approving it means risking his premature death. In both scenarios, the clan will lose a valuable ally.

When the decision is left to the clan's physician, Turner makes plans to manipulate her by taking advantage of her interest in him.

Will Bridget fall for the cold, calculated operative? Or will Turner fall into his own trap?

18: Dark Operative: A Glimmer of Hope

As Turner and Bridget's relationship deepens, living together seems like the right move, but to make it work both need to make concessions.

Bridget is realistic and keeps her expectations low. Turner could never be the truelove mate she yearns for, but he is as good as she's going to get. Other than his emotional limitations, he's perfect in every way.

Turner's hard shell is starting to show cracks. He wants immortality, he wants to be part of the clan, and he wants Bridget, but he doesn't want to cause her pain.

His options are either abandon his quest for immortality and give Bridget his few remaining decades, or abandon Bridget by going for the transition and most likely dying. His rational mind dictates that he chooses the former, but his gut pulls him toward the latter. Which one is he going to trust?

19: Dark Operative: The Dawn of Love

Get ready for the exciting finale of Bridget and Turner's story!

Dark Survivor

20: Dark Survivor Awakened
21: Dark Survivor Echoes of Love
22: Dark Survivor Reunited

Dark Widow

23: Dark Widow's Secret
24: Dark Widow's Curse
25: Dark Widow's Blessing

Dark Dream

26: Dark Dream's Temptation
27: Dark Dream's Unraveling
28: Dark Dream's Trap

Dark Prince

29: Dark Prince's Enigma
30: Dark Prince's Dilemma
31: Dark Prince's Agenda

Dark Queen

32: Dark Queen's Quest
33: Dark Queen's Knight
34: Dark Queen's Army

Dark Spy

35: Dark Spy Conscripted

36: Dark Spy's Mission
37: Dark Spy's Resolution

Dark Overlord

38: Dark Overlord New Horizon
39: Dark Overlord's Wife
40: Dark Overlord's Clan

Dark Choices

41: Dark Choices The Quandary
42: Dark Choices Paradigm Shift
43: Dark Choices The Accord

Dark Secrets

44: Dark Secrets Resurgence
45: Dark Secrets Unveiled
46: Dark Secrets Absolved

Dark Haven

47: Dark Haven Illusion
48: Dark Haven Unmasked
49: Dark Haven Found

Dark Power

50: Dark Power Untamed
51: Dark Power Unleashed
52: Dark Power Convergence

Dark Memories

53: Dark Memories Submerged

54: Dark Memories Emerge

55: Dark Memories Restored

Dark Hunter

56: Dark Hunter's Query

57: Dark Hunter's Prey

58: <u>Dark Hunter's Boon</u>

Dark God

59: Dark God's Avatar

60: Dark God's Reviviscence

61: Dark God Destinies Converge

Dark Whispers

62: Dark Whispers From The Past

63: Dark Whispers From Afar

64: Dark Whispers From Beyond

Dark Gambit

65: Dark Gambit The Pawn

66: Dark Gambit The Play

67: Dark Gambit Reliance

Dark Alliance

68: Dark Alliance Kindred Souls

69: Dark Alliance Turbulent Waters
70: Dark Alliance Perfect Storm

Dark Healing

71: Dark Healing Blind Justice
72: Dark Healing Blind Trust
73: Dark healing Blind Curve

Dark Encounters

74: Dark Encounters of the Close Kind
75: Dark Encounters of the Unexpected Kind
76: Dark Encounters of the Fated Kind

The Children of the Gods Series Sets

Books 1-3: Dark Stranger trilogy—Includes a bonus short story: **The Fates take a Vacation**

Books 4-6: Dark Enemy Trilogy —Includes a bonus short story—**The Fates' Post-Wedding Celebration**

Books 7-10: Dark Warrior Tetralogy

Books 11-13: Dark Guardian Trilogy

Books 14-16: Dark Angel Trilogy

Books 17-19: Dark Operative Trilogy

Books 20-22: Dark Survivor Trilogy

Books 23-25: Dark Widow Trilogy

Books 26-28: Dark Dream Trilogy
Books 29-31: Dark Prince Trilogy
Books 32-34: Dark Queen Trilogy
Books 35-37: Dark Spy Trilogy
Books 38-40: Dark Overlord Trilogy
Books 41-43: Dark Choices Trilogy
Books 44-46: Dark Secrets Trilogy
Books 47-49: Dark Haven Trilogy
Books 50-52: Dark Power Trilogy
Books 53-55: Dark Memories Trilogy
Books 56-58: Dark Hunter Trilogy
Books 59-61: Dark God Trilogy
Books 62-64: Dark Whispers Trilogy
Books 65-67: Dark Gambit Trilogy
Books 68-70: Dark Alliance Trilogy
Books 71-73: Dark healing Trilogy

MEGA SETS

INCLUDE CHARACTER LISTS

The Children of the Gods: Books 1-6
The Children of the Gods: Books 6.5-10

TRY THE SERIES ON

AUDIBLE

2 FREE audiobooks with your new Audible subscription!

PERFECT MATCH SERIES

Vampire's Consort

When Gabriel's company is ready to start beta testing, he invites his old crush to inspect its medical safety protocol.

Curious about the revolutionary technology of the *Perfect Match Virtual Fantasy-Fulfillment studios*, Brenna agrees.

Neither expects to end up partnering for its first fully immersive test run.

King's Chosen

When Lisa's nutty friends get her a gift certificate to *Perfect Match Virtual Fantasy Studios*, she has no intentions of using it. But since the only way to get a refund is if no partner can be found for her, she makes sure to request a fantasy so girly and over the top that no sane guy will pick it up.

Except, someone does.

> **Warning:** This fantasy contains a hot, domineering crown prince, sweet insta-love, steamy love scenes painted with light shades of gray, a wedding, and a HEA in both the virtual and real worlds.

Intended for mature audience.

Captain's Conquest

Working as a Starbucks barista, Alicia fends off flirting all day long, but none of the guys are as charming and sexy as Gregg. His frequent visits are the highlight of her day, but since he's never asked her out, she assumes he's taken. Besides, between a day job and a budding music career, she has no time to start a new relationship.

That is until Gregg makes her an offer she can't refuse—a gift certificate to the virtual fantasy fulfillment service everyone is talking about. As a huge Star Trek fan, Alicia has a perfect match in mind—the captain of the Starship Enterprise.

The Thief Who Loved Me

When Marian splurges on a Perfect Match Virtual adventure as a world infamous jewel thief, she expects high-wire fun with a hot partner who she will never have to see again in real life.

A virtual encounter seems like the perfect answer to Marcus's string of dating disasters. No strings attached, no drama, and definitely no love. As a die-hard James Bond fan, he chooses as his avatar a dashing MI6 operative, and to complement his adventure, a dangerously seductive partner.

Neither expects to find their forever Perfect Match.

My Merman Prince

The beautiful architect working late on the twelfth floor of my building thinks that I'm just the maintenance guy. She's also under the impression that I'm not interested.

Nothing could be further from the truth.

I want her like I've never wanted a woman before, but I don't play where I work.

I don't need the complications.

When she tells me about living out her mermaid fantasy with a stranger in a Perfect Match virtual adventure, I decide to do everything possible to ensure that the stranger is me.

The Dragon King

To save his beloved kingdom from a devastating war, the Crown Prince of Trieste makes a deal with a witch that costs him half of his humanity and dooms him to an eternity of loneliness.

Now king, he's a fearsome cobalt-winged dragon by day and a short-tempered monarch by night. Not many are brave enough to serve in the palace of the brooding and volatile ruler, but Charlotte ignores the rumors and accepts a scribe position in court.

As the young scribe reawakens Bruce's frozen heart, all that stands in the way of their happiness is the witch's bargain. Outsmarting the evil hag will take cunning and courage, and Charlotte is just the right woman for the job.

My Werewolf Romeo

The father of my star student is a big-shot screenwriter and the patron of the drama department who thinks he can dictate what production I should put on. The principal makes it very clear that I need to cooperate with the opinionated asshat or walk away from my dream job at the exclusive private high school.

It doesn't help matters that the guy is single, hot, charming, creative, and seems to like me despite my thinly-veiled hostility.

When he invites me to a custom-tailored Perfect Match virtual adventure to prove that his screenplay is perfect for my production, I accept, intending to have fun while proving that messing with the classics is a foolish idea.

I don't expect to be wowed by his werewolf adaptation of Red Riding Hood mesh-up with Romeo and Juliet, and I certainly don't expect to fall in love with the virtual fantasy's leading man.

The Channeler's Companion

A treat for fans of *The Wheel of Time.*

When Erika hires Rand to assist in her pediatric clinic, she does so despite his good looks and irresistible charm, not because of them.

He's empathic, adores children, and has the patience of a saint.

He's also all she can think about, but he's off limits.

What's a doctor to do to scratch that irresistible itch without risking workplace complications?

A shared adventure in the Perfect Match Virtual Studios seems like the solution, but instead of letting the algorithm choose a partner for her, Erika can try to influence it to select the one she wants. Awarding Rand a gift certificate to the service will get him into their database, but unless Erika can tip the odds in her favor, getting paired with him is a long shot.

Hopefully, a virtual adventure based on her and Rand's favorite series will do the trick.

Copyright © 2017 by I. T. Lucas

All rights reserved.
No part of this book may be reproduced in any form or by any electronic or mechanical means, including information storage and retrieval systems, without written permission from the author, except for the use of brief quotations in a book review.

NOTE FROM THE AUTHOR:
Dark Guardian Found is a work of fiction!
Names, characters, places and incidents are products of the author's imagination or are used fictitiously and are not to be construed as real. Any similarity to actual persons, organizations and/or events is purely coincidental.

FOR EXCLUSIVE PEEKS AT UPCOMING RELEASES & A FREE COMPANION BOOK

Join my *VIP Club* and gain access to the VIP portal at itlucas.com
To Join, go to:
http://eepurl.com/blMTpD

INCLUDED IN YOUR FREE MEMBERSHIP:

YOUR VIP PORTAL

- Read preview chapters of upcoming releases.
- Listen to Goddess's Choice narration by Charles Lawrence
- Exclusive content offered only to my VIPs.

FREE I.T. LUCAS COMPANION INCLUDES:

- Goddess's Choice Part 1
- Perfect Match: Vampire's Consort (A standalone Novella)
- Interview Q & A
- Character Charts

IF YOU'RE ALREADY A SUBSCRIBER, AND YOU ARE NOT GETTING MY EMAILS, YOUR PROVIDER IS SENDING THEM TO YOUR JUNK FOLDER, AND YOU ARE MISSING OUT ON **<u>IMPORTANT UPDATES, SIDE CHARACTERS' PORTRAITS, ADDITIONAL CONTENT, AND OTHER GOODIES.</u>** TO FIX THAT, ADD isabell@itlucas.com TO YOUR EMAIL CONTACTS OR YOUR EMAIL VIP LIST.

Check out the specials at
https://www.itlucas.com/specials

Manufactured by Amazon.ca
Bolton, ON